BONES FOR BREAD

The Scarlet Plumiere Series: Book 2

By L. L. Muir

For Linda,
My editor —
May these imperfections
not drive you to drink!

Muir

P.S. Stanley says "hi!"

Bones for Bread © 2013 Lesli Muir Lytle

All rights reserved

This book is a work of fiction. The names, characters, places, and incidents are products of the writer's imagination or have been used fictitiously and are not to be construed as real. Any resemblance to persons, living or dead, actual events, locales or organizations is entirely coincidental.

ISBN: 978-1491293805

Cover Design by Kelli Ann Morgan
www.inspirecreativeservices.com

Interior Book Design by
Bob Houston eBook Formatting

"Come," he repeated and stepped back.

It was just enough room. She brought up her knee with unrepentant force. He yanked on her wrist, pulling her to one side as he turned his body in the opposite direction, but it could not save him. At least, not all of him.

It could have been surprise, as much as pain, that made him release her. Two steps and a leap put her on the horse's back. After she was well out of his reach, she dared a glance over her shoulder and found the man standing, but bent, with his hands on his knees. Standing was a fine thing; he'd be able to get out of the cold at least.

She slowed her horse and could not resist one last taunt.

"Go home. Go home and remove yer hands from all things Scottish, aye?"

His head snapped up and even though she was turning away, she feared his glare was far too familiar.

I only imagined it, she thought, while her clever mount wove through the trees for which she had no attention. The other one, the man who haunted her dreams and stole her sleep, would have no business in Scotland, surely.

Unless. Her heart tripped at the thought of it. Unless he came looking for me.

BONES FOR BREAD

The Scarlet Plumiere Series: Book 2

By L. L. Muir

Published By
Ivy & Stone
www.llmuir.weebly.com

To Dorothy

For your honesty of life,
your blindness in love,
and for passing it all down.

You are my hero.

PROLOGUE

The Pipe and Spittle, Brigadunn, Scottish Highlands – 1816

The nervous wench set a pint just within his easy reach and scurried away like a wee mousie from a cat.

He snorted. It must have been his rare-seen smile that frightened her, but he couldna hide his glee for all the tryin' in the world. Though the rain be fallin' sideways on the far side of the tavern door, it was a fine, fine day indeed.

He took a celebratory swig and used his sleeve to wipe the bubbles from his stubbled lip. The course cloth of it dragged across his face and he grimaced. If any man in Brigadunn deserved to wear finer clothes, it was he. But he couldna walk away from the role he played, at least not for a wee while anyhow.

But soon.

Soon.

He took another drink and let the suds alone, avoiding a second reminder of the rags he wore, favoring a happier thought.

He couldna understand why the Fates would deal so generously with him. After all, he was a ruthless man down to the bottom of his boots. He'd spilled more blood than Paddy had spilled beer, and truth be told, there was a time he would have let his own mother freeze if it meant her shawl would earn a bit of silver. So why would his enemy be delivered into his hands like a boon from Heaven?

As the warm drink disappeared down his gullet, he wondered at what sort of pagan god might have taken notice of him. What noble service might he have performed, accidentally, that would inspire some deity to bless him?

He could think of nothing. Truly.

Perhaps he was favored for being such an enterprising man. Wasn't it written in The Bible that God preferred a soul who could help himself? So mayhap it had naught to do with the Fates, and all to do with God using a mortal arm to exact a bit of vengeance on the wicked—or at the very least, a man as ruthless as he.

A sign is what it was.

God was delivering his enemy to his very doorstep. What choice did he have but to do God's will? If he and the Almighty were of a mind, there was a tree somewhere in the glen destined to feel the weight of the Right Honorable Earl of Ashmoore.

Or rather, his lordship's weight and then some, for don't a body weigh a bit more when it be swingin'?

He laughed when he imagined the look on Lord Ashmoore's face when he realized not all his enemies lay in France.

CHAPTER ONE

The North of France, two years before. . .

They're coming!

Blair swung her heavy plaid skirts into an alley as the three English gentlemen stepped out of the tavern, their faces pinched in frustration and not from the glare of the afternoon sun. She was fair certain she wore the same expression—since *she* sought the same people *they* sought, their bad luck was hers to share.

She held her breath as they passed by, headed for their horses. Their steps were sharp and nearly in unison, as if they'd marched together so often that walking in cadence was a habit. Just as it was her heart's habit to speed its rhythm as she anticipated getting caught.

For weeks, she'd observed the men, followed each errand, and listened in on every conversation she could. Sometimes accompanied by a common man, the three had combed a full circuit of the moderate town surrounding the Chateau de Sedan, with Blair following at a careful clip. And it had come to nothing.

What they all needed was a fresh wind of hope to fill their sails. And if they didn't get some soon, she wondered how much longer she could keep trailing behind them, hoping they could see something she could not.

The gentlemen had just met with Etienne MacDonald, the Marshal of France himself. The aging man had sworn upon his life that if hostages were being held near his beloved Sedan, he would know it. They'd taken the man's word and decided to look elsewhere.

Her eyes closed against the wave of disappointment pushing at her breast. The medieval chateau had looked so imposing, so sinister. She could easily imagine a large dungeon where hostages were locked away until their ransoms were paid. Even easier to imagine was the marshal filling the role of villain—but only until he'd spoken. There was nothing but honesty in his speech. Nothing but sincerity in his eyes, and he'd not even been looking her way.

Damn the man.

Her heart was weary, her body as weak as the soup she'd hovered over while eavesdropping. But the image of her brother, suffering in some bastard's pit, prodded her on. If she allowed her mind to dwell on the fact that his ransom date had come and gone, she wouldn't be able to keep her legs beneath her. Better to keep them moving, aye?

She sighed and peeked out of the alley. It was safe to follow.

If the men moved their arses, they could all return to their rooms in Charleville before the gloamin'. Rather than leave first and risk missing some detour, however, she had no choice but to wait and follow. But oh, how she wished she could collect her horse and give it its head. How she longed to scream her frustrations to the wind as it whipped her cloak out behind her and dried her tears even as they fell.

Instead, she would follow from a wee distance, as she had for more than two weeks now. And no doubt she'd end the day with picking her way along the dark streets of Charleville, hoping her feminine form would be none too obvious, hoping she would never need to clear her blade from her skirts and harm anyone. Though, today harming someone might be just the thing to soothe her spirits.

The gentlemen turned into the livery and she counted to twenty before she crossed the street to the less reputable looking stables where she'd left her own mount. She could have patronized the more respectable business, but it would do no good rubbing shoulders, even casually, with these men. They had proven to be more wary than most, and she was a mite surprised they hadn't confronted her by now. They'd noticed her in their shadows. There were far too many glances in her direction to be accounted for otherwise. But perhaps they failed to see her as much of a threat.

She was not a threat, of course, to anyone but those who'd taken her brother. To them, she would be the Angel of Death. They would not be the first men she'd killed, but they might be the first to be deserving. It would be easier if they were deserving. Surely, they wouldn't be allowed to haunt her if they were villains of which the world was well rid.

As they often did, the faces of those men she'd felled in battle rose to the fore of her mind and waited for her to bid them leave. But this time, she shook them away with a single toss of her head. She was weary enough for one day.

Thankfully, they didn't hang about to argue.

As Blair came around the corner, the stable hand jumped to his feet, but relaxed when he noted it was her. The slow considering look he gave her, from toes to nose, would have made most women turn tail and run. She was not most women.

The fool took a bold step toward her.

She took a menacing step toward him.

"My horse," she said firmly, not taking her gaze from his. "Now."

He narrowed his eyes.

She narrowed hers.

Amused, he waited.

She gave him nary a blink.

Finally, he dropped his chin in a half nod, then did as he was bid.

She mounted before reaching for his payment—a single coin she fished from a small pocket in her cloak. She couldn't help but smile at his disappointment, that he'd heard no chime of other coins on her person. There was no use of him asking for more.

She tossed his payment in the air. He released the bridle in order to catch it, and she turned the beast to go.

By the time she reached the street, she could still see the last two gentlemen riding out of town. Had the larger man taken a grand lead? Or was he still about? Had they sickened of being followed and meant to confront her on the road between them?

Her mount shifted its weight beneath her while she considered. But if she wished to reach Charleville—base camp, so to speak—she could not dally long. She drew a deep breath, huffed it out. Then she nudged her horse, urged it to the right, and entered the eastern flow of carts. She rode two blocks before turning, then continued a block to the north and turned west.

She sensed no one behind her as she left Sedan, but her imagination summoned myriad possibilities in her mind. By the time she reached Charleville, her head was fair spinning with foul deeds that might have happened along the road, leaving her spent and wearier for it. She would need to find a way to bridle her imaginings, however, for as soon as she found her brother and got him safely returned to Scotland, she was going to be alone for a fine long time. For it was certain she wouldn't be returning with him.

She'd never be welcome home again, but Martin would. And didn't young Finn need someone besides their aging father to look after him?

She entered Charleville long after the sun had set. Her grasp of time had been far afield all the week. But at least the buildings here were familiar to her. And well they should be, after a month of coming and going, first on her own, then following the Englishmen. For weeks she'd searched the area around Charleville, finding nothing. Then, when the English had arrived, themselves searching for kidnappers, she'd felt in her soul she was in the right place. But their two weeks of searching had turned up no more than hers had.

So frustrating, like looking for a lost shoe near its mate. You know it's there. It has to be there. But for all the looking, you canna see it.

Behind her, a foot shuffled against the cobbled road and she saw in her mind a figure made of shadow rising up to steal her away to some faery hill.

"Ridiculous," she muttered. Wasn't it always herself who chided her fellow Scots against wasting their lives with foolish superstitions? Of course it was. If they could but see her now, shaking and silly over childish fancies, they would chase her from the village.

She forced her mind onto pleasanter thoughts. Again, a dark figure rose in her imagination. This one was not so sinister, but made her heart race at the same clip. The Englishman in black. The tall one who could wrap her neatly in his arms and pull her into the recesses of his soul if she wasn't careful.

She could not resist glancing around her, wondering— if he appeared, there, in the dark street behind her—would she run?

CHAPTER TWO

Blair left her horse in the hands of a capable lad, then walked through the rear entrance to the Hotel Place Ducale. Although she had rented a room in the same establishment as the Englishmen, there was little risk of rubbing shoulders with them there; they'd let a suite of rooms on the second floor, she'd let a small maid's room on the ground floor for which she was charged no mouse fee. After all, who could guarantee there would be no vermin below stairs?

She was relieved to see all three of the gentlemen's horses being wiped down in the yard. The men, she expected, were tucked in nicely at the auberge around the corner where they usually took their meals—and their libations. The wise thing to do would be to follow them there, to eavesdrop on their next plan, but she was wilted as a thirsty thistle and wanted only her bed.

The disappointment of the day was tugging at her heart and if she got to sleep quickly, she might avoid her now-regular nightmares. And another day would bring another chance at finding Martin.

No matter how discouraged the Englishmen were at night, they were always up with the sun with a new plan, a new place to look, a new lead to follow. They had yet to fail her since the day they'd arrived in Reims, the day she'd realized they, too, were searching for kidnappers in the area. And because she had run out of leads herself, she'd attached herself to their tailcoats—from a distance, of course—and thanked God she had been given new hope of finding her brother. All she needed to do was keep them in sight and pray they succeeded where she had failed.

Heaven forgive her, she was even too tired for proper prayer. Tonight, she would have to leave the worrying to her trio of heroes.

When the attendant mumbled a greeting, Blair found herself leaning on the polished hotel desk, staring into a faraway corner.

The fellow looked down his nose at her, as he'd done each time she'd asked for the key to her room. Apparently he could not forgive her for that first night when he'd suggested he join her in her room for a drink—and she'd laughed. But tonight, there was a bit of a sneer to one side of his nose.

He placed her key on the counter, then pulled his hand back quickly, as if he were afraid she might touch him. What she was tempted to do, if she weren't so weary, was to free Wolfkiller from its sheath, slice the nasty man's cravat in half, then sheath the blade beneath her skirts before the man could catch a flash of candlelight. For the time being, she would simply have to enjoy the fact that she could do it.

She scooped up the key and laughed as she walked away, surprised she had the strength for even that.

The single sconce in the servant's hallway had not been lit. Her room would be the fourth on the left, far enough into the darkness to give her pause. If it were any other day, she might insist the attendant come light the way for her, just to cause him bother, but with her small haven so near, she could feel her pluck quickly draining from her. Her legs wobbled to get her attention—they would get her to the door and no further. A walk back to the lobby was out of the question.

No matter. She could feel her way. And getting the key in the lock would be a simple trick. She'd done it dozens of times. She could do it in the dark.

Blair walked into the shadows and reached out for the wall, counting the doors as she passed them.

One.

Two.

There should be a table.

There was.

Three.

Four.

She couldn't bluster away the image of that shadowy creature standing behind her yet again, lying in wait for the moment she would turn her attention to unlocking her door. Her heart jumped and bumped in her chest as she struggled to find the keyhole. She'd expected the task to be so much easier.

Finally, the key slid home and she turned it. Refusing to act the ninny, she walked quietly inside and closed the door behind her, as if a scream wasn't building in her chest and demanding to be released.

Locking the door in the dark was a simple feat. She blew out her breath in controlled silence, then pressed her back to the door. Her hood was heavy as she lifted it from her hair and pushed it onto her shoulders. Next, she freed a heavy comb from her nape and shook her head, welcoming the cool air into her curls.

"So," came a dark voice from beside her. "*Vous este une femme.*" *You are a woman.*

As she jumped away, her hand went immediately to her skirt pocket. Her fingers stretched through the hole inside which led to a scabbard secured to her thigh. She wrapped her fingers around the hilt of Wolfkiller, but before she could pull the blade free, hands grasped at her, then arms descended around her, encircling her, holding her arms to her sides.

"Whoa, there. *Vous n'este pas dans danger, madesmoiselle. Je vous assure.*" *You are not in danger. I assure you.*

An Englishman, no matter his lack of accent. The mixture of English and French made it clear enough. The hunter had become the hunted; they'd noticed her after all.

Fighting would hardly be wise, but struggling came naturally. They wouldn't hurt her. She'd been watching them so long, she felt as if she already knew them. But she'd be damned if she would concede control of her person to anyone.

The one she fought against had to be the large one they called Ash who always wore black and spoke not half as often as his friends—the man whose posture tensed when she came near, the man who invoked a bit of tension in herself, truth be told. And the more she struggled, the closer he held her.

She stilled, the realization much more disturbing than being held against her will. She was pressed against his chest, her head turned with her ear against his heart. Heaven help her but he was a tall drink. And wide as well. She was squeezed up against the center of him but there was room to both sides. He could likely hold two of her just as easily.

A rather stirring scent tickled her nose and not at all unpleasant. She refused to take a deep breath of him, however. Not only would she give away the fact that he had some effect on her, but she suspected she might enjoy his scent so much she'd never be able to scrub it from her memory. And scrub it she would. The horrors of war and the search for Martin were memories she soon planned to load onto a ship with her brother and send away.

Blair huffed, as much to expel the stranger from her nose as to let him know she was finished with being held down.

"Parlez Anglais?" he asked.

"Oui." She let him know two things with her strained answer, that she did speak French, and that he was holding her too tightly.

He loosened his hold, but only just.

"Forgive me, Mademoiselle. For all I knew you would run me through with your impressive blade before I had a chance to speak."

Impressive? When had the man ever seen Wolfkiller?

It was a question she would not voice. Instead, she asked, "The lobby would not do well enough for a conversation?"

He laughed, his low voice rumbling deep in his chest and into her own.

"I'm going to move you away from the door, now. I'll not have you escaping before I have the chance to light a candle. And I must remove your weapon. Surely you can understand why."

She took up struggling again, but it impeded him not at all.

Slowly, but easily, he moved her hand away from her pocket, then grasped her wrist with his other hand, completely controlling her with one arm alone. Slowly, without a bit of conscience, he slid his free hand down along her side.

She gasped. "Ye wouldna dare!"

His hand froze, but she suspected it wasn't her words that gave him pause, but her accent. He'd thought her French and she'd just let her brogue slip what with the shock of having a man dare to put his hands on her. He took a slow breath, then another, his chest inflating against her each time he did so.

"I beg your pardon," he said, but his hand resumed its path down her side. When his fingers searched the folds of her skirt for her pocket, she fought with everything she had left, finding to her surprise that his presence inspired more strength than the bit she'd walked through the door with.

But she couldn't simply stand there and allow him to find the hole in her pocket.

She could no longer afford to fight like a lady.

"Get yer hands from me ye great bloody bastard!"

If he was shocked by her language, it failed to slow his search. He spun her around and pressed her against the wall with his body, still holding tight to her hand, which pinned her arm between her body and the wall. She screamed, for all the good it would do her. Any who heard her voice would likely assume she'd seen a wee mousie, or a rat.

The lack of comment from his friends told her they were not in the room.

She was alone, in the dark, with the man they called Ash. The fascinating one. The man who slayed the dragons of her nightmares and stomped out the evil faeries who'd taken her brother and had come for her.

The man whose hand was roaming up and down her leg!

He finally found the pocket, then reached *beyond* it, and she realized the man must have been watching her closely indeed to know where her best weapon lay.

Then she remembered his first words to her. "*So, you are a woman.*"

He hadn't been surprised she was a woman. He'd *known!*

She clamped her mouth tight and bucked against him, then froze when she realized such a move would be the most foolish of all.

The weight of him was suddenly gone, as was the weight of her dagger. She hadn't even noticed him touch her leg. Also gone were his hands and the heat from his proximity. Blair was simply grateful for the darkness that concealed her blush, for she *was* blushing. Her cheeks burned as if she'd laid a hot coal to each of them.

"Seat yourself," he said quietly, his voice further away, perhaps near the table with the candlestick and flint box—against the far wall.

Since the only seat was the bed, he couldn't be surprised when she remained standing. Instead, she began inching her way silently toward the door, intending to run. She began searching her pocket for the key.

Of course she'd been prepared for a confrontation with her Englishmen. If it came down to it, she'd planned to ask for their aid in finding her brother, explain why she believed the men who took Martin were the same men who had kidnapped their friend. But at the moment, she could only be outraged at being. . .handled. Though she could not honestly say he'd caused her any pain, she was fashed at being handled so. . .completely. He'd taken all control from her. She would never forgive him for it.

She'd been relieved that the creature in the darkness had proved to be this man and not the hotel attendant, or some other Frenchman with evil intentions. And that relief, combined with her outrage, then combined again with her uncontrollable fascination with him, left her emotions fairly rioting in her chest.

Even if there were a proper light and proper seat, she had no intention of carrying on an intelligent conversation when the last thing she felt was intelligent. She wasn't certain she could speak clearly enough to berate him, let alone discuss the reason she'd been following him. She might well end up in a puddle of tears.

No. Better to run and fight another day, when she was in fighting condition. Perhaps after she'd had a good night's sleep, a good meal. . .and her brother at her side.

Her traitorous boot scratched the floor.

He struck a flint. The sparks arced, and then died.

She had to get out before the light caught!

"If you continue toward the door," he growled, "I will have no choice but to tie you to the bed before I continue. And I'll do it even though I have your key."

She held her breath in surprise, then chided herself for believing him. He was a gentleman, after all. No gentleman would—

"I advise you not to test me on this."

Blair stomped her foot—a habit from childhood she sought to leave behind, but resurfaced when she was particularly frustrated. It only served to embarrass her.

He chuckled darkly and resumed his assault on the flint.

She frantically searched her pockets, but found nothing. Then she groped for the door and pulled at the doorknob to no avail.

When the flame took to the candle, she pulled up her hood, tugging it too far forward for the light to reach her face. She drew her cloak tightly about her before she turned back to him. She'd be damned if she'd allow him a good look at her, and he'd be damned to Hell if he tried to put his hands on her again. But even Hell wouldn't be able to hold him, she thought. If she killed this man, he would haunt her mercilessly. And she was haunted enough.

Heaven help her—when had she become such a monster she would think so lightly of killing a man?

She pushed the thought aside. In her current predicament, examining what was left of her soul would need to wait.

He lifted the candle.

She turned her head aside.

He sat the candle on the table. When she turned back, he gestured toward the bed.

"Sit."

She didn't move.

He huffed out a breath, then pointed to bed again.

"Please, sit. I assure you I shall remain standing. You have my word as a gentleman."

Again, she made no response. His honor be damned.

Finally, he nodded, as if he'd given her permission to refuse his direction. She nearly sat just to spite him.

His attention fell to the dagger in his hand and he lifted her precious Wolfkiller into the weak light to inspect it.

"Viking," he murmured.

"Yes."

"You wouldn't know its name, I suppose?"

"Wolfkiller."

His brows rose. One corner of his mouth lifted. "Where did you come by it?"

If she said nothing, he might well believe she'd stolen it and assume it only fair to take it from her. But if she admitted she inherited it, he might learn who she was. And her secrets were the only things she could keep from his control.

"It's mine," she finally said, in the same tone she'd used with the stable hand in Sedan.

He nodded, as if he'd just worked something out in his mind. He laid the weapon on the table as if it had become too much of a distraction for him, then flipped the triangular hilt once so one of the three edges of the blade lay flat.

He glanced briefly at her skirts in a way that made heat flush through her body to the roots of her hair. But when she realized where he was looking, she suspected he wanted a close look at Wolfkiller's scabbard, and that was all.

She folded her arms in what she hoped was a clear message—*someone will get hurt if ye try.*

He shook his head and shooed the idea away with his hand, smart man. A lock of hair across his forehead vied for her attention, but she resisted.

And there they stood, facing off. Her back was to the door that would not open. His back was to the small window that looked out upon the stable yard, or rather, would have if one could see through the dirt. As the only covering for the window, however, the dirt was fine where it was.

The bed was small and wedged against the wall to allow enough room for the door to swing wide. Her large bag sat at the foot. She might have hidden it beneath the bed if she didn't fear small animals might make off with her things while she was out during the day.

The hearth was a square of blue miss-matched tiles that barely reached her knee. The hole in the middle had no grate and might hold a single log, though it didn't look like it had been used for quite some time. The only other piece of furniture was the small table. The only source of warmth was the candle.

Well, the candle and the tall man standing beside it.

She was suddenly embarrassed by the room, as if it defined her somehow, and not as someone who would ever have conversation with her noble visitor.

He turned his head to the side. "I feel it my duty to inform you, lass, that by holding your cloak so tight around you. . ."

When understanding dawned, she let the cloth loose and leaned back against the wall, refusing to show her mortification, hoping her knees would hold out until she could get the man to leave. Then she would drag her bed over to the door and tie the knob to the bedpost. She'd no ken how he'd gotten inside—

Unless the attendant had let him in! No wonder the other man had smirked at her when she'd asked for her key. She'd laughed at his advances, then turned out to be the sort of woman a rich man would seek out for. . .

Well, no wonder.

"I'll take my dagger, if ye please," she said, bringing his attention back to her. She realized he'd looked away while she'd adjusted her cloak.

Ever the gentleman. Well, the gentleman had bloody better give her back her weapon!

"You may have it when our business is concluded," he replied. "I would not leave you defenseless."

No, of course he wouldn't *leave* her that way, but as long as he was there, it was how he wanted her.

"Oh," she said, "and haven't ye done just that?"

He waved away her concern.

She wanted to break his flippant fingers.

He lowered his chin and stared into her eyes as if he knew exactly where they were in the shadows of her cowl.

"You have been following us since we reached Reims. You will tell me why."

Blair's wee spit of anger died. She didn't have the strength to keep it up. But no matter, it was foolish to make war with the man when she so desperately needed his help. Perhaps it was her own desperation she was angry over.

Wedging herself against the door was the only detail that kept her from puddling on the floor. Well, that and a bit of stubborn pride in her bones. Eventually, she gave that up too.

"My brother was kidnapped near here. I was instructed to take his ransom to an abandoned monastery, but no one approached me. I felt someone watching, but none would answer when I called out."

"Did you have the money?"

He sounded skeptical, which she found slightly offensive. She wished she could tell him she had money aplenty, but there was no reason to lie. One look about her room was enough to tell him the truth.

"Nay. I had no way to raise a ransom, but I thought perhaps they might be willing to negotiate. In any case, when I overheard ye and yer friends talking of another kidnapping, I hoped your man and my brother had been taken by the same lot, that if ye found the villains, I'd find my brother."

"And your brother's name?"

She shook her head. "I'll not have ye tossing it about where the kidnappers might hear, aye?"

"You can trust me not to." His voice rang with promise, the timber of it rattled her very bones.

She ignored both. "I'll not be in yer way. But I will follow ye about, aye? As long as there is hope. . ."

As she spoke, his frown deepened.

Finally, she shrugged. "Ye doona believe me?"

He shook his head. "I believe you, lass. We had just hoped. . ." His voice grew faint at the last and he cleared his throat. "We had hoped you had been sent by the villains. That you might finally approach us with new ransom demands. That we might be able to find him. . .through you."

She grimaced. "When it was *I* who hoped to find my brother through *ye*."

He stepped forward suddenly. She jumped in reaction, then calmed when he held out the hilt of her dagger. She took it, then turned to the side while she slid it through her pocket and into its sheath.

He stepped back again and released a heavy breath as if he were trying to blow out an entire candelabrum of candles. Since he seemed to have something of import to say, she gave him her attention.

"We have only one place left to look, I'm afraid. We'll leave at first light. If we find nothing by tomorrow evening, I do not know what we will do."

Blair stepped forward, closing the distance between them, then pushed back her hood. "Ye canna give up. Ye're all the hope I have."

He smiled, then reached out to slide a finger along the side of her cheek, quite near her rather visible beauty mark. And the thought struck her—perhaps they were called beauty marks because she felt rather beautiful when he touched her there.

"Well, I cannot crush the hopes of a fellow countrywoman, can I?"

She tried to ignore the way her body vibrated in time with his baritone.

"Nay, ye canna," she teased. "I'm certain there is a rule, somewhere."

He smiled all the way to his eyes, but never removed his finger from her face. "I must confess I'm relieved you are not in league with the blackhearts. It would have been a pity to hang you."

Her breath caught. "Would ye truly hang a woman?"

"I would bring anyone to justice who dared harm a friend of mine."

She smiled. "That sounds rather nice."

He frowned. "I just admitted I would see a woman hanged and you see something nice about it?"

She laughed. "No. It must be nice to have a friend such as ye. Someone who would so fiercely protect ye against all others, as a brother would."

"As I am certain your brother will protect you once again."

She tried not to roll her eyes at the thought. Poor Martin had been the one needing the protecting. How her father ever thought her brother should go to war without her watching his back was a mystery. But if she hadn't been so crowding him, her brother might never run off to gamble that night—the night he'd never returned.

"And of course," the Englishman's voice demanded her attention once again, "*we* can protect you well enough I should think, until your brother is found."

She smiled her appreciation, if only for the token of hope. Then for the life of her, she could think of nothing further to say. He seemed to have the same problem. And still, his finger remained.

Their gazes locked. Their breathing adjusted to the same cadence. And finally he drew the digit out toward her chin, which she lifted without thought. His face was slowly lost in shadow as he leaned down, slowly, as if he might press his lips to hers.

Fascinating.

She held still and breathed ever so carefully.

When he was close enough for his own breath to flutter across her cheek, he paused. It was impossible to tell what he might be thinking. But then suddenly, he straightened.

She'd been around war enough to know a retreat when she saw one. But still he couldn't seem to release her completely, allowing that finger to drop to her cloak, just over her collar bone, where it toyed with the curl of hair that lay against it. Then his touch was gone.

The contact was far too brief for her liking, even though it left her quaking on the inside. His hands disappeared behind his back, but he held his ground.

"The air is getting cold," he said.

"Aye. It has a chill about it," she chirped.

It was not entirely unpleasant, she admitted, standing and watching each other breathe in and out. He looked no more uncomfortable than she, but must have felt the need to fill the silence.

"I expect it to rain tonight," he said. "Likely tomorrow as well."

"Aye." She bit her lip, waiting for him to explain what the weather had to do with their mutual quest.

"You will remain here tomorrow. Stay by the fire."

She rolled her eyes. Hadn't he noticed? She had no fire. And she wasn't the sort of Scotswoman to take instruction from bloody anyone, let alone an English *man*— the unification of their countries be damned. It was a fact she could not remember the last time she did another's bidding, including her father's.

When she gave no reply, he opened his mouth yet again. "I will come to you tomorrow night and report what we discover. You have my word."

She raised a brow.

He lowered his chin and searched her eyes.

"Give me your name," he said softly.

Blair gave her head a slight shake that her hair was eager to exaggerate.

"Give me your name or I shall name you myself." He tilted his head. His dark eyes crinkled at the corners and he bit his lip, no doubt to keep from smiling.

She laughed, then shook her head again in earnest. If he planned to knock on doors tomorrow, she didn't want him tossing her name about for any reason. It might endanger her brother if the kidnappers discovered her snooping about.

"Fine." He folded his arms, then lifted one hand to rub across the lower half of his face. He tapped his lips as if deep in thought. "I shall call you. . .Scotia."

She shrugged, wondering if he might take hold of her again, wishing he had a reason to do so.

He looked a wee bit disappointed in her lack of excitement for her new name. He then dropped his hands to his sides and looked at the door behind her.

"Well, Miss Scotia, we are headed for Givet Faux in the morning. Until the Reign of Terror, it functioned as a prison, and I assure you a former prison is no place for a. . .woman."

He'd nearly said lady, but had stopped himself as if he dared not insult her. Of course it was his pause that insulted, but what could she expect, following them about like a spy, living in a mouse hole without a fire? Not the behavior of a proper lady, that. But then, she'd never been one. Her father might have called her Princess, but that, too, was about as appropriate for her as the name Scotia.

"I expect you to be here when we return," he said seriously. "If we do not return with Northwick and your brother, we shall make our next plan. Agreed?"

After a moment's consideration, she said, "I'll be happy to sit in on yer next strategy meetin'. Thank ye."

Although he stood perfectly still, she sensed he'd like nothing more than to put her over his knee and spank her until she saw reason. She nearly felt sorry for the man, he seemed so frustrated. But of course she would not wish him to lose sleep over her, especially the night before he might be chasing villains on her behalf.

There was nothing for it but to lie.

She sighed dramatically.

"Fine," she said. "I surrender. A day of rest in front of a warm fire sounds too lovely by half."

He gifted her with a charming smile she suspected he did not share often.

"I'll arrange it," he said and stepped around her, toward the door.

"Arrange what?" She demanded, suddenly afraid he might take all control from her again. Was he planning to have her locked in her room? Heaven knew he could likely afford to arrange anything he wished.

"Your fire, Scotia. It seems the hotel has been a bit lax in your care tonight. I'll make certain your meals are delivered as well. Of course, you would be more than welcome to spend tomorrow in our suite."

She shook her head. She understood that he was merely offering the use of his finer rooms only while he and his friends were away. But the last thing she wanted was to start earning the reputation her father expected, even if it were only in the eyes of a small town near Belgium, or simply in the eyes of one hotel attendant.

She considered protesting his offer of food and fire, for surely, if the meals were delivered and she was not there to eat them, the food would go to the mice. And come whatever the weather, she was not about to lie abed and grow soft while her brother might be languishing in Givet Faux, or whatever the place was called. If this man and his friends stumbled upon the nest of vipers, Blair was going to be there to make certain Martin Balliol was rescued from harm. If a certain English gentleman wished to berate her afterwards for not staying behind tending a fire that didn't need tending, then so be it.

But there was no need to ruin the man's sleep over it. Let him learn the truth tomorrow, that she was not easily swayed by a gentle touch or a pat on the head.

She smiled and gave a courtly curtsy to her would-be gallant and led him to the door. He pulled her key from his coat pocket, unlocked the door, then pressed the warm metal into her palm. He walked out into the darkness, but if he turned back, she didn't wait to see it.

As she locked the door behind him, she hoped his scent might linger just until she drifted off to sleep, for the memory of his presence, and his touch, might serve to keep her warm while the sheets lost their chill.

But she wasn't bloody swayed.

CHAPTER THREE

Dawn rode in on a wave of rain that threatened to turn the stable yard into a permanent pond. Ash shrugged off the notion of bad omens. They would find North today. They must. He refused to return to Hotel Place Ducale with empty hands yet again.

He took a tight hold on the cinch and pulled up. The horse before him stamped in protest and he realized he'd put too much of this morning's frustrations into his task. He tossed up his hands and gestured for the groom to finish the job. No sense punishing an animal for the sins of a foolish woman. And that was precisely what he'd been doing—punishing everyone because that woman, that Scottish imp, had left the hotel long before he'd ever stirred from his bed.

Thunder crashed. The horses murmured nervously. Ash stood under the eaves and witnessed a new wave of rain double the size of the pond in less than a minute, flooding all paths out of the yard.

He wondered where the imp was hiding, waiting to follow his little band out of town. He almost wished she was out in the open, suffering the wrath of heaven on her head for not staying put as she was told. As she'd promised to do!

But that was not strictly true. She'd agreed that his suggestion had sounded lovely. She hadn't agreed to abide by his dictates.

Damn the clever wench.

Damn the lovely clever wench.

He should have known she was not French. Only a stubborn Scot would have followed them across France in miserable weather.

A stubborn Scot with dazzling red curls.

He imagined all those curls to be black and straight about now, dripping with the weight of the rain. And a little river of water trailing down the side of her face, catching on that unnerving beauty mark, then continuing down to that long pretty neck.

Damn her if she caught a chill!

The thunder crashed again, though much further away, and like a colt called by its mother, the rain looked up and hurried away. Soon there was little more than a drop or two to keep the wide puddle from settling.

Pity. He wouldn't mind a bit of wet if it meant it would chase Scotia inside somewhere to sit by a fire and await his return. He tried to convince himself she would do just that, for he needed his wits about him today instead of worrying over the relative comfort of a strange woman who did not know well enough to take what was offered.

Her room had clearly not seen a fire in quite some time. He'd found no food stuffs in the place before he'd inadvertently doused his candle. And yet the woman had come in straight from the road, with no apparent intention of leaving again in search of her supper. What gentleman could have continued to call himself a gentleman and left her cold and hungry?

He'd ordered that mousy fellow to take her enough wood for a week's worth of fires and three meals a day until she quit the place, even if she chose to stay on another month. It was the least he could have done for someone on his same desperate quest. But she'd had the gall to cancel his orders!

Of course she had sound reason for following him and his friends. Odds were high that if her brother had been kidnapped in the same area to which their own search had led them, both North and the brother had been taken by the same villains. But rescue was a cause best left for men, not some far-too-lovely wench with only a dagger for defense—and that weapon not easy at hand.

He tried not to think about where that same dagger might reside at that very moment.

Before mounting, Ash resisted the urge to strike a blow to the wood beam against which he'd been leaning. If she were watching from somewhere nearby, he refused to display his frustration. No doubt she would assume herself to be the cause. No doubt she would preen over her success at having moved him to a show of temper.

No one moved the Earl of Ashmoore to anything.

Well, anything but revenge, that was, for laying hands on his friend.

He breathed deeply of the cool moist air and forced all thought of the woman behind him. Of course *behind him* was exactly where he'd find her, just as soon as they left the periphery of the city.

His mind should be on Northwick!

And as they set out for Givet Faux, he sent a thought to his friend.

Don't give up, North! We're coming!

~ ~ ~

Ransoming of soldiers was a despicable practice, but Ash acknowledged it was not the most despicable. Even more vile was the act of sending ransom demands to the families of those soldiers who had fallen in battle. If those blackhearts could get payments from those families before the battle reports were received, they could make a pretty penny without the need to capture, secure, and feed anyone at all.

But Northwick hadn't fallen in battle. He'd been with his battalion in Brussels when Napoleon surrendered, and the Four Kings—North, Stanley, Harcourt, and Ash—were to meet in Paris. North had never arrived. Nothing would have kept him away unless some*one* kept him away.

Ash and the others had learned of the ransom demands only after the exchange date had come and gone. But they'd been hopeful a second demand would be made. Ash had men posted at all North's estates, watching for just such a message. As time passed, however, he'd stopped expecting that message from England.

Scotia's brother was in similar straits. His ransom demands had been delivered to her, which meant the villains knew she'd been traveling with the young man. When she'd gone to the location of the exchange, however, no one had shown themselves. She'd admitted it—either they no longer had her brother to give her, or they knew she wasn't able to pay and so hadn't bothered to meet her.

Even so, she hoped. But he wondered if the thing for which she hoped. . .was revenge.

As they neared the outskirts of Charleville, Ash allowed Stanley and Harcourt to take the lead. It was possibly the first time he had done so. But if they were about to find North, shouldn't he be rushing forward, anxious to know, one way or the other? Was he so fearful that they were about to exhaust their last bit of hope?

As they struck out on the open road, however, he acknowledged the true reason he had lagged behind—so he might turn back unnoticed, to see if a certain caped figure followed behind.

He was both disappointed and relieved as he watched her enter the roadway a quarter of a kilometer after they'd passed her hiding spot. At least he knew where she was, he told himself. Of course he was disheartened the rain had yet to dissuade her, but his lips tightened in a slight smile for a woman who was not easily dissuaded. Too bad her stubbornness did not lean toward more genteel pursuits. Wallpaper she simply must have. . . A young man's eye she must catch. . .

Stanley's curse brought his attention forward again.

"Damn me, but there she is again," he said, gesturing over his shoulder. "I'd begun to think she was some charm of bad luck and if we set out today without her, it might be the day we find North."

Ash held his tongue. He'd told his friends all about their exchange the night before. Or, at least everything but how close he'd come to kissing the woman. But no use in confessing something that never happened.

Harcourt looked back as well, then looked at Ash, then at Stan.

"Perhaps she *is* our good luck charm. After all, we've been searching for over a month and since she began following us about, we've found one lead after another."

Harcourt had always been the most cheerful among them. Ash only hoped his cheerful friend would find something encouraging to say if this chateau turned up no Northwick and no new leads. For it was a certainty, this was their last hope.

It was only a matter of time before a cunning man like Napoleon escaped Elba, and if they were called back to the army. . .

He shook his head and refused to consider the possibilities. Besides the worst and unacceptable outcome—not finding Northwick—he also dreaded the need to explain to a lovely Scottish woman that her brother was likely lost to her.

It was indeed fortunate for everyone involved that Napoleon had surrendered. If he hadn't, Ash and the others would not have been together when word came of Northwick's abduction, and consequently, his parent's death. The couple had been travelling to Hull, to make the crossing to Zeebrugge to pay their son's ransom, when they were attacked and their carriage overturned. If it weren't for the coachman surviving the attack, Ash might not have learned of the abduction for months. By then, the villains might well have given up hope and disposed of an Earl for whom they would receive no ransom.

If Stanley, Harcourt, and he had learned of it all while still engaged in battle, Wellington might have had to deal with the desertion of three of his officers, for they would have put North's safety over the fate of the coalition, no question.

Yes, it was a fine thing, providential even, that the Emperor had agreed to his containment on Elba Island when he had. Ash prayed that by the time the ambitious man found a way to resume the war, Northwick would be safe, and by God, sound.

Everhardt entered the road and smoothly brought his horse alongside Ash's. He lifted a hand in a habitual salute, but when Ash gave a quick shake of his head, the man lifted his hat and scratched his head before pulling the hat back in place and dropping his arm.

"Not the right place for saluting, I'm afraid," Ash said.

Everhardt nodded. "Right you are, my lord."

Ash waited for Stanley and Harcourt to fall back within earshot before he asked, "Did you find someone?"

"Yes, sir." Everhardt spoke low, but clearly. "He claims to live inside the place. Says the keep is in the control of a Frenchman who claims his family owns the property, and there is a Scot that acts as an enforcer of sorts. It's an auberge of sorts, housing for soldiers down on their luck and unable to go home just yet, he says. A bunch of deserters from all sides, it sounds like." He paused. "Perhaps it's housing one or two men who are not allowed to leave, my lord."

Ash nodded, acknowledging the man's effort to lift his hopes.

"Anything else?" he asked.

Everhardt nodded again. "He said the gates are not locked. No guards. Just the one Scot. A body can walk right up to the door and knock."

"I suppose we'll have to do just that." Ash looked first at Stan, then at Harcourt, who grinned before he turned back to face the road.

Stan frowned. "Did the man say why they call it the Palais des Morts?"

Everhardt smiled. "He did, Your Grace. Said it's called the Palace of the Dead from days of The Plague."

Stan continued to frown, but now it was aimed at the road behind them. It took no imagination to know what he was looking at.

"Still with us," he said. "Are you certain we can't dissuade her? It hardly sounds like the kind of place to allow a woman."

Ash shrugged. "I cannot stop her, Stanley. Feel free to try."

His chest clenched suddenly at the thought of his overly handsome friend slowing his mount to have conversation with his Scotia. Of course she belonged to no one, least of all him, but he'd rather enjoyed being the mediator between her and his friends. No need for them all to get chummy.

But contrary to his unspoken wishes, Stan did slow his horse. Ash, Harcourt, and Everhardt continued on. Though Ash usually sought to keep North's possible condition from his mind, to keep from going mad, he now summoned the memory of his friend's face, to remind him why they must continue on their quest and disregard the safety of a woman who refused to keep herself safe. Besides that, who was he to begrudge Stanley's attempts to persuade the chit to turn back?

The Palais des Morts, as the locals called it, could only be another five kilometers north. They'd come at least that far already. It wouldn't be long now.

The more pleasant name for the keep was the Givet Faux—a smaller replica of the citadel called Charlemont, at the true city of Givet, and ten kilometers even farther up the River Meuse. It was supposedly built as a jest, but soon it became clear that it was meant to lure innocent travelers and merchants who were yet unaware of the true site of Charlemont. Goods and supplies meant for the large citadel and the city of Givet were sometimes waylaid at Givet Faux, the false Givet, if travelers were strangers to the area. And with Givet Faux lying in the direct path between the great city of Reims, France and the Belgian border, there were plenty of victims who fell prey to the pranksters. After a while, however, word spread far enough and wide enough that most travelers kept to the lee side of the Meuse when passing by the notorious keep.

With such avoidance, the settlement hadn't been able to sustain itself and had corrupted into a den for the corrupt. A perfect home for kidnappers, no question. But what den of vipers would be guarded by a single Scot? This was the question that kept his hopes from rising too high.

Of course he wasn't in the habit of worrying over the size of his opponents, but if a single man protected an entire castle, small or not, he might be a challenge even for the notorious Earl of Ashmoore, the deadliest gentleman of the ton.

He smiled at the memory of the night Northwick christened him with the title. He'd knocked unconscious five pugilists in a row before stopping for a drink. And after that drink, he'd taken on ten others. Later, their carriage had been attacked by five well-armed men and he'd insisted on taking on the lot of them himself. His friends had refused, and faced the band by his side, but it was the knife from Ash's boot and his already bloodied fists that had taken all five men to the ground. None would have died from their wounds but the largest man who refused to cease his attack until he had ceased breathing.

"Sometimes an animal must be put down," Stan had said.

Harcourt had attributed Ash's ability to Battle Fever that must have still been raging in his blood from the previous bouts.

Northwick hadn't cared the why of it. He'd merely been grateful to be standing beside the deadliest gentleman of the ton and not opposite him. And the sobriquet had stuck.

Perhaps he should merely have it announced at Givet Faux that he was on his way. Perhaps they would flee and leave Northwick sitting on the front steps with a written apology pinned to his coat.

What a sight that would be!

Dear God, please let North be alive, he plead for the thousandth time. *Let us not be too late!*

He'd nearly forgotten about Stanley and was about to urge his horse to a gallop when he heard his friend rejoining them from behind. Stan's face was flushed. In fact, he appeared upset.

Ash glanced over his shoulder to find the dark form of Scotia still trailing them, but a bit further back than she had been.

"What did you say to her?" he demanded, then hoped he hadn't sounded as defensive to his friend's ears as he had to his own.

"Stubborn. . . Ridiculous. . ." Stan shook his head and took a breath.

"What did she say?" Harcourt asked, slowing to come alongside their handsome friend.

Stan rolled his eyes. "How the bloody hell should I know? When I stopped my horse, she stopped hers, refusing to come nearer. When I started toward her—slowly, mind you—she turned her horse and retreated, watching me over her shoulder as she went. When I stopped, she stopped. It is as if there was a long stick between us that would not allow us to get even a step closer than we were." He frowned at

Ash. "You never said she was disfigured. Is there perhaps something wrong with her face that she would be embarrassed to have me see her?"

Ash shook his head, then laughed. He glanced back again and found her following at exactly the pace of their little band, then he laughed again.

"Do not take it too much to heart, Stanley," Harcourt soothed. "It must be that to some women, you are simply too handsome to bear."

The jibe served to cheer his fair-haired, too-blessed friend. Harcourt was pleased, as usual, with his own wit. And Ash was pleased his Scotia, whom he determined to stop thinking of as *his*, had yet to be exposed, face to face, to the perfection that was Stanley, Viscount Forsgreen, the future Duke of Rochester. He also realized how long it had been since the three of them had known a reason to laugh.

God willing, there would soon be another.

CHAPTER FOUR

The morning's ride was tearing Blair apart, but not for the reasons it should.

Of course she was filled with equal parts hope and dread—hope she was about to find her brother, and dread she was not. But what distracted her was another pairing—a wish and a fear.

She wished the large one wanted a word with her half so urgently as the blond one did, but apparently her dark visitor had nothing to say to her that morning. Her fear, of course, had everything to do with how angry he must be that she'd gone against his wishes—er, dictates, truth be told. The poor man was simply in the learning stages—learning she did as she damn well pleased.

No doubt he'd imagined her knitting by the fire in all patience until he got around to remembering her, got around to telling her whether or not he'd found her brother.

All patience, my arse.

Of course she'd been treated thusly all her life. No man wants to admit that a woman might defend herself just as well as he could, and in her case, better—except for the previous night's encounter in her room, when it would have been a shame to harm such a pretty man who wanted nothing more than a conversation. After examining the memory all morning, she could come to no other conclusion for the mercy she showed him. Any other man might have suffered a hot candle to his eye for daring to lay hands to her person or her blade. By all rights, it should have been *he* who searched frantically for the key, to escape *her*.

In the end, he'd turned out to be no different than most men when he'd insisted she allow him to make arrangements for her. Most men wanted to prove she was witless while at the same time proving themselves to be gallant heroes. Most men she'd known were fools.

The question was, how foolish would these Englishmen turn out to be? When she insisted on accompanying them inside this Givet Faux, would they make a fuss, or not? She could hardly wait to find out.

Her mount stumbled, then danced to one side. Had it sensed her anticipation?

It came to a halt, complaining as it did so.

She quickly unhooked her right knee and slid to the ground on the left, next to a raised hoof. She hoped she'd acted quickly enough, before the animal was badly hurt. Thankfully, the beast stood still while she bent beside it.

Embedded in the pad of its foot, and held tight by the well-worn shoe, was a large rock with jagged edges that had cut into the pad and drawn blood. She removed the stone. The foot was bruised, the beast in pain and shouldn't be ridden.

She patted the leg, then released it. She straightened, then glanced down the   road where the three gentlemen, and a fourth—the man they called Everhardt—had stopped at the top of a small rise. They had turned their mounts to face her, most likely when her horse had complained.

Her difficulty was obvious. The fact she did not remount should have been explanation enough. She could not ride her horse. Which meant she must needs ride behind one of them. They would, after all, arrive in the same place, just as they had every day in the past weeks. Surely they realized. . .

Ash nudged his horse forward and in doing, nudged her heart into beating rather faster than usual at the thought of sitting so close to him, with her arms around his middle. But after a few steps, he reined his beast to a halt.

She could nearly hear his thoughts as he thought them.

If I do not rescue you now, I get what I wanted in the first place.

She tried to convey her own message with the lift of her chin.

Ye canna stop me, so I suggest you take me with ye.

He lowered his own chin, staring at her like a bull preparing to charge, and answered her with a slight, nearly imperceptible shake of his head.

She stomped her foot before she could refrain. Cold water splashed beneath her skirts onto her thick woolen socks, reminding her that acts of temper rarely worked to her advantage.

She glared back at the man, but shrugged to mask her roiling emotions. She then turned and plucked up a tuft of grass, combined it with a ball of soft mud, and bent next to the horse once again. With one hand, she lifted the foot into view; with the other she pushed the soft mass against the wound. When she was hopeful it would stay in place, she stood and urged the beast forward. By the time she tossed a defiant glare at the men on the hill, they were gone.

Leading a wounded animal along, it took a good half hour before she caught sight of Givet Faux. The curtain wall of the modest-sized citadel had crumbled away enough to reveal four horses in the bailey. Everhardt stood beside them. The other three Englishmen were nowhere to be seen.

Blair could hardly beat on the door and demand to be admitted, though she wished to do just that. Equally unwise would be to interrupt whatever plan the men had hatched between them. The only option to her now was to wait and see if the men emerged with their friend or her brother. The fact they'd left their man outside led her to hope for less violence than she'd envisioned. But neither could she imagine how courtesy might win the day. Of course she prayed they were successful. And if they were, she might even forgive them excluding her.

Martin was all. If Martin were saved, she could forgive anything.

She imagined them emerging with her brother and the image gave her permission of a sort, to hope, to believe that Martin was actually inside. She was usually so careful not to get her hopes up, but this place was just too right, too accurate a depiction of the evil fortress housed by men evil enough to take her brother.

Somewhere from the recesses of her heart, she heard a small warning, like the warbling of a bird, a warning not to expect too much.

She shook the warning away as she led her poor mount into the trees that ran up the near side of the keep. Of course she would not stand before the steps with her arms flung wide, but she would be close enough to get to her brother quickly, especially if they all came out fighting.

Finally, she found a deeply shadowed spot from which she could watch the front door and Everhardt. Whatever happened, he would react first. She would have to settle for reacting to him.

And she waited.

Everhardt mounted one of the horses. The rains returned and intensified. He dismounted and wedged himself beneath one horse's neck.

At least the poor man would have the luxury of one warm shoulder, she thought as she pulled her hood forward, then stood to avoid a small channel of water growing beside her. As for Blair, she was perfectly warm thanks to her tightly woven dress and cloak. The wool repelled the rain and kept all of her warm but the tip of her nose.

The rains subsided, and still they waited.

Everhardt had apparently deemed it long enough and pulled a sword from his side, then headed for the entrance.

Blair's heart jumped into her throat and she considered calling out to him to wait for her, that she'd join him. But the opening of the keep's doors froze her feet to the spot.

She wasn't brave enough to look, yet she was unable to turn away. The only compromise was to close her eyes slightly, to peek out her wet eye lashes. Her fingers gripped her own arms beneath the cloak, her fingernails biting into her skin, but she could not help herself.

The blond they called Stanley emerged first and paused at the base of the stairs. The distance was too great to see his expression. His hands were raised, but only because he was pulling on a pair of gloves.

The second man to emerge was Harcourt. He moved quickly down the steps. Blair had rarely seen the man without a smile on his face, but there was no flash of white teeth as he turned in her direction, headed for the horses. Stanley turned and followed.

Blair inhaled once, then twice, refusing to think while she waited.

The tall black form of Ash appeared. He walked slowly, took his time descending the steps. Perhaps he was waiting for his friend and Martin to be brought to him! Behind him, two men emerged, one a great deal larger than the other. They remained by the door. Were they, too, waiting for the others to emerge? Had they been so mistreated they needed help?

If she had to judge, she would guess the big man at the door to be even larger than Ash. His expression was also unreadable, but she could tell he was watching the dark Englishman closely. Everyone was watching him.

Instead of turning toward the horses, Ash walked straight ahead to the crumbling wall and took to the steps, that portion of the wall still intact. Once at the top, he put his hands to his hips and surveyed the valley of the River Meuse, as if the keep were his own castle and he was taking some measure of his surrounding kingdom. When he looked her way, her breath caught. It was if he were looking into her soul, as if, through all those trees and shadows, he knew just where she was standing.

He gave the slightest shake of his head, just as he'd done on the road. He knew her question, and the answer had been no.

But perhaps this time he was telling her not to show herself. That was reasonable. Perhaps he predicted she would run to Martin's side. . .

She shook her own head then, to stop the ridiculous thoughts from multiplying inside it.

He knew her question. *Was Martin inside?*

And the answer was *no*.

He didn't want to tell her face to face because they'd have to agree there was nowhere else to look. And maybe if they never said it aloud, it wouldn't be true.

Tears distorted his image, but she would not look away.

He continued his survey of the hillside, then dropped his arms and descended the damaged steps. Once he was mounted, the four men left Givet Faux without so much as a backward glance. As soon as they disappeared over the rise in the road, Blair numbly turned back to the keep. The smaller man slapped the larger one on the back, then the pair went inside.

The rain returned, speaking to her in hushed whispers, intent on conveying so much, yet saying nothing. She could think of nothing better to do than listen. The small channel of water at her feet began to grow again and she felt it trickle against the side of her boot, but she couldn't care enough to move.

It may have been minutes, it may have been hours, but finally the numbness wore off and she forced herself to look away from the doors from which her brother would not emerge. Martin was not inside. The reunion she'd envisioned would not happen today. It was the same disappointment as yesterday. Nothing had changed.

And yet, everything had changed.

"This is our last hope," came Ash's deep whisper from the night before.

"This was your last hope," the rain mocked as it diluted the salt-water washing down her face.

If the rain was right, if Martin was lost to her, she was a boat drifting at sea. No sail. No oar. Tied to nothing. Holding to nothing. . .

Blair looked once more at the crumbling wall, saw again the black-clad figure of Ash, watched the slight move of his head from side to side. Only this time, she imagined him mouthing the words, "No hope."

She tried not to think too unkindly of him. She'd run out of hope herself before she'd stumbled upon the men in Reims. Who was she to judge?

For the past few weeks, it was if she had been living off their faith and determination. They carried both around like giant pockets full of coins. She'd reached in, day after day, to take what she needed. But today, there was no clink of coin upon coin. No use of her asking for more.

Gone.

A wave of pain washed up inside her body and when it hit her chest, she crumbled to her knees and silently wailed her brother's name.

Martin!

Martin!

Why did he not wail back, to tell her where he was?

Martin!

She shook her head, pounded her fists on the wet mud, refused to believe he was dead. In her head she screamed her refusal to God and demanded He bring Martin back to her.

A wave of dizziness washed over her. Delirium. The journey, the quest, had worn her to the bone. She needed sleep. If only she could sleep, tomorrow she could find her

head and a direction to search. If she was but a drifting
boat, with no Martin for an anchor, she had nothing else to
do with her time but search. When she'd allowed herself
such thoughts, she'd imagined that if all hope was lost, the
searching would cease. But what else was there to do?

She swallowed and forced down the self-pity that rose
like bile from her stomach.

No. She needed no pity. Just because the Englishmen
had given up, did not mean she had to give up as well, aye?
If her choices lie between mourning her brother and hoping
unreasonably, she would hope unreasonably.

She closed her eyes to calm herself. In the darkness,
she saw again the shake of the dark one's head. But this
time, she denied his pity. He'd best save it for himself.

"Forgive me, Martin," she said aloud. "A weak
moment. But the moment has passed."

From the east came a rumble of thunder. She chose to
think of it as a fine answer.

CHAPTER FIVE

What gentleman would leave me behind with a lame horse?

He'd known where she'd been standing. He could have circled back around for her, bloody man.

Suddenly warmed by ire, she rose to her feet and gave her beast a pat for his patience. Over her shoulder, she heard a squeak and turned.

The front doors had opened again. She told herself not to expect Martin to walk out of them, but she'd forgotten to tell her heart, which tumbled and fell in her chest when a small dark man emerged. Though she saw no others, he seemed to be arguing with someone just inside. He gestured to the rainy sky, then at his boots. A moment later, his shoulders fell and he turned down the steps. The doors closed behind him.

He tucked something inside his shirt, grimaced once more at the sky, then struck out for the road on foot. What interested her most was the fact he was walking south, and swiftly, as if he would like to catch up with the men on horseback.

"Ye've as much a chance as I do," she whispered, and set off in the same direction.

She moved through the trees the way she'd come, but soon the whinny of another's horse brought her up short.

After a moment of waiting, she moved on carefully, though silence was hardly necessary with the rain knocking about in the leaves.

A dark chestnut mare stood tethered to a tree. A fine white handkerchief dripped from a branch above its head. If it weren't raining, the white flag would have been easily seen from the road.

He hadn't left her after all.

As she untied the flag, she gave God thanks the dark little man hadn't noticed the horse first. She'd traveled approximately a kilometer when she passed the man. He was splashing along in the mud. As she left him behind, he called out to her in French that it was cruel for her to ride away with two horses and leave him in the rain. Of course, it would have been foolish for any woman to stop for a strange man on such an ominous evening, even if she were capable of defending herself; she assumed the man would understand.

The storm moved on and the sun came out for one final appearance, dancing on a stage of dark pink clouds that poured over the edge of the horizon, slowly dragging the sun over with it. Blair's neck grew sore from her constant glancing sideways to watch. It cheered her like nothing but Martin's face could have done.

But the face that haunted her all the way back to Charleville belonged to another man altogether.

~ ~ ~

The wall sconce in her hallway was graced with a new candle, and a poor man's candelabra held a trio of fatter candles while protecting the solitary table from lustrous beads of wax. No doubt the attendant expected some worthy to grace the servant's hall. She only hoped he'd be wrong since again, she was of two minds about coming face to face with Ash. After all, what could they possibly have to speak about? His lack of hope? Her refusal to give up?

Indeed.

Still, as she turned her key, she held her breath and waited to see if a handsome gentleman might be waiting to wrap his arms around her once again. Which he was not. But there were signs of him everywhere.

Obviously, he'd repeated the orders she'd cancelled. The fire carried on a crackling conversation with itself on its new grate. A flagon of wine and a single glass rested on the table next to a large pillar candle, and the entire room smelled of warm wax and smoky wood. There was no lingering smell of the man himself. A note sat propped against the candle.

Please join us for supper at the auberge.

It was simply signed with the letter A.

The last thing she wanted was to sit by the fire and torture herself with images of Ash standing on a wall, shaking his head—especially when she could torture herself with his presence instead. So she donned her only other gown, another wool dress, this one with a bit more green than blue to the plaid. She put on her cloak, hoping the damp would never reach her clothes, and banked her fire.

Blair stepped outside into the gloaming and turned to the right out of habit. As she was passing the shadowed alley that led to the stables behind Hotel Place Ducale, she nearly jumped from her skin when she realized the dark little man was standing in the shadows, the one she'd passed on the road and ignored when he'd called out to her. His back was turned, but she recognized the shape and unusual size of him.

Another man joined him, then nervously glanced her way. She turned her attention back to the sidewalk and moved on. Her curiosity would not allow her to go farther than the corner, however, and once there, she pressed her back against the stone wall and edged her nose as near to the alley as she dared, to listen. If someone passed her, they might suppose she was standing under the eaves seeking shelter from the ever-pouring rain.

Her ears strained to catch the conversation. The men spoke in French. One was not happy with the price he was paid, but gave up his information because it was raining and he was too fatigued to argue.

"The English nobles you seek are around the corner in the Auberge Ducale. Where else would they be?"

Blair turned and fled toward the door of the glorified tavern. She hadn't quite decided whether or not she would join the English lords or ask for her own table, but she was determined to discover the little man's business, even if she had to sit upon Ash's lap in order to hear it. She hoped more had gone on inside Givet Faux than could be explained with a simple shake of a head. And if so, perhaps the next clue to follow would come from this little man.

Her heart jumped at the possibility, but she reined it in like a silly colt. There was only one thing to do. One task at a time. To find the gentlemen and get close enough to hear their conversation with the dark little man.

She moved to the far right aisle of the large tavern and approached the gentlemen's usual table. One look at the trio, however, and she realized she could not possibly join them. Neither would eavesdropping do her any good.

They were drunk.

CHAPTER SIX

With all drinks being poured and spilled in the large tavern, it was a true feat to have the smell of it wafting from one's table instead of the bar. But they'd managed it. When they failed to glance up at her, she moved on to the seat in the corner to her left. It was her usual spot and, on those nights she came to spy, she tried to be in it before the men arrived. It was a dark corner. Her cloak helped her blend in. Often times the serving woman peered into the shadows to make certain she was there before asking her order.

She slid around the table and into her favorite shadow making nary a sound. Since the men were oblivious to her, and the nearby tables were unoccupied, she looked her fill.

The men were seated in their usual arrangement. Ash, always with his back to the wall, faced the aisle. The other two sat at his elbows. The table contained bottles, glasses, and food—no one reached for the food. With the lead they'd had, they couldn't have eaten much of anything if they were already so deep in their cups that most of their heads were bowed.

She had seen them drink before, but never like this. And she knew, with an invisible blow to her middle, that she'd been right. They were out of ideas. Out of plans. They were giving up.

"Oh, madame, I did not see you zere," said the serving woman, suddenly blocking her view. "What shall I bring you zis evening, eh?"

Blair asked for whatever they had that was hot.

"And may I hang your cloak, madame? Near the fire perhaps?"

Considering how drunk they were, she doubted anyone would recognize her, especially if she kept her back against the seat and her red curls in the shadows.

She handed the cloak over, ignored the way the woman's eyes bulged when she got a look at her hair, and scooted as far back as possible, feeling far more exposed than she'd expected. But the woman had been right. Her cloak was wet and wanted hanging. And if the dark little man entered, he would still not recognize her.

Somewhere near the entrance, a man argued with a woman. The woman gasped and Blair could hear her footsteps as she ran away. A heartbeat later, the dark little man appeared, walking toward the gentlemen's table.

She leaned forward to listen, knowing the little man would be hard to understand, especially if he turned his back to her. But he didn't stop at the table. He walked right past it.

Was he blind? Hadn't he been asking where to find them? Were there so many similar sets of men dining or drinking in the auberge tonight, then?

He scurried through a door at the corner of the wall, then disappeared like a rat. The door closed silently behind him and a shiver rolled through her.

Blair looked back at the table where both of Ash's friends had lain their heads on their arms, while he sat back in his chair with the crown of his head resting on the wall behind him. With the candle on the table doused, it was impossible to determine whether he was sleeping or staring at her. For all the movement, they might all be dead.

The notion was impossible, but she panicked just the same.

She tried to remember what the little man had done as he passed the table. His nearest arm had been visible. She remembered recoiling at the filthiness of his sleeve. But what could he have accomplished with his other hand? A *silent* shot from a pistol? Impossible.

She pushed her table away and stood, willing the big man's eyes to widen with recognition. They did not.

She glanced at his body. Impossible to tell if he'd been wounded. Blood would hardly show well against the black of his clothing.

Deciding there were things more important at the moment than her anonymity, she stepped around her table—just as Stanley let out a snort.

She froze.

He turned his head to the other side and rested it once again on his arm.

Alive.

The big man didn't move, but she assumed he was in the same sad condition. And if they were all unharmed, then what had the little man wanted?

Again, she looked at the table while she wavered on her side of the aisle.

Had he simply stolen a bite of food on his way past? Had he been so certain noble men would have food on their table for the taking? If so, why had he paid the man in the alley for telling him where they could be found instead of purchasing food for himself?

Her eyes rested on a folded note next to a plate of rolls. Had it been there before? Was it their bill?

Her view was blocked by the serving woman once more.

"Ees somesing wrong, madame?" She looked from Blair's hands and back to her face.

"No. Nothing wrong. Something smells good, aye?" Blair sat and pulled the table back toward her so the woman could set down a bowl of soup.

"A bit of mulled wine for you, perhaps? And your cloak is certain to dry quickly."

Blair nodded. The woman smiled and turned away. Then she walked to the men's table, put one hand on her hip, and looked them over. Blair prayed she wouldn't start taking dishes away lest she think to take the note as well.

Finally, with a shake of her head, the woman reached up and took hold of a thin curtain and pulled it across the front of the table, creating an alcove. Perhaps she could expect a good tip if she allowed them to sleep it off.

For a moment, Blair was disappointed, but soon realized that curtain would give her some privacy as well. She took a few bites of her soup while she considered the steps she would take to get behind the curtain. Then she took a few sips of the wine to bolster her courage.

Anything for Martin.

Satisfied the shadows would hide her absence as well as it hid her presence, she slipped around the table once again. No patrons were facing her direction as she glided silently across the aisle. She did pause for a peek behind the material, however, to see that her heroes were still sleeping.

They were.

So she slipped around the curtain and paused again. Though she was fair to certain her heart could be heard by all and sundry, none of the men stirred. The conversations of other patrons went on without interruption. Footsteps neared, then passed without pause.

Blair looked down and realized her skirts might be seen below the hem of the curtain, so she stepped around Harcourt's chair, deeper into the alcove. She tried not to dwell on the fact that she'd also stepped away from a quick escape.

For Martin, she reminded herself, and reached for the note. It hadn't been sealed, so there was no fuss and no noise made when she opened it. Unfortunately, it was too dark to read it. She closed her eyes for a wee moment and listened to the heavy breathing around her. The fumes from their drinks swirled against her nose and she coughed.

Stanley's snoring stopped, as did her loud heart. She opened her eyes but found no one looking back at her, but the fact she could see them so well meant her eyes had already adjusted, praise be. She peered at the note once more. The letters were barely visible, but she managed by deciphering them one at a time. The hand was legible.

The message was brief.

> *Gentlemen,*
> *10,000 English pounds.*
> *27th day of June*
> *The abandoned monastery south of Charleville.*
> *Or an unspeakable death for your friend.*
> *Waste no time.*

Finally! Dear God, finally!

She hugged the note to her and silently wept. But before the first tear fell to the floor, she realized, though this was a miracle, it wasn't hers at all.

She knew where *Northwick's* kidnappers were. Not Martin's. It was possible these villains would not bother with any but wealthy officers. After all, what profit could be gained from kidnapping soldiers for whom they see no ransom?

She refused to continue the thought. This was her only, last, and best hope of finding her brother. She must assume there was only one band of kidnappers in the area, only one place her brother could be, since she'd fairly turned the district topsy-turvy with her searching and found no trace of him. Givet Faux truly had been the last stone to turn. And if Northwick and Martin were not inside when the others had searched, then it was likely they were being held nearby.

Her problem now? If these blackhearts did have Martin, this note still meant little hope for him.

These Englishmen had another two weeks to either gather the ransom or rescue their friend. And the former might be the simplest. Divided between the three of them, it was not such an impossible number. A little over three thousand pounds each. Easy enough for a future duke, an earl, and a Marquis, not to mention Northwick's own money.

Easier, say, than fighting their way into Givet Faux.

In fact, they might believe paying the ransom would be the safest way to get their friend back unharmed.

But Martin? Martin's ransom had not been paid, would never be paid. Even if the kidnappers realized she was unlikely to afford the ransom and had, instead, sent a ransom demand to their father, there was no telling whether or not her father received a ransom note, let alone read it. But if they were waiting for a payment from Scotland, it would at least have bought Martin more time.

Villains would surely not feed a hostage indefinitely. If Martin was still alive, it wouldn't be for long. Not long at all. And his only hope resided in his blade-wielding sister, who could only do so much.

But a trio of English gentlemen, trained for combat, was a boon.

What Blair needed were three *alert* and vengeance-minded men to help her raid the place, not careful men who might look for a safe and peaceful way to get their friend back.

She needed them as determined as she was. They needed to believe the danger to Northwick was immediate. They would need fire in their bellies to do what she required of them. Therefore, *they could not know about the ransom note*. They could not know they had two weeks to act, for Martin couldn't wait two weeks.

If they attacked the keep and found nothing, the English would still have time to gather their money and meet the ransom demands. If they didn't find Northwick, she would tell them all. They would still have hope. Surely they would forgive her if they still had hope.

Harcourt mumbled. She hid the note behind her before looking down, but the man was still asleep. A quick look around the table proved the others were equally unconscious, but still she watched them as she made her way to the curtain and escaped. Then she moved quickly to the large fireplace.

She would have tossed the note in straight away, but she worried she might forget a detail, so she read it yet again. The message took up only the top half of the parchment, so she tore it off. Waste not, want not.

She prepared to toss the message into the flames, but paused once more.

It was a betrayal, to be sure.

She imagined the look on Ash's face when he discovered it, but her brother's face pushed its way to the fore.

She took a deep breath and fed the fire.

"Anything for Martin," she muttered as she watched it burn.

"Have you finished, Madame?" Blair jumped at the woman's sudden presence.

"Oh, uh, no, I haven't. Could I trouble you for a pen and some ink?"

"*Certainment*," the woman said, turning away. "Do you need parchment also?"

She held up the blank half of the note. "No. I have what I need."

Quarter of an hour later she sat before an empty bowl, an empty cup, and a finished note of her own.

> *Our villains are at Givet Faux.*
> *Meet where you left me your horse.*
> *Sundown. Thursday.*
> *I will enter without you if I must.*

That would give them half a day to sleep off their drink, she reasoned.

A new set of customers were led to the table next to Blair's and she cursed under her breath. With the curtain still drawn, she could hardly walk past their table and toss the note on the rolls. The little man had been foolish to do so in any case—if the Englishmen staggered away without a good look around, they would have left the note behind. It might have been tossed out with the rubbish and ended as a snack for a pig!

For all his trouble, all that distance in the rain, the little man must have been exhausted indeed to toss the note and run off. Perhaps he was not welcome in the auberge and ran out before he could be tossed in the street.

Foolish man.

But now, here she was contemplating the same dilemma.

How to make certain they read the message? And get away besides? For indeed, she did want to get away without a fuss. If they woke, alert, and found it tonight, they would no doubt come looking for her and demand to know how she'd learned the truth. She'd much rather face them just as they are about to rescue their friend. Perhaps they'd be much less interested in her and her sudden information if they are moments away from the prize.

Yes, facing them the following night would be much better. Besides, with Ash looking into her eyes, she was afraid she might tell him anything he wished to know, that a forced rescue of their friend was not necessary. And he could not know the truth. Not until she had a chance to save Martin.

She would confess then, and gladly.

Probably.

She laid her coins on the table then sat back in the shadows with nothing else to do but twist the ring on her finger and wait for an idea to present itself.

The ring was a gift from Martin. He'd come across it somehow—gambling she suspected—and presented it to her on a night she was feeling particularly homesick, the night before his brigade attacked Bergen op Zoom. The face of the ring was molded into the shape of an owl, like her own pet owl, Shakespeare.

It was far too big for her, of course. A man's ring, truth be told. But she'd tied a bit of cloth around it to keep it hugging her finger. There was likely room for a bit more cloth. . .

There was likely a bit more room—

A *man's* ring.

The man whose finger she imagined it on was seated across the way with his head lolling against the wall.

If she slid the ring on a small finger, she could also fit the little note. The ring would secure it! He'd be sure to get it whenever he roused himself.

Blair ignored the people now seated at the table nearby and lifted the curtain aside. If they were curious, they said nothing. Again, she walked around Harcourt's chair and stepped close to the dark form of Ash. His head hadn't moved. His eyes were closed. If she weren't in a hurry, she would have liked to stay and study the man's face until he awakened. Pity she could do no such thing. It was an interesting face tipped back and relaxed instead of glowering and stern.

She sighed and gave her head a shake. His left hand rested on the table. Long fingers. Well groomed. No rings.

Ever so gently, she placed the note along his smallest finger, then looked back at his face. He hadn't moved.

They must have been devastated indeed to get so drunk they could not defend themselves. If they were expecting Everhardt to stand watch, they should have informed the man, for as loyal as he seemed to be, he would never have left them alone as they were.

She breathed on the ring to remove any chill, then lifted his finger and slipped the ring over both it and the note. She added pressure to get the ring to slide further than the knuckle.

In for a penny, in for a pound.

She slowly lowered the finger back to the table and glanced up at his face once more.

"Dinna lose it, ye drunk bastard," she whispered, then she peered closer, for if she wasn't mistaken, his eyes were slightly open.

His fingers suddenly wrapped around her own! She froze, half bent over him. To rise, she would need to pull her fingers free, but he was holding them too tightly.

"Scotia," he said. "I am dreaming you."

She tried to keep from smiling in relief.

"Yes. Ye are," she said soothingly. "But if ye doona close yer eyes, ye'll wake, and I'll be gone."

His eyelids lowered again. His hold on her fingers slackened. She was almost disappointed.

"Kiss me, Scotia," he whispered.

She rolled her eyes. The bloody man was awake. The last thing she wished to do was to reward him for teasing.

She waited for him to realize she wasn't a fool.

And she waited.

And he never opened his eyes.

Perhaps he was asleep. There was a slight rattle to his breathing. Was he snoring? Or pretending to?

Ash's hand remained lax on the table. The note and ring were secure. And his lips were so near. If he was awake, she was already in trouble. If he was asleep, she could get away with. . .

Before she allowed herself to consider further, she kissed him!

With his head tilted back, she simply lowered her mouth to his, careful not to touch him with her hands lest she wake him. The texture of him was at once soft and hard. His lips gave no resistance at all, but the prickly flesh around his mouth seemed so much more solid than hers. Of course she'd been kissed before by a bounder or two, but never long enough to examine the difference between the roughness of a man's chin against the softness of her own chin. Although his lips seemed as tender as hers, she had the immediate impression that men were separate creatures, built from unique material altogether.

Blair half expected his hands to come up and grab her.

She half *wanted* just that.

She pulled away, but then kissed him again, allowing him one more chance to kiss her back, she supposed. It was a silly thought, considering how desperately she wished to get away before he woke.

When still his lips did not move, she straightened and narrowed her eyes.

He bloody well had better be asleep, she grumbled silently. And with her face aflame, she fled.

CHAPTER SEVEN

Ash woke in the night with a horrible pain in his neck, surpassed only by the pain in his skull. He rolled his head one way then the other to be certain it was indeed his neck that hurt, not that the ache in his brain wasn't simply spreading throughout his body.

Definitely his neck. He'd fallen asleep against the wall.

Bloody hell.

The sound of dishes rattling brought him up straight in his seat. Stanley and Harcourt sat to either side of him blinking at each other.

They'd drunk themselves under the table, or near enough, it appeared.

He cleared his throat, to say something or other, but he forgot. Dear Lord, he was still drunk? Then he remembered why they'd taken to Brandy in lieu of food.

Napoleon has escaped. We are out of time. I have failed Northwick.

"Brandy!" he said loudly and giant church bells clanged in his head.

"Ash," Stanley spit. "Do shut up, for pity's sake."

Harcourt laid his forehead on the table and stuck his fingers in his ears. The curtain was pulled aside and an old gentleman handed cups all around.

"What is this?" whispered Stan. "Hair of the dog?"

The old man smiled. "Brandy to see you to your beds, messieurs."

"Excellent," Ash said. "My compliments to the chef."

~ ~ ~

Hours later, with the pre-dawn cast of blue around his curtains, Ash woke again. In his bed. Fully clothed. He very carefully removed his loud clothing and louder blankets from the bed, then went back to sleep. . .when removing his loud skin proved too difficult.

~ ~ ~

"Oh, I say," said Stanley. "Sunlight is far too hard on my eyes just now, Ashmoore. No need to add to my pain."

Ash opened one eye. Stanley stood at the foot of Ash's bed where, coincidentally, his own head hung. He lifted the offending orb and followed Stanley's gaze to find himself splayed out, nude. "I'm going to need some Brandy. Just tip it into my mouth." Ash resumed his posture, hanging his head back where he'd found it, but also opening his mouth in anticipation.

"What you need, old sock, is more clothing," said Harcourt from the doorway. "That bit on your finger is not covering anything what needs covering."

Ash lifted his right hand, then his left and found, to his dismay, a ring he'd never seen before, and a bit of parchment formed to his finger.

"So there is the little devil," he growled. "Failed all night to lay my hands on that noisemaker."

He pulled the ring off, then dropped the paper to look closer at the ring itself. "It is an owl," he mumbled. "The cursed thing may well have been hooting all night."

Harcourt laughed, then winced.

Ash rolled, very carefully, to his side. "I was not jesting about the brandy."

His friends ignored him.

"Did you win it in a wager?" asked Stan.

"Hardly," he replied. "I was not wearing this ring yesterday. I have a vague memory of someone placing it on my finger while we were drinking our suppers."

He was grateful no one brought up the subject behind their drinking. They were about to leave Northwick to his fate, abandon the search, and all because a little Frenchman had tried to escape Elba Island. May God have mercy on their souls.

"Brandy," he demanded. "Or you are not my friends."

Stanley made a cursory search of his pockets. "Plum out. It was grand knowing you old man."

"Goodbye, then," sang Harcourt as he slouched to the floor.

No brandy then. Jolly.

Inspiration came to him then. "Where is Everhardt?"

"Here, my lord," came a quiet voice from the parlor room.

"Six bottles of the best Brandy you can find, man. Now," Ash said carefully.

Stanley moved off to sit in the sole chair beside the dressing screen. "Did you mean to say six? Not an easy number to be divided by four—er, three, I meant to say. . ."

They were used to splitting any number of things four ways, between the Four Kings. And the simple necessity of changing his calculations was more than Ash could stand. Damn him if he would ever play cards again, either, for each time the King of Hearts was played, he'd likely dissolve into a weeping woman. Either that, or he'd draw steel and begin taking on all comers.

Of course he'd prefer the latter, but the mere chance of the first reaction was enough to send him back into oblivion, where it was safe.

He sat up quickly, and after the room settled into a slow roll, he made his way to the piss pot. Unfortunately, as the previous night's drink left his body, something niggled at the back of his mind. Something he needed to remember, or needed desperately to forget.

Someone tossed his small clothes over the screen. He offered no thanks, for although he might agree to don his breeches, he meant to go nowhere. Possibly, ever.

"I'll need six bottles for myself, Stanley," he finally said. "The pair of you should have ordered some as well."

And still something niggled.

He stumbled to the corner where he'd apparently tossed his saber, ignored the pressure of his head, and retrieved it. He slid it from the scabbard and winced at the sound it made.

"Here, now," said Harcourt, attempting to slide back up the doorway and failing. "What will you need that for?"

"To kill Everhardt, if he returns too slowly."

No use shaving, Ash decided an hour later, and reached for his shirt, stretching high to retrieve the blasted thing from a dormant chandelier hanging over his bed, the tip of which hung like a heavy arrow over the center of his bed—a heavy piece with far too small a chain. One day, he was certain, the chain would fail and some unlucky chap would forfeit his life. Or perhaps a couple might be summarily separated in the dead of night.

Unbidden came the image of Scotia lying next to him beneath the foreboding pendant—yet another image a tall whiskey would chase away.

Where was Everhardt? And where had Stanley hidden his sword?

Perhaps when his man returned, Everhardt might remember whatever it was he was forgetting. While there were plenty of things he was forgetting on purpose, he sensed this mysterious item was not something to relegate to that list.

He pulled the sleeve over his left arm, but something caught and pulled at his finger.

That ring.

He slipped the shirt off again and took a good look at the carved image. The fabric could easily have caught on one of the owl's little ears.

Why the bloody hell would someone have put it on him? And why the devil wasn't Scotia around to watch for silly details like that? He would have been able to send for her, ask her what she might have witnessed. She was supposed to have joined them for dinner. He determined to take her to task for not accepting his invitation.

Or had she?

Feeling a bit unsteady, he placed his backside on the bed, then winced and shut his eyes to the glare coming through a window that hadn't been there the day before. Was he in the correct room?

In the orange darkness behind his eyelids, he saw the upholstery of the auberge, the same-colored curtain drawn around him. He imagined Scotia coming to him from the shadows, leaning over him, lowering her lips to his.

Scotia. His phantom.

Was it possible the woman was nothing more? Had he conjured her to push him along as he searched for Northwick? To make certain he never gave up? And now that he had no choice but to give up, would she never appear again? With her little piece of paper—

He jumped to his feet. "Help me find that paper!"

Ignoring the pain in his head outright, he bent beside the bed and fell to his knees. The item he'd forgotten, the message from Scotia, whether she was real or not, would be important, at least to him. Eventually, his friends joined in the search. They tossed the bed clothes aside. They looked everywhere. Even in the chandelier.

Where the bloody hell? He'd held it in his hands. He'd heard it rustle against the sheets. The note was no phantom, even if the woman was.

But that wasn't right. She was real. He'd touched her.

"I suppose," Stanley said, "we can simply summon the chit and ask her what it said."

Ash stilled. "The chit?"

"Our shadow, of course," said Stan. "If someone left you a ring and a note, I'm certain it was her. She was seated just across the way, if memory serves, which is doubtful, I admit. If she didn't leave them, she'll know who did. If she did leave them, she can give us the message again."

Ash's brandy-soaked mind had forgotten—his friends had seen her too. They'd discussed her on a daily basis for more than a month. Of course she was no phantom.

"But why leave a note?" asked Harcourt. "Unless she was going away and would be gone by the time we sobered. . ."

Ash's stomach dropped. He might never see her again? Why should it affect him so? The woman could mean nothing to him, after all. They would both return home with their hearts broken for the men they'd been unable to find. They would never belong to the same circles. It would be strange indeed if he ever found himself in Scotland. Considering her accent, she was far north of Hadrian's wall. When the devil would he ever have occasion to visit the Highlands?

But even if they happened upon one another again, he could not have her. No woman deserved to be shackled to the Devil's own. She was far beyond his reach as his own redemption. There were simply some things that could never be.

So it made no matter if she was gone. Surely. But even so, he found himself praying. *Just let me see her one time more.*

"Here it is," sang Harcourt. His friend had tossed the bedclothes back onto the bed. "It must have been caught in the blanket."

Ash forced his breathing to calm.

"Well, man," Stan said. "What does it say?"

"She meant it for you, I am certain." Harcourt handed over the precious scrap.

Ash took it from his friend's fingers and opened it. He read the message silently. His heart stopped. He couldn't breathe. Dear Lord! How close they'd come to failing North!

His body convulsed as he gorged himself on hope. He gulped air between waves of elation. She'd done it. They'd hoped she would somehow lead them to Northwick, and she'd done it!

She must have seen something after they'd left Givet Faux. . .

"Ash, please!" Stanley tugged on his elbow.

Everhardt knocked on the parlor door then opened it before bending down to lift a sturdy box of dark bottles and bring them inside.

"We won't need those," Ash managed to say, then passed the note to Stanley.

The latter read it quickly, then choked out, "Coffee. We need coffee." Stan then handed the note to Harcourt and sat on the floor. Ash thought it wise to do the same.

"Everhardt. Leave the brandy," said Harcourt as he lowered himself to the bed. "We'll need both before the day is done."

Ash had orders for Everhardt as well.

"Find her," he said, "before she does something foolish. Sit on her if you must until we can find our clothes and our heads."

Everhardt shook his head. "I regret to tell you, my lord, she is already gone."

CHAPTER EIGHT

Blair suppressed a shiver when the late afternoon breeze rushed around her ankles and up her skirt. Though there was fresh snow on the pine boughs as she'd picket her way back through the trees that morning, the sun had made quick work of it. The white was gone.

Beneath her layers of wool, she'd managed to be overwarm, but not for long. The sun had passed the tips of the forest in which she hid and if the smell in the air was to be believed, there would be snow again tonight. She only hoped by the time it began to fall, she and Martin would be long gone from this place.

She refused to believe he was not inside.

All night she'd wavered between excited anticipation and anger at herself; thrilled by the hope of finding her brother after all, and angry she could not force her thoughts to quiet so she could get some sleep. She would need a clear head if there was fighting. If she were overly fatigued, she'd be no more effective than a drunken English lord.

For the hundredth time she chided herself for not having the courage to face the trio and explain what she'd seen and show them the ransom note. But she could not change horses mid-stream. She would see her plan through, allow the gentlemen to believe immediate action was necessary. When all was said and done, she'd face the consequences. Consequences were not her greatest concern at the moment, however.

The note had been securely attached to Ash's finger, but what was her guarantee the note would be read?

None.

She wasn't any cleverer than the dark man after all.

Wrapping her cloak tighter around her legs, she reclined beneath the boughs of an aspen and resolved to imagine herself back in the Scottish Highlands, to listen to the rustle of the newborn leaves, and sleep.

Sleep.

Please, sleep.

~ ~ ~

The gloaming was settling in with the lovely pink hues of sunset at her back. The wee forest surrounding her had blocked the sun for the past two hours. The truth came upon her slowly, like the stretching of the shadows. . .

She must enter the keep alone.

Though she was thirsty, she decided against drinking the last of her pouched wine, for she would need her wits about her if she was to talk her way through the door. After that, she was going to need a great deal of luck.

First, she secured her horse. If she managed to find Martin and even get him out the door, they would need the beast quick to hand.

Next, she tossed back her hood and twisted her mass of curls into knot and secured it to her crown, both to keep it out of the way once the fighting began, and to attempt a more alluring look for the role of a whore. Truth be told, she could not think of any other way to gain entrance. A respectable woman travelling alone would raise suspicions. A whore looking to earn a coin might well be expected to look for that coin wherever men gathered.

Once she got inside, she would do whatever necessary to get her brother out intact and leave the worry over her soul for another day.

A deep breath. Then another. Then she moved to the edge of the trees and looked beyond the crumbling wall to the path that ran alongside the miniature citadel and around to the front door. In spite of the chill air, she untied the laces at the top of her bodice, pushed the fabric off her shoulders and allowed her cloak to drape off her elbows. It would have to suffice.

She set her first boot onto the short grasses that stretched between her hiding place and the path, but it was pulled back sharply when a hand came around her waist and another clamped firmly across her mouth. Neither of her feet touched the ground as she was whisked back into the trees.

She held onto the arm that held her head against her assailant's chest, but she did not struggle.

She had no ken if a whore would struggle, and if the man were from inside the keep, she must act as expected. On the other hand, if he were one of the Englishmen come late to the party, she didn't want to hurt the man. And judging the distance from the ground, it was the large one who carried her.

Or perhaps the large man from the keep?

Her blood ran cold with the unknowing.

She was lowered to the ground and unfriendly faces surrounded her. But at least they were English faces she knew well enough.

"Good evening, my dear," said Harcourt.

She gave him a small nod.

"You're bloody lucky we caught you," the blond said.

"Lovely to see you again, as well, Stanley." Then she nodded at the man standing just past the blond. "Everhardt, isn't it?"

The man nodded. Stan and Harcourt exchanged a private look, then laughed. The hand about her waist slowly dropped away and she turned to find Ash looming over her, but she refused to take a step back. Instead she glared up into his dark face.

"Ye're late!"

"No, we are not," he growled. "You were impatient."

He said it as if he believed it to be the worst of sins. Considering the way he glared at her bare shoulder, however, it was possible impatience was not the sin he had in mind.

She followed his gaze, but didn't right her clothes, rather enjoying the fact she had drawn emotion from him. Heaven knew she'd suffered enough emotion on his behalf.

"Have you a better idea for getting inside?" she asked.

He nodded. "*We* have."

It was the way he'd said *we* that gave him away. They didn't intend to let her go with them.

She shook her head and backed away, then, when he reached for her, she lunged to the side, eluding his grasp.

He sucked air between his teeth. He didn't appreciate her defiance, poor man.

He smoothed his expression, then lunged for her again. She turned the other way, spinning her skirts out of reach just in time.

She put a tree between them. By the time he got to her side, she was gone again.

"It's the skirts, she taunted. Four inches too short keeps a girl from tripping," she teased. "Perhaps that knowledge will help you someday."

His friends laughed quietly, but made no move to help him catch her.

"I'm going inside," she announced, then stopped running. With hands on hips, she stood her ground. He stopped only a foot away but left his hands at his sides. While they glared at one another, his friends gathered close.

"*You* will stay with the horses," he finally said.

"Five blades are better than four." She cocked her head, daring him to argue with her reasoning.

"You would be a liability."

She refused to be moved by the gently given statement.

"I can fight as well as any man," she assured him. "I'm nay weak."

Ash shook his head. "Not weak, no. But a weakness. If they took you, we could do nothing but surrender."

She rolled her eyes. "Is it not the same with any of ye? If they threatened the pretty blond," she nodded toward Stanley, "would ye not also surrender?"

The blond in question straightened, as if he were offended somehow. But after a moment, he relaxed and nodded.

"I can make it much easier for you to accept my assistance," she said with a smile.

Ash raised a brow.

"I will simply accept *yers*. For I will be going inside to collect my brother. Ye may come if ye wish. But we should save our fighting for the enemy, should we not?"

"Mmm," was all he said. He took a step back, then reached forward, beneath her skirts.

Taken completely off guard, and fearful of falling, she threw her weight forward and leaned a hand on his back while he tugged at her layers. She moved both hands to his shoulders as he began to rise with the fabric in hand. Then he quite roughly pulled the back of her dress up before her and tucked it into the band of her waist.

She looked down to find her legs still covered, though barely. He'd essentially turned her skirts into pantaloons.

"Like the fishwives," he said. "And you'll stay behind me always. One look at your silly legs and I'll be distracted. Distraction is death. Our first priority is Northwick. You, then your brother. In that order. Do you understand? We will leave you behind if we must. If you insist on coming along, you must be prepared for it."

It saddened her to admit it, but he was right. Their friend was their first priority. But it also made her more certain she'd made the right decision to burn the ransom note. Had she not, she believed they would have headed to London to collect money instead of coming with her for Martin's sake.

CHAPTER NINE

Ash had been horrified to find her already gone, then down right jubilant that he'd caught her before she'd made it out of the woods. Getting his hands on her had been an unplanned boon. But his relief hadn't lasted long. She was a stubborn woman, but she had a bit of spring in her step, and a sharp tongue. He only hoped her blade was as sharp and that she might know how to use it.

It was a fact, women who carried weapons were usually well-versed at using them. And during the few times he'd followed her, when she believed she was following him, he'd sensed her cunning, observed her sleight of hand when checking for the weapon at her side. Brief little touches that likely assured her the weapon was still there. More than a few times she'd reached for it, reconsidered, and moved her hand away again. But never once had she seemed timid about the blade so near her skin.

As this was no time to be thinking about that skin, he shook the image from his mind, only to have it immediately return. Her room had been black as pitch when he'd searched her skirts. It was impossible to expect him not to imagine every detail of what he felt. And then, after they had a flame to see by, he'd been mightily impressed by the weapon itself.

Wickedly sharp, artfully honed—a mystical weapon with an evocative name. Much like the woman herself. And now he had no choice but to trust that her ability would match that art, since he was powerless to stop her. A woman like that would only find a way inside if they left her tied to a tree.

Worst of all, if she did make it out alive, she would never look kindly on him afterward. Once they stepped inside the keep, he would once again turn into the deadliest gentleman of the ton. And how could any woman see him as anything more than a monster afterward? Especially if she were standing behind, watching his bloody work.

Although he was desperately afraid she would not come out of Givet Faux unharmed, he was beyond the ability to worry about her now. He regretted it. Braced himself for it. But he could not afford to dwell on it.

As Stanley drew the layout of the interior, Ash watched her face, waiting for those fleeting glimpses she took of him. Enjoying for the last time that light of interest as their gazes connected for a heartbeat. Then her attention was back on Stanley and his drawing in the dirt.

She had no such looks for his over-handsome friend, he noticed.

But neither would she have such looks for him when the night was through. No. Once the morning brought light to his bloody work, she would have a different expression for him—if she dared glance his way at all.

He tried to tell himself it was for the best, that any woman who might reach for his heart would lose her fingers. For ultimately, he had no choice but to release the monster within. If Northwick was indeed inside those walls, the surest way to get all four kings out alive was to make certain the villains did not. As soon as the mêlée began, the red haze would descend and he would welcome it. After more than a month of searching, it would be a satisfying end.

Once again, she glanced up at him. This time, there was suspicion. Did she think he might have left without her? Of course she did.

He shook his head and she smiled as if she'd read his thoughts.

Dear Lord, don't let her read all of them.

"We've been going over what we remembered from yesterday, when they allowed us to look about the place," Stan was saying. "We found the inner walls to be circular, like the outer walls, obviously, except for here."

He had drawn a large circle. Inside the front entrance was a large hall that took up the center of the building and ended half way through. To the right, he drew a large triangular solar with the outer edge curved to mirror the citadel wall. On the other side of the hall, he drew its mirror image. The rear half of the circle contained the kitchens, again with the outer wall rounded, the pantries mirroring the kitchen, but where the rest of the wall should have been round, it was straight, where a row of servants rooms ended.

"You see, there is a large section unaccounted for here." Stanley pointed to the last triangular section that completed the circle. "There is also a passage that encircles the front half of the building. Approximately seven feet wide, for defense. I remember it ending in a passage to the kitchens on the left, but on the right, it ended with a large cabinet that filled the wall."

Harcourt knelt and pointed. "We believe there is a passageway behind the cabinet, that hostages could be hidden in the space unaccounted for. We were welcomed to see the rest of the space, including the cellars beneath the kitchen, where we found a pit, but no one in it. No signs of recent use."

"Yes," Stan said, coming to his feet. "There are god-awful smells in some of the rooms, but those were accounted for when we met some of the occupants. It is an understatement to say this mission will not be pleasant, Miss. . ."

The woman smiled and shook her head, obviously in answer to Stan's request for her name. Then she glanced at Ash and her smile widened. Her teeth a surprising white in the deepening darkness.

"I suppose ye could call me Scotia," she said.

Scotia, you fool.

Perhaps it would be better, in the end, if he did not know her true name. It would keep him from looking for her if he ever made a trek to the Highlands. Although it was unlikely their paths would ever cross again, he had the strangest feeling they would.

"So, what is our plan?" she asked, looking into his eyes.

"After we get the door open, we turn to the immediate right and head for the cabinet," said Harcourt. "We expect to have resistance from both the front and rear as we make our way forward. Two on the attack, two on the defense. I suppose the place for you would be in the middle."

"With no one to fight," she huffed.

Ash leaned close. "Avoiding our backswing should keep you sufficiently entertained, madam."

She gave him a quizzical look for a moment, then nodded and looked away.

"Thank the Lord for small favors," he murmured.

She laughed, but did not look back. Her attention was turned to her skirts where she reached for the weapon, likely to determine whether or not their arrangement would interfere with her ability to draw it quickly. To his relief, and her own, she pulled the blade from her pocket with no trouble.

Harcourt stepped forward, took hold of her wrist, and held the blade up between the two of them. It was a rare occasion when the man was serious, but this was one of those times.

"Once our blades are drawn," he told her, "you won't have much reason to sheath it again. Do you understand?"

Ash appreciated the man's attempt to intimidate the woman one last time, but his friend hadn't seen that fire in her eyes at close range.

"We fought at Bergen," she said quietly. "Dinna worry for me."

"Bergen?" Harcourt looked Ash's way. "Bergen op Zoom?"

The ill-fated attack on the fortress north of Belgium, led by her countryman, Sir Thomas Graham, had suffered heavy losses. It had been a bloody affair ending in too many dead and even more taken prisoner. The mere idea of her being present at the battle made him sick to his stomach. But that wasn't his sole reaction—he was also relieved. At least she wouldn't faint at the first sight of blood.

"My brother served in the 73rd Highland Brigade under Gibbs. I. . . I watched his back."

Ash could hold his tongue no longer.

"Just how did you watch his back?" he asked.

She smiled and held up the unique blade. Its three sharpened edges shone even in the darkness. Unique and deadly. It wasn't that a blood-thirsty woman appealed to him, but at least she would be less frightened by him. Or so he hoped.

Stanley piped up. "And your brother was taken captive—"

"Outside Reims," she snapped. "By all means, talk war, gentlemen. I'll just go collect my brother on my own, then, shall I?"

It was a fact they had to race to catch up with her. Damn if he wasn't stepping up to the tall doors when he remembered North. Instantly, his mind turned away from the woman at his back to the task at hand. His heart beat at the inside of his chest as if it, too, would join the fight. Stan's arm came across to stop him as the door opened wide. And a close thing too, as he was already prepared to carry out the sentence of death for all who dared to threaten his friend.

"Back again?" asked the large Scot. He stepped back and gestured them all inside. "Did you need a place to stay the night, then? I'm certain Jean-Yves could name a fair price. . ."

The man's attention fell on Scotia.

"You!" He dragged a pistol from his belt and trained it on her as he backed into the hall.

His face twisted in horror as if she were the devil incarnate come for his soul.

CHAPTER TEN

Then men surrounding her seemed as stunned as she was. The plan was forgotten.

"I assure ye," she said quickly to the room at large, "I do not know this man."

The big Scot's horror turned to a hurt frown and the end of his pistol dipped.

"You doona ken who I am?"

She shook her head and turned to Ash. "I do *not* know this man."

The Scot, now angry, bent his tongue against his teeth and gave a whistle that might have drawn the stones of the keep down on their heads. She gave up her grip on the hilt in her pocket and covered her ears. Though her noble guards winced, they were able to arm themselves before the mind-numbing ricochet died. And a good thing too, as the room filled with ragged men armed to the teeth.

The Scot had disappeared. She spun about and found more villains behind them, but thank heavens her guard knew what they were about and had slid into the formation they'd planned from the start.

Strangely, it seemed more like a country dance with everyone lined up, waiting for the first note of music.

~ ~ ~

Ash fought the demands of his stomach, which insisted on emptying its contents immediately.

The Scot knows her!

She was one of them. Or had been at some point, perhaps? Either way, it seemed they'd been led, quite handily, into their own abduction.

What a clever woman, to distract him with her searching gaze, to engage his senses, and then deliver him to the hands of her accomplices. If they were unable to get North out, at least they would clap eyes on him soon. At least they could all suffer together.

As the moment slowed, he glanced about him, sensing the enemy, predicting who would first break formation and come for them. His eye caught on a scrap of paper nailed to the hall entrance, the inner edge of the archway under which they stood. *Rents due Saturday*, it read. But it wasn't the notice but the parchment he recognized—the message she'd attached to his finger was a perfect match for it.

How silly he'd been, leaving his horse for her, that she might ride comfortably away from her nest of fellow vipers. But if she had been inside the day before, why would the Scot be surprised to see her? And why would she still be standing at his back instead of rushing away from the reach of his blade?

He could not make sense of it. But no matter. He would certainly know where she stood if he felt the cut of Wolfkiller in his back. But until he did, the fight was on.

"To the plan?" Stanley asked casually.

"To the plan," Ash replied.

And the villains came at them.

~ ~ ~

Blair held Wolfkiller in her right hand and lifted her left leg to slip the skean dhu from her sock, a sock that was conveniently exposed thanks to her slap-dash pantaloons. But Ash had been right about the backswing of their blades.

And it only took a minute of dodging about to convince her it was a dangerous place to be. As she slipped out the side of her would-be sanctuary, the men adjusted without thought, as if they sensed too much space at their backs. If she changed her mind and wanted back between them, it was too late.

A man ran at them from around the bend in the wall and looked temporarily disappointed to find only a woman to engage with, but after she knocked his sword from his hand, he became content to fight her. The weight of his weapon was no match for Wolfkiller, however, and he was quickly overcome.

Over her shoulder she called, "Are we killing them, then? Or just wounding them?"

A black shadow moved around her, obstructing her view of her opponent. She held her blade in check as the man might well be Ash. When the man moved away again, her opponent lay motionless, staring unseeing at the ceiling, his throat. . .a river of blood.

She turned to find the gentlemen all engaged with the enemy. Ash was closest to her, but he never glanced her way. Then their little war machine moved on and her dead opponent was beyond her sight.

Bodies dropped at the Englishmen's feet in time with some silent rhythm. Engage, kill, step back. Engage, kill, step back. Harcourt and Everhardt pivoted behind her and she was again wedged between the pairs. But with no one to fight, she made herself useful by either moving Ash's and Stanley's opponents out of the way so the other two, walking backward, wouldn't trip over them, or, when the bodies were too heavy to move, warning them where to step. Though it was difficult, she tried not to look at their faces so they might be readily forgotten.

Blair kept pace as they moved deeper into the right corridor and headed into the darkness A single sconce burned just before the bend, but its light was too weak to illuminate the mob within its reach. Someone lit a torch, which temporarily blinded her, but it was a blessing. At least she could keep from harming her companions.

When there was light enough to see it, the passage was a curved, slick sea of red, fifty feet long. A giant, bloody Saracen's sword with bits and bodies lying near its edges. She slipped a dozen times but was careful not to make a sound as she did so. One look over his shoulder at the wrong moment and a man could be killed for his concern.

Because of the curve of the passage, she could not see them all, but assumed they'd left twenty of the enemy in their wake by the time the cabinet came into sight. One of the doors stood ajar and light came from inside.

"There is a passage," Stanley called out. With only ten feet left to the corridor, he'd finished off his last opponent and was free to look about him. He took Blair by the elbow and moved toward the cabinet, then pointed at a trail of blood that led up to it, then into it. Ash was still in the fray, wrestling a man against the wall. The other two were fighting the final man attacking from the rear.

Blair and Stanley listened and waited, but no new villains emerged. After a quick peek behind the still-closed door, Stanley went in first. Blair glanced back over her shoulder as she stepped inside.

Ash was no longer occupied. His gaze slid over her, then to the cabinet. His eyes were different, as if they belonged to another man. He seemed not to see her at all. Perhaps the dim lighting made her part of the shadows.

"Come," Harcourt said to Ash, then hurried to join her.

On the far side of the cabinet, they stepped onto stone once again. Stanley was waiting at the top of a staircase. Beside him lay the trail of blood, the drops were wider, thicker, as if the bleeder had moved much slower here than he had in the hallway.

The five of them stood in a circle and took a quick inventory of each other. They shared a smile—a silent celebration over the fact they were all still standing. No one appeared injured, though they were all covered in blood.

Her mind staggered at the reality—all that blood had been coursing through bodies only five minutes ago.

Harcourt put his arm around her waist and gave her a squeeze.

"Steady, lass," he whispered.

She took a deep breath and nodded, then straightened away from him. They could not think of her as weak. They should not be thinking of her at all.

Ash's friends were watching him strangely. Were they worried about him? Why? Hadn't he proven himself the most capable among them?

"There must be something important down there," Everhardt said, "to guard it so fiercely with so many men."

The comment served to wash away her thoughts of blood and ghosts, guilt and innocence. She moved next to Stanley, her mind suddenly consumed by the prospect of finding Martin. Anxious for just that, she forged on.

"Wait!" Stanley called, but she ignored him.

With her blades to hand, she picked her way down the steps, entirely aware of the trail of blood showing her the way. Everhardt soon caught up with her and took the lead. She tried not to see him as an impediment to reaching Martin, but she was hardly reasonable at the moment. Her insides shook with a mixture of excitement and dread, but her hands were steady. No one looking at her would imagine the emotion raging in her chest.

The stairway bent back on itself and the lower portion had twice the steps of the upper. The distance between the walls was substantial enough to accommodate swordplay, but there were no takers. Following Everhardt's lead, she took three or four steps, paused, then took three more. And still no one came. Had they all rallied in the corridor without leaving any behind?

The stairs were partially lit by oil torches that sent a black ribbons of smoke heavenward. The bottom step ended with dirt. The same trail of blood they'd followed down the steps were no longer visible. Somewhere near they would find a wounded, unpredictable man, but it was the possibility of finding Martin that kept her from hesitating.

Ash suddenly moved past her, out into the shadowy room beyond. She supposed he was suffering from the same excitement she was—the possible reunion at hand. She imagined he was as compelled to shout Northwick's name as she was to shout for Martin.

She listened to the men move around her, tried to keep track of where they were, and realized Ash had disappeared.

No one moved. Stanley stood to her left. Harcourt to her right. Everhardt disappeared up the stairs for a moment, then returned with a lit torch. The ring of light grew to include Ash, who stood over a man who had curled into a ball against the wall.

"Dead," Ash said, though his voice was course, like a shovel sliding beneath a pile of coals.

The light moved away, then grew as Everhardt moved about lighting torches. The body at Ash's feet, besides a bloody sleeve, had the now familiar slash across its throat. Ash moved away toward the countless iron bars that were now visible along the far wall.

A woman screamed, then whimpered. Blair moved left with the rest, following the noise.

Small cells lined the wall that most likely ran the same length as the keep's large hall. A cold fire pit sat at the end farthest to the right, but Blair was certain any heat from it was never intended to reach the cells or their occupants. The wide space before those cells held no new villains, but there was movement on the other side as a dozen tattered creatures came forward to peek through the bars. None of them were women.

The whimper repeated. Farther to the left.

They hurried to the last cell. A woman was kneeling next to a pallet upon which lay the thin body of a man. The light failed to reach more than his hand, but it was enough. Blair had held Martin's hand enough to know it.

She forced herself to breathe deeply, to hold her tongue until she heard what the woman would say. There was no sign, besides her weeping, to say the boy was dead.

"Please, don't hurt us," the woman begged in English through a thick French accent. "My boy and I. We have done nothing wrong, *messieurs*."

"Don't believe a word!" shouted another captive. "She's one of them!"

"Non!" She pressed her hands together and turned toward the now-open cell door, walking on her knees, casting a pleading glance at each of them in turn. "They only hate me because I would not bed with them. You must save me from this hell. And save my son!"

Blair pushed her way past Ash, who was blocking the opening and faced the woman.

"He is alive?" she asked the woman.

"Oui."

Blair's heart soared. Martin was alive. He was here. And if this lying woman were just out of the way, she could get to him!

"What do you think, Stan?" Harcourt asked. "Do we believe her?"

Blair stepped around the woman, then picked up Martin's hand. It was warm! And his breathing was steady! He was unconscious, but he was alive! No matter how much tending it would take, she would have her brother back!

She schooled her features as she turned, leaving Martin safely behind her as she and Wolfkiller faced the rest.

"Believe her if you wish," she said. "But I tell ye this man is *my brother*, and our mother's been dead these long eight years." She looked down at the woman whose face was already twisting with hatred. "And even when she was alive, she wasna French."

The woman screeched as she pulled back a blade from the lace at her wrist, Blair's weapon began its descent toward the woman's shoulder, above her heart.

The black form of Ash loomed forward. The blur of his arm left no doubt he'd been the one to dispatch Blair's first opponent of the day. He'd been the black cloud of death, as he intended to be again. But Blair had already set Wolfkiller in motion.

Too late. There was no pulling back.

Time slowed.

Sounds and sensations collided.

The whisper of Ash's blade sliding through flesh was interrupted by the uglier sound of Blair's gruesome weapon puncturing a shoulder, then crunching bone—

Then the ring of a bell as Spanish steel struck Viking substance. The jolt in her arms, her body. The hilt tearing from her hands as the force knocked her away. The complaint of the steel as it surrendered and snapped.

The whistle of the blade flying free.

Orange flames licked the dying woman's face as rage smoothed away into nothingness. And, as it did so, the orange face was painted into Blair's memory. This one, she would not forget.

When the woman tipped to the side and became a puddle, Blair turned to find her avenging angel pulling the wayward end of his blade from the back of his forearm. Stanley and Harcourt were already at his side. One with a torch, the other pulling his cravat from his neck.

"Damn me," Stanley said as he ripped away Ash's sleeve, "but I didn't think you bled old sock."

Ash cleared his throat. "Only when I shave, to prove I can."

Blair was relieved to hear Ash's voice returned to normal, relieved his friends could care for him so she could finally turn her attention to Martin.

Harcourt laughed. "You do realize, it took *you* to wound you."

"Don't forget the Viking," Ash replied, nodding at her and not her weapon.

Everyone laughed at that. So, with a smile on her face, she knelt beside her brother. He hadn't roused. His breathing was smooth, as was his brow. Everhardt knelt beside her and looked her brother over, then he opened the sleeping man's mouth and sniffed.

Did he think her brother was drunk?

He looked over his shoulder at the others. "Laudanum." To her he said, "He'll be right as rain in a day or two. Once we get him outside, we'll discover why he needs it."

"I'm surprised they would give him something for his pain," she thought aloud.

"I hate to interrupt, my dear," said Stanley. "But we cannot dally." He pushed a rather clean Wolfkiller into her hand. "Everhardt, can you bring him?"

The man nodded. "Go on, my lady. I've got him."

She nodded her thanks, took a final glance at Martin before following Stanley out of the chamber. Harcourt held the torch while Ash unlocked the other cells. At each lock, he called out.

"North?"

But there was no answer.

As each prisoner was released, he'd praise and thank Ash, then gather with the rest at the bottom of the stairway. None of them dared go up.

As Ash opened the last cell, only to find it empty, he roared and slammed the bars shut.

His friend was not there. Her heart broke for him, knowing how she'd have felt had they not found Martin.

"My lord."

Two men stood with arms locked around each other's shoulders, shoring up their thin and battered fellow. Neither looked fit enough to stand on his own.

"My lord," one of them growled, no doubt his voice was dry from lack of water. "Lord Northwick. In the hole. Four days ago." He raised a shaking arm and pointed to a spot beneath the stairs. Ash and his friends rushed to the spot where a stone lay on the ground for no apparent reason. Together, they moved it to the side. As soon as the hole below was uncovered, another parched voice called out. "Here! Ici! Je suis ici!" *I am here!* "Aidez moi!" *Help me!*

"North!" Ash roared. "North! Good God, man. We've come!" He looked up at Stanley. "We need rope." Then he looked around until his eyes found Blair. The tears in his eyes said all that wanted saying. He shook his head once, as if to say he could not find the words. She answered him likewise.

The smell of death emanating from the hole told the tale. It was likely Lord Northwick was the only man to be removed from it. Alive or dead.

Long minutes later, a filthy, shaking man was removed. As he was wearing nothing but a pair of pants, Ash removed his own shirt and put it on his friend, then he pulled his coat back over his own bare shoulders.

Blair tried not to watch. Of course she could not help herself.

Ash pulled a small flask from his pocket.

"It is only water," he told the man. "Can you stand? Can you lift a blade? Would you care to kill a few of your captors?"

"Gladly," said the other, and handed back the flask.

Harcourt offered North a blade and together he and Ash helped the poor man stand. Harcourt then positioned himself beneath Northwick's left shoulder.

"I can fight well enough with my left," he said cheerfully.

Blair had to admire them for never once wrinkling their noses, even a wee bit. She was determined try to keep her expression composed, but it was almost as difficult as keeping her eyes off Ash's bare chest. Of course, the memory of that chest helped distract her from the poor man's smell.

"They're gathering," said Everhardt, nodding up the stairs.

Blair imagined another pack of villains coming down the steps. The idea that some of them might realize the danger and slip away raised a wicked heat in her breast. She wished someone could follow behind them, herd them like cattle past their fallen comrades and into the talented blades of the English nobles.

Then she thought of a way to do it.

She ran back to the woman's body in the cell where they'd found Martin. Without hesitation, she pressed a hand to the woman's bloody neck. Next, she wiped it across her own. Then once more. Her skirts were already covered with the stuff from slipping and falling in the blood-covered corridor. It would have to be enough. There was no time for more.

"Someone protect my brother," she said as she ran toward the stairs and disappeared up the dimly lit steps before anyone could stop her.

CHAPTER ELEVEN

She's mad!

To run alone toward an enemy of untold numbers, when she could have stood with allies? Why?

Ash tried to postpone the thought, to keep his mind from even considering it, but the words pushed to the fore—*she might yet be the enemy.*

If she was not the enemy, the blackhearts would be cutting her down the moment they saw her. If she was not the enemy, following her, dividing their ranks, might mean death for them all.

At the moment, it would be better for her if she *were* the enemy.

Either way, it was time. Even if he had no other reason to fight his way out of the keep, Ash refused to allow that oubliette to become his grave.

But how close Northwick had come to that fate! If not for the woman. . .

He certainly owed her anything she might ask in payment—anything but running after her to certain death.

He'd already steeled himself. If they threatened her, he would not be swayed. She'd been warned. She chose to come in any case. Her death would not be his fault. If he could exchange his life for hers, he would do it, but not unless his friends were safe. And they were not.

A low rumble came from the opening. Everhardt stepped back to join him and Stanley to create a formidable front line. Ash took a moment to roll his shoulders, to flex his fighting arm. He allowed the red haze to descend once more, his thoughts becoming a series of blade strokes. His lungs filled with the scents of blood and death.

Ah. Here. I know this place. There is nothing to fear in this place. . .but me.

The bastards dawdled on the stairs, then came in a rush. Those at the fore brandished their weapons wildly, their eyes bulging with fear. In three moves, he put a pair of them from their misery, but allowed Everhardt and Stanley a man or two on which to dull their blades.

The next line tried to turn and flee but two others were backing down the steps, preventing their escape. But why backward?

A woman's voice caught his attention, but she did not sound distressed—she was bellowing Scottish war cries. Of course it must be Scotia, but again, he had no time for her distraction, not even time enough to be pleased she was still alive. Somehow.

The last two men finally turned and ran down the final steps and all but skewered themselves on his and Stanley's blades. He had just pulled his sword free from its human sheath and raised it for the next villain when Scotia stepped into the opening. Her blade was held triumphantly toward the ceiling. It was christened with only a drop or two of blood. He was simply glad to know the blood across her throat was not her own.

"I draped myself along the steps and feigned death. They walked right past me. Then I blocked their retreat, aye?"

Her celebration was brief. Her smile changed to concern and she ran immediately to her brother. She thanked the prisoner who had stationed himself beside the unconscious man.

"The dead woman was the only one to tend after this one," said the prisoner. "He was never allowed to wake for long—only time to eat a bit. But some days, they'd come for him. They'd blindfold him, take him above stairs, bring him back, and drug him again. We never understood it."

Ash was simply relieved the brother was still alive. A weeping woman was the last thing he wished to deal with, now that he had Northwick at his side again.

He suddenly realized he had yet to see her weep. Considering everything she'd done and seen this day, it was simply a matter of time. He only hoped that when the hysteria came, her brother would be aware enough to comfort her, just as she was currently attempting to comfort her sleeping brother.

She sheathed her blade, then pushed the boy's hair away from his face and Ash could almost feel her fingers doing the same to him. He shivered and rubbed his forehead, erasing the phantom caress.

"We need to leave," Stanley murmured. He was frowning at Scotia.

Ash was still wondering how the big Scot had known her, but they'd have to discuss it later. As soon as they were away from that place, he would have an answer for that and more, no matter how he had to go about getting it. If this woman had been an accomplice, nothing could save her from his swift justice.

And the truth of it squeezed his heart.

There was no one to impede them as they moved their party up the steps and into the passage. All prisoners, save her supposed brother, were able to walk. Everhardt carried the young man over his shoulder while Stanley protected him from the fore and the woman from the rear with a small dagger. Only one torch burned, so the bodies lying about the floor were little more than lumps to walk around. Drying blood pulled and sucked at his boots as he walked. Stealth was impossible.

Amid the sticky steps and labored breathing, a loud click rang out against the stones. The cock of a pistol.

Everyone froze. To the left, a large shadow rose from the floor and became the large Scot, pistol in hand, aimed at the woman.

Another click.

A second form appeared from around the curve in the corridor. It was Jean-Yves, the proprietor, who had so generously allowed them an extensive tour of the fortress the day before.

"With renewed expectations of ransom," the Frenchman said, "we were about to pull Lord Northwick from the oubliette, but *la*, you have accomplished this for us." He shook his head and made a tisking sound. "But now, we may as well put him back, since none of you are able to send for that ransom. A pity. But perhaps there are those who will pay your own ransoms, no?" He smiled. "You will return to the dungeon. Now."

None moved.

None but the big Scot.

He inched closer to the woman, shaking the end of his pistol to gain attention. "Turn yer arses 'round or the woman dies." He knocked her small knife to the ground, then pulled her over to his side of the corridor. She moved stiffly, as if she truly feared the man might fire.

Ash smirked. "Fine. Kill her. She is one of you. What does it matter to us?"

Scotia gave a short gasp, but said nothing. The fleeting worry in her eyes—was it from the threat of death or the disappointment of discovery? When he'd accused her, he had only been trying to distract the villains. He hadn't truly believed it. Now he wasn't sure.

"One of us?" The Frenchman scoffed. "Too absurd." He gestured to the Scot, then to the woman. "Kill her then."

The Scot slid behind her, his weapon aimed under her raised chin.

Ash took a step forward, but froze when the Frenchman lowered his aim to Ash's heart. If he were to die here, for any reason, he could not save North.

"Uhn, uhn, uh," taunted Jean-Yves.

All eyes turned to the Scot whose beard raked over the woman's shoulder. "It breaks my heart that ye doona ken my name, lass. Indeed it does."

Scotia looked down, to the right. Ash could see the temptation in her eyes. But with the man's pistol arm wrapped around her right side, she could not reach her blade.

Ash could not choose her over his friends. He could not. Even if he believed her innocent, he could not help her. Unless something distracted the Frenchman. . .

"Pity," the Scot murmured next to her ear. "But I see no future together—"

"Wait!" Ash demanded.

The Scot's gave a crooked smile and pulled the trigger. The blast rang loud in the constriction of the corridor. A small puff of smoke lifted into the shadows like a ghost. The woman remained on her feet. The pistol still aimed. . .where the Frenchman's form toppled forward.

Ash moved the moment Jean-Yves' arm lowered, but the Scot was prepared with a blade already at the woman's throat, winking in the light of the torch. The big man hissed until Ash stopped his advance.

"I'll spare her," the Scot said. "All ye will stay inside. When I'm certain I'm not followed, I will release her. Unharmed," he added.

The woman tried to speak, but he stopped her with a bite of the knife. With the blood previously smeared there, she already appeared mortally wounded.

"Agreed," Stan said, then leaned casually against the wall and waved a hand toward the open doorway behind the pair.

For a moment, the Scot hesitated. Then he lifted her feet from the ground, and in four quick steps, they were gone. The door closed in their wake.

CHAPTER TWELVE

The Scotsman prodded her quickly up the rise behind Givet Faux. In the darkness, she could not tell where he held the blade. She only felt the bite of it if she walked too slowly. After they cleared the rise and could no longer see the round roof of the fortress, he allowed her to stop to catch her breath while he grinned, obviously pleased by their escape and doubtful they'd be followed.

Since he had yet to notice the second skean dhu in her other sock, she pulled at the fabric tucked in at her waist and allowed her skirts to drop into their rightful place.

"Why did ye do that?" he demanded.

"Too tight," she said.

He nodded, then gestured for her to start moving again. Soon they began their descent on the far side of the rise. After walking the next ten minutes through a damp forest, the trees grew farther apart. She could hear the distant worrying of horses. Eventually, they came upon a low building. If he was going to kill her, it would be here.

She tripped and rolled to an awkward stop, then reached for that last dagger.

It was gone.

"Up then, Princess." He gestured with his dagger. "Believe me when I tell ye I can throw a knife as sure as I can drive one home. Ye stray out of reach and I can still

make certain ye'll never make it home to again to
Scotland."

The sneer to his words caught her attention. Besides
the fact he'd called her Princess. Once upon a time, her
father had called her just that. Could this brute be someone
from home?

She stood and faced him, tried to gain a better look at
him in the light of the stars. Even without the moon, it
seemed brighter there in the woods than it had indoors with
candles and torchlight.

She imagined him without the beard. Wondered at the
jaw hidden beneath. Tried to place his eyes. Quickly went
down a list of lads she'd known.

He hesitated as well, perhaps sensing what she was
about. His eyes looked earnestly into her own, as if he were
willing her to remember.

Still she remembered nothing.

She shrugged. His face fell, then he grabbed her wrist
and turned toward the low building.

"Perhaps you could tell me where we've met before,"
she said.

He dragged her roughly forward so she entered before
him. She heard the pop of his jaw as she passed him. When
he said nothing, she thought it best to leave him be.
Obviously she'd insulted him by not recognizing him, and
he would not risk being insulted further.

The low building turned out to be a stable. The Scot
was confident enough to light a lantern and hang it on the
wall.

Did he want the Englishmen to find them?

"Saddle this one," he said, pointing at a broad-backed
mare.

She dared not question him, though she hoped he
would allow her to have her own horse. Or perhaps, now
that he was so insulted, he'd be going on alone and she'd be
left in a puddle of her own blood.

It was strange, she thought, as she lifted the saddle from the floor and settled it on the nervous beast, that of all the bodies falling to the ground, never to move again, she never once worried she might be joining them. That was, not until she found her sock empty. But she admitted the truth of it—her fearlessness hadn't come from a knife in her sock, it had come from her companions. Or rather, one companion. It was Ash who'd made her feel invincible.

At least, until he'd decided she was the enemy. . .

Her heart clenched at the memory of him standing in the corridor, looking down his nose at her. She'd suffered the same heartbreak when her father had promised to disown her if she followed Martin to war, then again when she'd discovered Martin's ransom demands. The last time had been over a month ago, just before the Englishmen had shown up, when she'd given up hope of ever finding her brother.

She'd half-expected her heart to break yet again that day, but for another reason entirely. She'd come to expect only her father and brother could cause her that kind of pain—never a stranger with whom she'd barely conversed, and a bloody Englishman at that.

How had he gotten close enough to her heart to break it?

She bore down and pulled the cinch tight. The horse grunted.

"Stand back," said the Scot. He stepped up to pull on the saddle. "Stronger than ye look," he mumbled. "I'd best mind that."

"Aye, ye better," she snapped. "Do I get a horse? Or would ye rather trust me at yer back?"

At the moment, she felt like a wounded, cornered animal and she was anxious to have this battle over and done. She gave not a damn if the man had wounds of his pride to lick.

"Look here, Princess," he said, advancing on her, pressing her up against the wall. His body pinned hers while he took his fine time breathing in her face. "Ye'll not speak to me so and expect no cost fer it. Ye breathe because I allow it. And at the moment, that's generous."

His breath smelled of blood. His lip was split. Since she'd not noticed him in the fray, he had to have come by it from one of his own men. Perhaps the Frenchman had been killed for more reasons than she'd imagined.

She glanced up into his eyes, curious to know what he and his accomplice had fought over.

His beard moved as his lips curved with a smile. He'd apparently taken her curiosity for something else.

"Ah, ye recognize me now, do ye? Princess?"

She dared not deny it and gave him a slight nod.

"So ye'll fight me no more?" He pushed his forehead against hers. His black eyes searched for her soul.

She slyly raised the corners of her mouth in a knowing smile, then she shook her head.

"Ah, Princess," he whispered and pushed his lips against hers.

As disgusted as she was by his breath and the odd lump in his lip, she allowed it. Kissing him back would have been impossible. She only hoped that whomever he'd mistaken her for wouldn't have been eager for him either. There were redheads aplenty in Scotland. And if much time had passed, he likely misremembered the woman's face. Unless she wanted to die, she must keep him believing, at least until she got her hands on another weapon.

"Won't we travel too slowly on just one horse?" she asked carefully.

"Nay, Princess. They'll be heading for the city, to a doctor. They have what they came for. No need to chase after me. And by the sounds of it, they didn't have much use for ye, either."

Blair ignored the reminder, ignored the kick to her stomach, and realized she did have a bit of hope left after all. If Ash really believed she was party to Northwick's kidnapping, he would come for her, if only to kill her. . ..

CHAPTER THIRTEEN

"Come now, Princess," the Scot said softly. "Another kiss before I put you in the saddle, aye?"

Before the man could put his lips on her a second time, Ash's brought his blade between them and pulled. The sharp blade slid through sinew as easily as flesh. Of course he might have been a bit too enthusiastic, since he nearly took the man's head from his shoulders, but he couldn't find it in him to be contrite. In fact, he couldn't find a tender feeling anywhere in his enraged body at the moment, and a good thing too. It wouldn't be easy to kill the woman. Best to just have done with it and go.

"About bloody time ye arrived," she said.

He paused to consider his response and whether or not it would be bad manners not to clean his blade before using it on the fairer sex.

"Are you not ruffled in the least," he asked, "that a man has nearly been decapitated as he leaned in to collect another kiss from you?" *Another* kiss. A *second* kiss. Because she'd already kissed the blackheart once before, damn her.

"Doona be a fool. He clearly mistook me for someone else."

She used the hem of her cloak to wipe at the bastard's blood smeared across her breast. She'd simply stepped back as his body had fallen at her feet, the cold-hearted witch.

"Clearly," he sneered. "But wouldn't he have discovered his error the moment he'd tasted your lips the first time?"

Her head shot up, her eyes wide.

"Tasted? I... Can you tell what someone tastes like?"

A deep breath was not enough to pull his mind back from where her innocent comment had sent it, so he leaned forward and busied himself cleaning this blade on the dead Scot's shirt.

When he stood again, gripping the hilt of that blade with intent, she seemed completely oblivious to her danger. She couldn't seem to keep her attention on anything but his lips. When she finally glanced down at his weapon, however, she instantly paled.

She shook her head and looked away.

"Ye decided I was the enemy long before the bastard kissed me." She wrapped her arms around herself, then reconsidered and forced them to her sides. "And of course, we're the both of us Scots." She swallowed. Her eyes shone, moist with tears. "Already yer enemy by blood alone."

He realized what she was trying to accomplish. She was trying to make herself angry at him, to keep her fear at bay.

She turned her back suddenly. Her head never bowed, but her shoulders shook slightly. She took a slow breath. Then another. He could hear her swallow. Could tell when she caught her breath again and held it. Then let it go.

For a full five minutes, he stood there, refusing to be moved by her silent tears, refusing to offer comfort to an enemy he was about to execute. But even so, his stomach clenched over and over while he waited.

But hadn't he been expecting her to cry? Hadn't he, minutes ago, been hoping her brother would be there to comfort her when the horrors of the day finally settled in her mind?

He was just about to take a step toward her when she again pulled up the hem of her cloak, wiped her face, then dropped it once more.

Then she turned. Her face was red but dry. She kept her eyes cast down.

"I'm ready," she said boldly, but her voice faltered.

She lifted her chin. Swallowed. The blood drying on her neck cracked along the edges, folded into little lines.

He adjusted the grip on his blade.

She closed her eyes.

"Inverness," she whispered. "Remind yer friend."

Inverness. Either Harcourt or Stanley had promised to get her brother as far as Inverness.

She was trying to distract him, make him believe the unconscious man was really her brother, that she'd been telling the truth all along.

"*She's one of them,*" he remembered the man say from the next cell. He'd likely been referring to Scotia and not the other woman. It was Scotia who condemned her, after all. And he'd carried out the sentence without question. Scotia who had killed the woman as surely as he had.

And it was Scotia who was toying with him now.

No! Not Scotia. Just a woman. An evil one with no name who would use her considerable talents to find other victims if he allowed her to escape.

Though she made no sound, tears leaked from the corners of both eyes and poured in opposite rivers toward the sides of her face.

"Please doona torture me, Englishman." Her voice was little more than a whisper sent skyward. A prayer.

A Scotswoman refusing to call an Englishman *my lord.*

Another rush of tears damped the edges of her hair. Curls had escaped their confines and lay beside her neck, but none would impede the sword. A sleek but strong neck. A neck he had, more than once, imagined kissing.

His wild imaginings were pushed aside by an emotion he couldn't identify—or wouldn't. And he finally acknowledged the fact that he would never harm her. Even if she proved to be the enemy.

"Ah, Scotia. What am I to do with you?"

She opened her eyes, lowered her chin, confused. He knew the very second she realized he wasn't going to kill her—she crumbled into a heap in the straw and sobbed.

She had believed it all along. *Well, and why shouldn't she?* demanded a voice in his head.

"You knew I would come?" he asked awkwardly. He couldn't console her, but perhaps he could distract her. "You never supposed I would take my friends and go?"

"I knew you would never let him get away unpunished." She pointed at the body that lay between them. "And you still believe I'm one of them, do ye not? If ye mean to hang me, I'll tell ye true I'd rather be done with it now."

"No," was the only word he could manage.

She nodded and pushed herself to her feet, then began brushing the straw from her horrid skirts. Realizing those skirts were beyond saving, she stopped. She was a bloody mess. Another tear slid off her cheek. She turned her back again and cried again, though silently.

He forced himself to stand his ground until he was certain what he would do. For only God knew what that would be.

Someone approached and he turned to find Harcourt enter the stable with his sword drawn. He glanced at the Scot's body, then sheathed the weapon. Obviously, his friend believed the Scotsman had been the only threat remaining. Ash couldn't bring himself to correct him for the moment.

"Here, now," Harcourt said. "She's crying." He took a step toward the woman, but Ash stopped him. She might prove to be innocent in the end, but he wouldn't risk his friend's life until he knew for certain.

"Give me your weapons, if you mean to go near her."

It was impossible to say whose gasp was louder—the woman's or Harcourt's.

She awkwardly moved to the wall and braced herself against it as if she could no longer stand on her own. Her curls trembled, as did his heart, but he dared not move.

"You can't mean it," his friend said, even while he unsheathed his sword once again and laid it upon the ground. He then pulled a knife from inside his collar and a dagger from his stocking. He handed them to Ash, though not without an admonishing frown before he hurried to the woman's side and wrapped an arm around her back.

Seconds ticked by.

"Bring her," Ash growled. His voice was harsh but every bit of him felt harsh when another man was touching her, even if that man were one of the Four Kings.

"No." Her voice rang loud against the low ceiling. The horses' ears flipped up and back. The saddled mare stomped nervously. Harcourt took a step back.

Finally she turned to face him. Even in the dim light, her face was red, dark. The look in her eyes had changed. It was as if another woman stood before them, no longer cowering in the corner, but filling it.

"If you mean to hang me, I suggest you find a tree and a rope. I'll not follow you another step."

For all her bravado, the fresh stream of tears gave her away.

"Bring her," he said again, then turned and walked out.

He'd taken half a dozen large strides up the hillside when he heard it—the absolutely inconsolable weeping of a possibly innocent woman.

CHAPTER FOURTEEN

The wagon they'd taken from the Palais des Morts had proven too jarring for some of the more seriously injured, so they'd had no choice but to stop and rest mid-morning. They left the road but did not halt until they were well out of sight of it. The party was split between those who feared more villains would come for them, and those who *hoped* they would come, if there were, indeed, more of them.

Blair was simply content her brother was safe. Everyone seemed certain the effects of the drug would wear off soon, but that was just the problem—the effects would wear off soon. Of course she wished to speak with him, to ensure he was well, to hear his voice and see his eyes alight with recognition. But it was a luxury she'd decided she shouldn't accept.

If she was to have any hope of Martin returning home without her, he *must* believe her dead. And if she was dead, she could not revel in reunion. She needed to get on her horse and put a great deal of distance between herself and the man who still didn't trust her. A man who might at any moment convince himself it was time to hang her after all.

"Do not be dismayed, miss," Harcourt said as he bathed her face. "Most women suffer a similar reaction to violent battle. Surely you remember it, if you were at Bergen op Zoom."

Blair closed her eyes and sighed. She'd barely gathered her wits about her and already this one was testing her. So much for thinking of him as the kind one.

"73rd Highland Regiment. Under Gibbs. Would ye care to know how many men I killed and what they looked like?" she asked pleasantly. "I assure ye I can describe them all. Each man comes to me at night to tell me about their wives and children. Or would ye care to know about the battle? Of course, I could have read all that in a paper, could I not?"

He paused in his ministrations to laugh, but went right back to washing her.

"I'm relieved you seem to have no wounds, miss."

"And ye think if ye keep calling me 'miss' I'll get impatient and tell ye my name."

He grinned. "And will you?"

"No."

"My given name, by the way, is Presley."

"Presley." She gave him the sternest look she could muster.

"Yes, miss?"

"I had never seen that Scotsman before in my life. I have no idea who he supposed me to be. The man lying over there is my brother. Though his features are distorted and swollen, I know his hands well. We worked beside each other all our lives. You'll find a scar on his wrist just here." She demonstrated on her own wrist. "From a wolf pup he raised. When the wolf turned wild and attacked him, I killed it with my blade. As its name is Wolfkiller, and is possibly older than Scotland herself, I doubt that was the first wolf it killed. I'd like it back, by the way. I've never traveled unarmed before."

Wolfkiller landed in the dirt beside her, followed by one skean dhu, then the other.

She looked up to see the dark one looming over her. She looked down quickly.

"Thank you," she murmured, then tucked the blade in the sheath that was currently strapped to her leg over the breeches someone had acquired for her from the keep. As soon as she was able, she would burn them, of course, but her dress was soaking wet and so completely stained with blood one would assume the original color was black. She tucked the daggers into her boots. Though equally blood-stained, she kept them on. One can never run quite as fast as when one is wearing one's own boots.

As if the big man had read her thoughts, he snorted and walked away.

A wee while later, she felt him staring at her from across the clearing. She usually looked away, but to give him a taste of his own treatment, she stared back. He didn't look away either. They were twenty feet from each other, and yet she could hear him breathing, feel her own lungs fill along with his. She was vaguely aware of a throat clearing nearby but she couldn't for the life of her turn her head.

Ash's eyes left her only long enough to glance toward a thick grove of trees to her right, then back again. He raised a brow. His message was clear—a challenge or an invitation, it made little difference. But what message would she be giving him if she walked into those trees? She gave her head a slight shake instead. He didn't seem to care for her answer and gave his best silent argument—a frown and a nod.

She rolled her eyes and turned to her left. All his friends were watching her. She hadn't noticed when Harcourt had moved away from her to join the others. To a man, they blushed and turned away. Martin was tucked nicely beneath a canopy of pines. She stood and tried to find a reason to walk away, but the blood rushing in her head made it hard to be clever.

Ash made no bones about coming for her. The look in his eyes was the same wild look he'd had in battle. But hadn't she proven herself? Why was he still bent on suspecting her?

When she realized all his attention was for her mouth, a fissure of chills ran up her spine. She felt a ridiculous urge to run, but she had a thimble of pride left.

In half a dozen strides, he'd crossed the clearing. Without pausing, he took up her hand and walked on, into the trees behind her. She had no choice but to scurry along beside.

Her body betrayed her, thrilling at the prospect of finally being alone with the man, even if there was still a slim chance he might be leading her away to her death. But she hoped it had more to do with that night he'd come to her room, when he'd come so close to kissing her.

As a distraction, she'd thought a great deal about kissing in the past few hours, ever since he'd mentioned the idea of tasting someone. Of course, he was the only one she thought of tasting.

And after she'd gotten a taste of him, she would have a brief chat with Northwick, then she would go. Since Everhardt had assured her Martin would recover, she had turned her thoughts to others who needed her just as badly, others she was unable to help until Martin was found.

She couldn't go home again. She'd never go home again. To her father, she was already dead. Martin was a grown man. After last night, she'd done all she could do for him. He didn't need to have his sister watching over him now that he was free and headed home. And Finn would be in good hands. Her duties to them were finished.

She could no longer set aside the cry for help coming from across the channel.

Her thoughts were pushed aside as Ash pulled her up a small rise, then down into the trees below. All the while, her boots thumped the ground in an awkward effort to keep pace. She wondered if he'd forgotten how short she was, if he'd forgotten her completely, since he never glanced her way after taking up her hand.

Finally, he stopped and swung her around to face him. His breathing was only slightly labored whereas she sounded as if she'd been running from the devil. He noticed, then nodded as if he'd decided to allow her a moment to recover, but his grip told her she would stay put while she did so.

There was barely a foot between them. It wasn't easy, but she looked at anything but him.

The pale trunks of birches surrounded them like cell bars. The past year's leaves were a brown blanket on the ground interrupted here and there with equally brown pine needles. And all of them were well on their way to being absorbed back into the earth. It all looked so comfortable.

She quickly pulled her mind back from the dangerous path they were headed for and faced Ash.

His eyes darkened even while she watched and she realized how completely fitting was his choice to wear all black. The black cloud at her side. Now standing before her. Waiting. But for what?

He moved forward, forcing her to retreat until her back was against a thick, rough trunk. All the while, emotions rioted across his dark, stubbled face. He crowded her and a branch bobbed next to his head. He reached up with one hand and wrenched it from the tree, then tossed it aside. That simple act of brute strength sent a fresh spike of chills through her. His face was inches from her and still he'd said nothing. What was he waiting for?

She opened her mouth to speak, but before she made a sound, his mouth descended. . .

And she found a new appreciation for silence.

Her fingers came up to the sides of his head as if she might be able to push him away—if she ever decided to do so. It surprised her to find that his hair was softer than her own thick curls. And who might have guessed that the rough scrape of a man's morning whiskers would feel so fine.

From a long and lazy distance came the realization that she could taste him.

Finally.

She became aware of his body pressing against her and she stiffened. He ended the kiss and pulled back to look in her eyes. In his, she saw a struggle still raging. Now they both breathed liked they'd race up that hill all over again. His eyes dropped to the rise and fall of her chest, then he growled and pulled her to him, dropping his head to her shoulder, pressing his lips against her neck.

The act brought on chills of a new kind, an overwhelming glory of just being alive, and a growl of sorts from her own throat. This was not the first time she'd seen a man kiss a woman thusly. She wasn't naive, but she'd always assume the women were pretending to enjoy themselves. She'd had no idea they'd experienced true bliss.

As the rush of sensations receded, she was almost disappointed when he kissed a trail up the side of her jaw and cheek to retake possession of her mouth. Again, she was swept away in a world of excitement just behind her eyelids. When he pressed himself against her this time, she forgot to be afraid.

A throat cleared nearby.

"Ash?" It was one of his friends calling, and he wasn't far away.

Ash ignored the man and continued to press his mouth to hers, doing decadent things with his tongue that made her instantly forget about the intruder.

"Ash, I'm sorry to interrupt, old man, but I thought it best if I. . .interrupted. I'm certain you'll forgive me for it in a day or two. Come on, now. Turn the lady loose. If you need me to knock some sense into you, I'm sure I can manage to lift my fist. At least once."

Ash's body straightened away from her first. Then he put a gentle close to the kiss that had been anything but gentle. For a moment, he rested his forehead against her own, but did not look her in the eye. He whispered, "Forgive me," then kissed her ear and stepped back.

Northwick stood before them propping himself up between two thin trees. If he'd had to throw a fist at his big friend, he'd have ended up on the ground. The poor man was determined to regain his strength overnight, but already he'd had to give up the saddle and ride in the wagon. The fact he'd climbed a hill to find them made her worry.

Ash picked his way through the brush to wedge a shoulder under Northwick's arm for support.

"As long as you understand I won't be thanking you for a day or two," he told Northwick.

"Understood." His friend laughed. "Shall we join her brother? He seems to be rousing a bit. Not yet awake, but. . ."

Odin's teeth! Martin couldn't see her!

"Wait!" She hurried to block their way while she thought of a way to postpone the inevitable. She looked at Ash. "I would like to speak to Lord Northwick. Alone."

Ash frowned and gave a single shake of his head. His nostrils flared when Northwick lifted his arm from Ash's shoulder.

"Ash, leave us." Northwick's order was firm, which surprised her. None of the others dared order the bigger man about.

Ash shook his head again. "I will not leave you helpless—"

"Go." North waved her closer. "She'll see to me."

Ash gave a rather impressive growl and stepped forward and kissed her, briefly. Then he marched away.

Blair opened her mouth to speak, but North held up a hand while he watched his friend disappear. Then he stepped back to the trees and leaned on one.

"Forgive him," he said. "When he's emotional, he fails to communicate well."

She nodded, even though she thought Ash had been communicating well indeed until Northwick had interrupted.

"I beg you, do not give up on the man. Giving up is the worst sin of all, I'm afraid." He gestured to himself. "Of course we are all of us guilty of that sin from time to time. But tell me, why do you fear your brother waking?"

She raised an innocent brow.

"I saw your reaction when I said the lad was stirring."

Blair sighed, then nodded. She liked this man. He was as kind as his friends, but in observing him all morning, she suspected Northwick had secrets like hers—ghosts, nightmares, perhaps. Of course it was no wonder if he did, after what he'd been through, but perhaps it meant he'd be good at keeping her secret as well.

He gestured to a dry patch of grass and she gave him a shoulder to lean on while they made their way to it. Then they sat. She felt the weight of the Viking blade and without thinking, she bent to release the straps that held the thing to her leg. Without pulling the blade free, she laid it, sheath and all, across her palms and held it out.

"This should be given to my brother."

He took her offering and silently laid it aside.

"Our father is a bit old," she began. "He's not the most pleasant of men, to be sure. A bit full of himself. One day, he'll rub up against the wrong man and he'll be humbled, I have no doubt."

North nodded, but still made no comment.

"We have a young brother, ye see. I wasn't thinking of him when I left. All I could see was Martin dying of wounds somewhere and never coming home. Now, with all this," she gestured to France at large, "I canna be contrite for it, aye?"

North nodded again.

"But now I must see to my wee brother. To make certain Martin returns home to care for the lad. And my father as well, I suppose. For I canna do it. I am dead to my father, and my father is far too proud to ever take back a word, once he's given it. No matter how he might have missed me. I swear it."

"But why must your brother think you are dead, lass?"

She sighed. "He'll not go home without me. He's said it a hundred times since the day he found me on his heels." She faced Northwick and took one of his hands in hers. "Can ye imagine how yer heart must break, walking up to yer father after years of bein' away, and have him turn from ye? Have him bar the door against ye, from yer home and family? From his own heart?"

"I can imagine something similar, yes," he replied.

She could almost see his own ghosts rising in his thoughts and it pained her that she'd summoned them, but she had to make him understand—he was her last hope. Martin was rousing. If she didn't leave soon, her next plan of action, and her own redemption, would be lost to her.

Northwick pulled his hand from hers, leaned back and braced himself. Then he sighed. "I do not believe you, of course."

She started. Panic rose in her chest. "What do you mean?" She thought she'd been so convincing. "What do you not believe?"

"An imbroglio between yourself and your father is hardly reason enough to allow your family to believe you dead. There must be something more." He winked. "Would you care to tell me?"

She gave him a good frown, but he only laughed.

"Do not take offense, my lady. I assure you your acting ability is admirable. But if you care for your brother enough to fight for him, to kill for him, I doubt you would let him mourn you without a compelling reason."

After considering, she decided she could trust him with at least a summary of the truth and told him so.

"While searching for my brother, I heard some news I canna ignore. There are. . .people. . .in distress, aye? People I believe I can help."

"People in danger?" He straightened, as if he were hale and hearty enough to go to someone else's aid when his own health was in question.

"Aye. People in danger. But the help they need canna come from just anyone, I'm afraid. I believe they need a hand from the likes of me."

He relaxed a bit. "Are you certain I can be of no help to you, my lady? I owe you all."

She smiled and patted his boney arm. "I have no doubt ye would help if ye could, milord. And I have no doubt Martin would feel the same if he knew. But Martin must go home. And I must go where I can do the most good."

"You will not tell me where? Or whom you must aid?"

She shook her head.

His brow furrowed. "Why is it you have not tried to explain this to our dark friend?"

She laughed lightly, then shook her head. "I am not certain, other than to say I have a difficult time of it, resisting yer friend. I canna think clearly when he looks at me. If he asked me not to go. . . He could muddle my purpose, and I cannot be muddled. Others would suffer for it. Do ye understand?"

Northwick smiled. "I believe he suffers from the same weakness where you are concerned."

Was it only a day ago that Ash had said she wasn't weak, but a weakness. He was *her* weakness to be sure, but was she *his*? It wasn't reasonable, this thrill she enjoyed at the very idea of it.

Northwick leaned toward her conspiratorially. "If it is a consolation, I have never seen a woman affect him so."

Blair gifted her frail friend with the sweetest smile she could muster. They grinned at each other like idiots for a long moment.

"My Lord Northwick," she finally said.

He pulled back from her. "Here now, I've been warned you grant no man title. You are up to mischief."

She shrugged. "Did they perchance tell ye that if not for *my* information, they wouldn't have found ye yet?"

He frowned. "They said something to that effect."

"So, in truth, ye owe me yer life, ye might say." She rolled her eyes coyly.

He nodded. "Indeed, I do, my lady. As I said, I owe you all."

She smiled at the honor he'd given without pause.

"I would thank you in whatever way would make you happy, I assure you," he said simply. She waited for conditions, but he added none.

She gained her feet as ladylike as possible considering her breeches. "I already have a promise from Stanley, that he'll see to it my brother is helped as far as Inverness. It would make me happy if you and all your friends would support the story that I died."

Northwick laughed. "Do you realize *Stanley* is Viscount Forsgreen, *His Grace*, the future duke of Rochester?"

She rolled her eyes. "Of course I do. I've been eavesdropping for weeks."

"Ah." He laughed again.

She pointed to Wolfkiller. "It would also make me happy if you gave this to my brother when you tell him. It will help convince him that I'm dead. Tell him I died of a fever. I won't have him torturing himself, thinking I'd died trying to rescue him."

"Done." His head bowed briefly, but solemnly.

"Will ye fair well enough, if I leave ye here?"

He waved her away. "Ash will be back shortly, have no fear."

She bent and kissed the man on the cheek, then looked to the trees. Without a horse, she needed to move fast.

"And what shall I tell him?" North asked quietly. Apparently he was grateful enough not to raise a hue and cry if she fled.

She considered for a moment. A dozen silly possibilities went through her head, but she discarded all but three.

"Tell him. . .tell him I was never the enemy. That he should wear a white shirt at least on the Blue Moon. Tell him I had to leave because. . .because I have many more men to taste."

CHAPTER FIFTEEN

Ash had everyone mounted and loaded and still they hadn't returned.

If she was suffering another bout of wailing, she would have to finish along the way. He was done with waiting.

He stomped through the trees to give her enough notice to compose herself, but as he crested the little rise he saw Northwick lying on the ground with a smile on his face. But Scotia was nowhere in sight!

As he bent over his friend, he noticed the Viking blade at his side and relaxed. Surely the lass would never have left without it.

"Northwick. Wake up, man." He held out a hand when North's eyes opened, then pulled him gently to his feet before collecting the weapon. "Where is Scotia?"

North smiled, but the smile dropped away along with Ash's stomach.

"She's gone, Ash. I'm sorry. She asked for a boon and I had no choice but to grant it."

Denial came easy. "She wouldn't leave without her weapon, surely. And a horse. She wouldn't be so foolish. . ." But then again, she'd believed he was going to execute her. Any smart woman would have run. He was the foolish one, not to have expected it.

He found it hard to breathe and turned away so North wouldn't notice. He searched the trees, trying to guess which way she'd gone. Even in thick woods, he could catch up to her quickly on horse. He'd beg her forgiveness. She'd grant it. They'd embrace for an hour or so, then they'd join the others on the road. He just had to get Northwick back to the others.

"She had a message," North said as Ash wrapped an arm around him.

"And what was that?"

"She said to tell you she was never the enemy."

Ash grunted, refusing to admit what he'd believed one way or the other, for it was true, he'd gone back and forth on the matter a hundred times.

"Did she tell you how she knew how to find you and her brother?"

"No. But I admit I never asked."

Ash grunted again.

At the top of the rise, he paused for North's sake.

"There is more," his friend said. "She suggested you wear a white shirt at least once in a blue moon."

Ash laughed. The fact that she'd thought it right for him to wear a white shirt gave him the ridiculous impression that she saw something redeemable in him. It was also a fact that until that moment, he hadn't realized why he'd always felt most comfortable in black clothing. And waving from the rear of his thoughts was the idea that if this woman could forgive him for misjudging her, then some minor mercies might also be within his reach. Of course, he'd have to find her first.

He sobered, remembering his friend was watching him closely. "Anything else?"

North grinned, then grimaced, then grinned again. The truth be told, Ash was glad to see the man enjoying himself, even at his own expense.

"Tell me," he said, then reached for North's arm so they could get moving.

North evaded him. "I think I'll stand back a bit while I tell you."

Ash folded his arms and waited, feigning patience. He toed the fragile start of a pine tree pushing its way out of the dirt.

"She said she had to leave. . ." North took another step back. "God as my witness. . .because she has *many more men to taste.*"

In one long step, Ash closed the distance and grabbed North's shoulders. He then turned his friend to face the way they'd come.

"Which way did she go, North?"

His friend laughed.

"Which way!"

Eventually, North got hold of himself and pointed.

Ash left him teetering on the knoll.

CHAPTER SIXTEEN

Two years later, Scotland

"I regret to report, Laird Ashmoore, that yer stock was taken last eve." Allen Balliol stood with hat in hand, though to Ash he did not appear the least bit regretful. Balliol had been making himself at home in the manor when Ash had arrived a week ago to take control of the cursed Scottish property. Being demoted to the position of shepherd had perhaps soured the man's disposition. But no matter.

Ash raised a brow. "I am sorry to hear that, Balliol. Pray allow the Frenchwoman to see to your wounds."

The man laughed, as did his two sons, one perhaps twenty years, the other half as old.

"I received no wounds, sir. They trussed me up, but dared not harm *me*. I supposed ye're unaware that Balliol is a royal family north of Hadrian's wall. . .yer lairdship." Balliol's chest lifted, as did his nose.

"Then allow the woman to treat the damage done by the ropes." Ash gestured toward the kitchens where the Frenchwoman, Fantine, proved daily that she was just as talented a cook as she was a healer.

Balliol frowned and waved his wrists in front of him. "No damage."

Ash folded his arms and narrowed his eyes. The older son took a step back, but his father stood his ground. The young one merely looked back and forth between them all as if expecting entertainment.

"So. You did not try to liberate yourself? To raise a cry?" Ash took a threatening step forward, which usually sent men running. The fact that Balliol remained unaffected, after losing a hundred head, meant the Scot would need to be cowed another way. Ash would have to make an example of him in order for the rest of his sojourn in Scotland to be relatively peaceful. For peace was what he'd come for, no matter what his friends back in London believed.

Balliol rolled his eyes and smirked. "I dared not struggle."

"I thought you said *they* would dare not harm *you*," said Ash.

The older son glanced nervously behind him, at the open doorway. The young one laughed. His father clouted him on the ear, though gently. And in the doing, Balliol exposed his weakness.

"It be The Highland Reaper's men that took 'em," the older man said with a roll of his eyes. "None can be expected to fight against The Reaper. Ye'll learn that soon enough."

Actually, I will not be the one learning today.

Ash looked at the boy. "Your name, son. What is it?"

"This is me own lad, Finn." Balliol took half a step to the side, clearly ready to protect the boy.

Ash looked at the nervous one. "And you?"

Balliol answered again. "Me oldest, Martin. Fought against Napoleon. Came home a hero."

Martin blanched. Ash would wager the young man had either told his father tales, or the father lied on his behalf. As expected, the question served to get the man's attention off the younger one.

"Come here, Finn."

The boy stepped forward eagerly, oblivious to his father's grasping fingers.

Ash took the lad's shoulder, led him to his side, then turned him so they both faced his father.

"Finn Balliol," he said, "you are my hostage until my animals are returned. Do you understand?"

The boy's eyes widened as he took in the significance of the hand on his shoulder. Then he looked at his father, whose face was rapidly turning purple. Finally, he looked up at his captor and nodded.

Ash removed his hand. "I will ask for your word of honor that you will not try to escape."

The boy's eyes went wider still. He frowned at his father for a moment, then down at his overlarge boots. When he finally lifted his chin, he nodded once, then avoided looking at his father altogether.

Balliol screamed in frustration and headed for his son, but a heartbeat later, Ash had a short blade at the man's neck.

"Ye canna have me lad! Take the other one, if ye mun!" Balliol was in anguish. The lad meant a great deal to him; he would learn quicker than expected.

"You cannot have my stock, sir. Return them and the boy will be yours again. Return them not, and the boy remains with me, to raise as I see fit."

"Ye bloody bastard!"

Finn came forward and wrapped his arms around his father as if he were afraid the man would press himself into the dagger. "Dinna worry, da. Just go ask The Reaper to give them back. And dinna forget the pony!"

Ash growled. "They have my horses?"

Finn shook his head. "They left you one so you could leave Scotland faster than if you walked."

Balliol squeezed a handful of his son's hair, then stepped back. The look he gave Ash promised vengeance. "Spill but a drop of his blood, I will kill you for it." With that, he headed for the door, but at the entrance, he paused without turning. "Feed him. He's wee yet." Then he was gone.

Oh, but Ash nearly felt sorry for this Reaper fellow.

CHAPTER SEVENTEEN

The Highland Reaper hurried from her tent to interview the runner. The man was seated on a log with his hands on his knees, trying to catch his wind, but jumped to his feet when she approached. With the false shoulders beneath her black cloak, none would guess she was a woman, at least as long as they never heard her speak. Of course, someone would, eventually. She just had to do as much good as she could for her fellow Scots before someone saw through the disguise. Or beneath it.

And when they did, she'd have to leave her beloved country again—if her neck was not in a noose.

Jarvill hurried to her side to act as her voice. She had spread word that The Reaper's throat had been cut while fighting in Antwerp, and that he was now reduced to whispering. Besides the excuse for her voice never to be heard, it also served to fortify the belief that The Highland Reaper was not an easy man to kill.

"Who are ye, then?" Jarvill demanded.

"Kevin Kjar, from Brigadunn," he gasped. "I've a message from Allen Balliol. Was told to speak only with The Highland Reaper."

"Oh, aye. Ye may speak to The Reaper alone if ye mun, but he'll give ye no answer save through myself or Coll. Which shall it be, then?"

"So, 'tis true? Ye can but whisper?" The man had whispered the last. Blair almost burst out laughing, but she was anxious to see what message her father would have for the famous outlaw.

Jarvill clouted the man on the ear and sent him into the dirt. "No one insults the man and lives." He then pulled a dirk from his belt.

Kjar put his hands over his head. "I meant no insult. I beg pardon!"

Blair kept her arms folded beneath her disguise and her hood pulled far forward. In the dim light of the gloaming, Death himself might be standing among them for all they could tell. But she was fair to certain Death would be a bit taller. The cushions she wore in the heels of her boots helped, but not much.

Finally, she gave one nod and Jarvill sheathed his blade.

"Yer a lucky mon, Kevin Kjar, make no mistake. Now, will ye give yer message or no?"

"I will! I will. And thank ye." Kjar kept to his knees, and folded his hands before him. "Balliol requires ye to return the beasts ye collected last eve. He says to tell ye that the Anglishmon has taken his son hostage until the lot is returned."

Blair's blood turned cold. She was grateful the shadows kept the runner from witnessing the anguish she could not manage to keep from her face. She breathed in, then out again. Breathed in, then out. Then she leaned and whispered in Jarvill's ear.

"Which son?"

Jarvill repeated her question.

"The youngest, Finnian," said Kjar.

"Bastard!" Jarvill gave voice to her own reaction. The man was as clever as he was loyal. He knew what she was thinking most of the time, bless him. "Where does he keep the lad?"

"At the manor house, inside, with nary a tie to bind him. Balliol believes the Anglishmon has cast a spell on wee Finn so's the lad will no' leave the house."

Blair turned and walked away so the man might not hear her if she failed to keep her lips together. Her father was such a fool to blame every difficulty on superstitions. How was she ever to help her people when so many were swayed by such nonsense? It wasn't just the young who needed educations, but at least they were teachable. It would be a start. And she would keep teaching them as long as she was able.

When she'd calmed down, she walked back to the runner. She told Jarvill what to ask.

"What has become of the lad's owl?"

Asking about the bird would raise no suspicion. Anyone who knew of Finnian Balliol knew he was the lad with the wee tawny owl—called Shakespeare—that regularly perched upon his shoulder. Few would remember the bird used to belong to the sister.

"Finn does not have the owl with him, sir."

Shakespeare would starve if Finn wasn't able to feed him. Depending on when he last fed, the owl might not last more than a week. But perhaps Shakespeare might remember *her* well enough. If they couldn't rescue Finn right away, she'd have to take the risk and collect the bird herself. If her father caught her, it would be disastrous. But leaving Shakespeare to starve was something Blair simply could not do.

"Do ye have any message, then? An answer for Balliol?" Kjar bowed his head as if bracing himself for another blow from Jarvill.

Blair whispered once again in her devoted friend's ear, then headed back to her tent.

Jarvill laughed. "Tell Balliol not to be holdin' his breath." Then he turned to follow. When he came even with her, he spoke quietly. "Please tell me yer not more worrit about the damned foul than yer wee brother."

To punish her friend for even thinking such a thing, she kept her silence.

"Oh, Saints preserve us, Blair. It's yer own brother. Surely ye'll not punish the lad to spite yer father."

"I have no father, Jarvill." She ducked into her tent where a single wee candle burned strong. It offered so little light no shadows could be cast against the walls, but at least she could see a mite.

She kept a candle burning at all times, and for a pair of reasons. First, it was The Reaper's reputation to never sleep. And second, she could not stomach the darkness alone. She never fashed when others were about, or even if she was on her own with a bit of light from the moon or stars. But since those days in France, if her candle sputtered out and left her blind, the ghosts would come. And all of them.

Blair shook her fear away and tossed her cloak across her pallet, then she turned her back to Jarvill so he might help her remove her false shoulders. They stayed put much better when they were laced from behind. After a few tugs, the contraption was loose enough to remove over her head.

"If I have no father," she continued, "then there is no one to spite. But I think I should go collect Finn as meself, and not The Reaper."

She reached for the cloak again. Jarvill draped it around her. Without the false shoulders, it dragged the ground.

"Aye?" said Jarvill. "And what if someone recognizes ye?"

"Then I shall make ghostly noises and frighten them away." She laughed quietly.

Jarvill wasn't amused. "I fear this Englishmon is no' the kind of mon who is easily frightened."

She laid a hand alongside Jarvill's face and looked into his eyes. She hoped he could see her smile with dim light from the candle shining upon it, for she truly wished to ease his mind.

"Jarvill, mavournin'. There is only one English peer I fear, and the English are a bit thick on the ground in this world. Not much chance of the new laird of Brigadunn Manor being the sole man who makes me tremble. Or would ye care to make a wager?"

Jarvill frowned, his slashing brows were easy to see despite the light.

"I wish ye'd tell me what that mon did to ye," he said. "I'd hunt him down, English or no, if ye'd but say the word."

It was high time she was honest with Jarvill. He was like the level-minded brother she never had. He might understand, even if she didn't understand much of it herself.

"Weel," she said. "I'll tell ye, but ye'll make yerself sick with laughing at me."

"That I'd never do."

"Fine, then." She stepped toward the opening in the tent. "It is not what he did to me, Jarvill. Or what he might do to me." She shuddered and lowered her voice to but her usual whisper. "But what he *does* to me."

They stood there for a long moment as their hearts beat and the candlelight swayed. If she waited long enough, the truth would come to him.

"Ye're wrong, Blair. 'Tis no matter for laughing o'er. No matter at all."

CHAPTER EIGHTEEN

The growling of the lad's stomach reached the dining room before he appeared.

Feed him. He's wee yet. And hungry, it seemed.

"Come, Finn. Your place is here, beside me." Ash pointed to the place setting to his right. "Whenever possible, you should sit with your back to the wall and no man can surprise you."

Eventually, the boy took his seat. Ash placed a napkin over his own lap. Finn copied the movement, then stared down at the empty plate before him with his bottom lip protruding.

"Have no fear, boy. Food is coming. Just ring this bell." Ash nudged the bell's miniature tray away from himself.

Finn tilted his head as if sensing a trick. Ash nudged the tray again. The boy grinned and picked up the handle. The crystal bell chimed delicately.

"Ring it a bit louder so the kitchen staff can hear it."

Perhaps he should have demonstrated, he thought, when the boy put his all into the task and forced Ash to cover his ears. When it appeared as though the child had misunderstood and intended to keep ringing the thing until food appeared on his plate, Ash sacrificed the hearing of one ear to reach over and still the boy's arm. Once the ringing ceased—all but in his head—he reached over with the other hand and plucked it from Finn's grasp. He then gave the bell a civilized shake and set it back on its tray.

Finn nodded in understanding, then his eyes flew wide when Fantine and Sarah, Fantine's fourteen year old niece, came through the door carrying a number of courses. Two footmen entered after them and helped serve. The aromas that circled the room set Ash's stomach to growling as well and the boy laughed. Once their plates were filled, the footman stepped back. The boy folded his hands before him and looked anxiously at his host.

Grace? Good God, does he expect me to say grace?

Ash's frown seemed to have no effect, so he had to resort to actual words. He opened his mouth, intending to tell the boy that he did not worry over the state of his soul and thus did not bother with prayers of any kind.

Instead, the words that came forth were, "Would you care to do the honors?"

The boy looked quite relieved, then proceeded to recite what was possibly the briefest rendition of Grace ever offered, and all before Ash even got his hands fixed together properly. Finn's small fingers began the frantic task of getting as much food into his mouth as possible before he might be told to stop.

Ash recovered from his surprise and found his voice. "Stop. For pity's sake, stop."

The boy held up his hands, but chewed and swallowed quickly lest he be told to spit it all out.

"Finn, listen carefully. No one will be taking your food away. You may have all you want. Your belly will never be empty while you are in this house, is that understood? I do not intend to starve you, but I expect proper table manners. If you but watch what I do, you will learn quickly enough."

Finn's head bobbed and he lowered his hands, though he looked doubtful.

"Let us begin again." Ash picked up his knife in one hand and his fork in another and waited for Finn to do the same. But after a cursory search of the space around his plate, the boy could only produce a spoon.

Ash looked at the footman, who stepped forward smartly. Perhaps the footman would make a fine butler.

"Bring Sarah to me," he said and pretended he hadn't noticed Finn sneaking a bit of roll into his mouth before putting his hands back in his lap.

Sarah swept into the room and gave a curtsy before twisting her hands in her apron. Though her aunt was French, Sarah had been raised as an English young lady. Now Fantine was her only remaining family.

"Sarah, did you set the table?"

"I did, sir." She added another curtsy for good measure. Any day now, the lass was going to be able to relax around him. Any day.

"It appears as though you forgot to leave a knife and fork for Finn."

The girl looked at Finn and gifted the boy with a wrinkled nose before smiling back at Ash. "I did not forget, my lord. I assumed you would not wish to provide the enemy with weapons."

Ash smiled. It was just as he thought. He'd heard Sarah and Finn bickering each time he'd stepped inside that day, but he'd expected they would have worked out their differences considering the effort they put into pointing them out.

"First of all, Sarah, I'd like to thank you for your consideration. You're as clever as your aunt, which is precisely why I brought you both with me to Scotland." He gave her a smile, which she returned with an even brighter one. "Secondly, I would like you to understand that Finn is not the enemy."

The girl snorted and gave Finn a brief, though pointed look.

"Neither is his father the enemy. Nor the people of Brigadunn. The land is temporarily mine, the manor house as well, but the country belongs to the Scots. I have the right to everything this land can produce. I have the responsibility to ensure that the both the land and the people thrive. If anything, I am the enemy. If I fail in my responsibility, I will be nothing but an enemy, I assure you."

From what he'd learned, the owner before Landtree had squeezed the place dry and left the people starving and in arms. The only curse on the supposedly cursed property had been English greed. Good God, but he felt as if he was back in the fourteenth century trying to convince the Scottish they should welcome English rule with open arms.

Sarah shrugged. "I do not understand what I might do to help you, my lord."

Wasted. A fine speech, wasted.

"Go and collect Finn a knife and fork."

The girl rolled her eyes and walked away. She could use a lesson in manners herself. Sarah's parents had been English nobility. Perhaps she needed reminding.

"And Sarah?" he called.

She stopped and turned back with her hand on the door. "Yes, my lord?"

"Starting tomorrow, you will be taking your meals with Finn and me. And if you promise not to throw them, you will also be allowed a knife and fork."

After a silent curtsy, she quit the room. When she returned with Finn's utensils, she was the very study of a noble young lady. Finn even noticed.

"Will there be anything else, Lord Ashmoore?" Her little voice shook, but he suspected it was a good sign.

"That will be all, Sarah. Thank you."

She curtsied to them both and sailed regally out the door. Perhaps the girl wouldn't need nearly as much tutoring as he'd imagined.

"Tomorrow morning, Finn, be certain you are in place to pull her chair out for her."

"Yes, sir." By his tone, one would think the boy had been ordered to the most disgusting chore imaginable.

Nursemaid. If he didn't hire one, Earnest Merriweather, Earl of Ashmoore, was going to be playing the part.

Halfway through the meal, the silence became tedious.

"Tell me of the rest of your family, Finn. What of your mother? Should we send 'round a note assuring her of your safety? Promise her you've been well fed?"

"I've no mum," Finn said around a mouthful of food. "She died when I was born."

Ash decided the lad had been given enough dining instruction for one day and decided further table manners could wait until Finn no longer worried that each meal might be his last.

He resumed the conversation over rolls and butter.

"Brothers and sisters, Finn?"

"Ye've met Martin." Half a roll disappeared while the words escaped.

Ash nodded. "No sisters then?"

"Just the dead one."

The boy had tried to sound flippant about it, but there was a sting there, in his eyes.

"So, just the three of you, then?"

"Aye."

The lad's eyes filled with tears. For a brief moment, Ash thought the lad might even stop chewing, heaven forfend.

"And this sister of yours. What is your fondest memory of her?" he asked. Truth be told, he couldn't recall a meal during which he'd actually encouraged conversation. He was typically a man of very few words. Why he felt the need to cheer this boy was a mystery.

After a deep breath, the boy's face lightened. "Shakespeare," he said.

Ash offered a genuine smile. "She read you Shakespeare?"

"Oh, aye, she did that, but I mean my pet owl, Shakespeare. She raised him, then gave him over to me when. . .when she knew she'd be leaving, about the same time Martin began nattering on about going to war."

"A pet owl, you say?" For a moment, Ash was reminded of the owl ring and the woman who'd given it to him, but he shook the memory away and gave the lad his attention.

"Well, ye see," Finn said, "an owlet isna so clever. It thinks the first thing it sees is its mum. And so Shakespeare thought my sister was his mum. She trained it so it would only feed from her hand. Would never e'en kill a mouse for himself, silly creature. But he's clever in other ways, of course."

Ash smiled, more than a little relieved the lad's tears were gone. "I'm sure he is."

Finn reached for another roll but paused and waited for Ash's nod of permission before taking one. Then he launched into a list of things he'd fed to the owl at one time or another. When he could think of nothing more to add, he looked down at his empty hands, obviously wondering where the roll had disappeared to, as if he didn't remember shoving little pieces of it into his mouth as he spoke.

Ash pushed the plate and last three rolls under Finn's chin. One would have thought it was Christmas.

It must have been the Highland air to blame, but he found himself curious. "Your sister knew she was leaving? Do you mean to say she knew she was dying? Was she ill?"

"Nay. She got sick long after she left." Finn took a drink, as if the last roll were stuck in his throat. Then he set the glass aside and continued on, a bit more cheerfully. "But wee Shakespeare would feed only from her hand, and so would starve without her. So at first, I would wrap my hand around hers when she fed him. After a bit, I would hold the meat and she would wrap her hand around mine. Eventually Shakespeare began eating from my hand with my sister standing off a ways. But then one morning she was gone and the owl had no choice in the matter, aye?"

"Sounds like a clever lass," Ash admitted. He felt his supper rising in his throat as punishment for letting his mind stray to another clever lass he'd known, once upon a time. He'd wasted three weeks of his life trying to find that particular Scotswoman. When he'd finally come home with his tail tucked, his friends had blessedly agreed to never again speak of her or their French nightmare. He only hoped his friends were doing a better job of forgetting.

"Och, aye, she was clever. Father called her something else, but I'll not repeat it. He told her if she left, she would be dead to 'im. When we came in from the fields one day, my sister had left us a cold supper on the table and a letter under the salt. Da tossed it into the fire without readin' it."

Finn's eyes were filling again.

"And where is this owl now?" asked Ash, hoping the bird was not dead as well. Why the hell hadn't he simply allowed the lad to eat in silence?

"He's back at the old home with me father, where we lived before movin' into yer fine manor. It's not far, so I never brought the bird here." Finn frowned. "I reckon he'll need to feed in few more days."

"Well, then, let's hope The Highland Reaper returns the cattle before Shakespeare gets peckish."

Finn swallowed. "And if not?"

Ash huffed. What did the lad expect, leniency for a bird's sake? If Finn Balliol didn't understand that he was the hostage of one of the deadliest men in England, it was high time he realized it. The Earl of Ashmoore could bend other men to his will with simple stare. He did not go about bending to the tears of children.

Although Finn's eyes were dry, his chin quivered, but only the once. His hands gripped the edge of the table. His back was straight as if expecting a blow. Perhaps the lad did understand after all.

Ash set his napkin aside, stood, and pushed his chair beneath the table.

"If The Reaper fails you," he said, "he'll fail the bird
as well." He toed the leg of his chair with a shiny boot,
unwilling to see what reaction his reply might have earned.
"But it just so happens," he continued, "that I'm rather fond
of that particular playwright. I'm certain there is something
resembling a mews here at Brigadunn."

He'd barely gotten the words out before he was
attacked 'round the middle. If the child had been fed better,
he might have knocked Ash to the ground with his
demonstration.

He refrained from encouraging the lad and held his
hands high lest he be tempted to rest them on the small
shoulders.

"Finn Balliol, I've done you no favors," he said
sharply.

The boy straightened and stepped back, biting his lips
to keep from smiling.

"You cannot expect my servants to construct this
mews, do you hear? You've hard work ahead of you. And
any scraps you feed to that blasted bird will have to be
earned."

Finn threw back his shoulders and stared ahead as any
soldier might. Ash paced before him like some
commanding officer caught up, if only for the moment, in
pandering to a child. He remembered all too fondly the days
of playing soldier, long before the realities of war and
blood, and the deaths of comrades changed his dreams. He
could not begrudge the lad enjoying the game while he
could.

"You will not leave the immediate grounds," he
barked. "And if I call your name, I expect you to appear
immediately. Remember, you are on your honor here."

"Yes, sir."

Ash was surprised the boy didn't salute, especially
when his own hand rose of its own accord. He pushed a
wayward lock of hair from his forehead and quit the room
before he was tempted to ransack the house in search of

miniature soldiers. He walked to the study in search of parchment, intent on sending for a small set of such toys for the lad, but before he'd so much as located a pen, he crumpled the parchment into his fist.

What in the world had he been thinking? The cattle would be restored and young Finn Balliol would be collected by his father. And he'd be damned if he was going to play soldiers himself. His time would be better spent considering the war in which he was presently engaged. . .

. . .the war with a man called The Reaper.

CHAPTER NINETEEN

Ash headed for the manor after making certain his mare was secure. If the outlaw decided to come take his last mount, the clever strategy would be to sleep in the stables. It would make their inevitable meeting more probable, and the sooner the better. After he had removed the so-called curse from the property, he could find a more hospitable place to spend his summer. He certainly wasn't ready to head back to London, but there was something to be said for a good night's sleep when one did not fear what one might wake to find in the morning. Or rather, wake to find missing.

He'd known the cattle would be taken as soon as they'd arrived, but he'd lain awake for two nights before The Reaper got 'round to collecting them. He thought it might be easier to sleep after the bait had been taken, but he doubted he'd rest much tonight unless he brought the mare into the house and slept on the animal's back. Even then, he would not be surprised to wake up in the morning to find that he'd been kidnapped right along with the horse.

Surely, out of spite, The Reaper would come for more instead of returning the rest, for why would the villain care for the fate of a single boy? Ash was not surprised to find himself affronted on behalf of young Finn. The lad was clever, fearless even, and if Ash was not careful, he would come to care for the lad.

Snow was coming. He could smell it. No matter that the skies had been blue all day, there was no mistaking the impression of change in the air. Indeed, so strong was that impression, he wondered what other change, besides the weather, might be imminent. Of course, in Scotland, there was little chance of spring making an appearance in March, but it was not the change of season that he sensed.

A shudder ran down his spine and he stopped in his tracks. Something was amiss. Perhaps The Reaper had come, just as Ash suspected he would.

He turned and looked back toward the stable he'd left only a moment before. Thanks to the moon riding low on the far side of the manor house, his dark form would not be easy to discern, even though he was standing in the open.

The items he'd propped against the stable doors leaned exactly where he'd positioned them. A large and noisome cart blocked the only other access to his mare.

He stood, still as death, and waited. Nothing moved. No breeze to usher in the storm. Even the moonlight held its position on the outbuildings.

He turned and looked at the house, expecting to see Finn still standing all forlorn at parlor's side windows, like a little boy who'd been forbidden to play outside. It was well past time for the lad to be abed, but Ash had told him he could make his own decisions, so long as he stayed put. A little responsibility was good for a body.

But Finn wasn't at the window. Deeper within the house, a light was doused. Nothing strange there, if it weren't for that shiver now tickling behind his ears. What if The Reaper had come, not for the horse, but for the lad?

Ash's legs burst into action, though he made little sound as he hurried to a window. He closed his eyes for just a moment so they might adjust to the darkness within. Then he pressed his head to the edge of the frame and peered inside.

Two forms stood in the entrance to the parlor. The first was easily Finn. No other young lads were about the place. The other looked to be Sarah. They were arguing again. Perhaps they'd never ceased. Ash had left the house an hour before to get away from the god-awful noise. Sarah presumed to boss the boy in spite of him reminding her, each and every instance, that she was not his keeper.

It looked as if Sarah had decided the boy should be in bed and was trying to drag him there. But Finn's bed was above stairs and she was trying to pull him toward the rear of the house, away from the staircase. She appeared to be of a size to accomplish the deed, but something was amiss.

Sarah was not a full head taller than Finn, was she?

Ashmoore wanted to clout himself on the head when he finally realized that the woman could not be Sarah. Neither could it be the larger Frenchwoman. The mass of hair should have given her away as well, or perhaps the woman wore a hood. It could not be Finn's mother or sister trying to rescue him, for they were dead. She simply must be in league with The Reaper!

Ash headed for the kitchen door at the back of the house, expecting to find the villain waiting there, surprised when he was not. But did he dare wait for the female accomplice outside, or confront her inside? He had no doubt their tug of war was due to the fact that Finn refused to be rescued, but the woman didn't seem to be giving him a choice.

Ash was grateful for well-oiled hinges as he entered the kitchens. The house was silent. Unnaturally silent. Unfortunately, he wasn't familiar enough with the place to avoid a large basket on the floor and the damned thing went skittering across the stones as if it were purposefully trying to give him away.

With stealth denied him, he ran for the front hall, awkwardly reaching out to feel the walls to either side of him. If the woman fired in his direction, she'd be hard-pressed to miss her target.

His heart jumped when a body slammed into him and wrapped its arms about his waist. Ash's hands came down on Finn's shoulders, but did not push him away.

"Finn! Are you hurt?"

"No," the child mumbled.

Then Ash realized Finn was impeding his progress on purpose!

He gently peeled the boy from his body and sat his bottom on the floor with a nice thump before he lunged for the door. He'd be damned it the ungrateful imp didn't stretch his legs out to try and trip him!

The moonlight lit part of the front lawn. Ash held onto the doorframe and searched for movement. No sense running out into the night if he ran in the wrong direction. But there, on the far side of the fountain, a shadow moved. As he ran full out, he had to remind himself that this was a woman. He'd have to be gentle, not knock her to the ground with his body.

She heard him coming and was on her feet and running down the sloping lawn before he reached the other side of the fountain. He expected to catch her before she reached the rose hedge that bordered the drive.

He was wrong.

And the hedge didn't stop her.

He very nearly forgot to keep running when she sailed over the rose bushes. With her cloak billowing behind her, he could almost believe she was a ghost, that her lower half had simply disappeared through the branches as she'd flown through it. If it weren't for the thumping of her boots across the drive, he might not have shaken off his foolish thoughts and resumed the chase.

She disappeared into the tree line, but he anticipated the angle at which she'd entered and made up some ground. And a good thing too—she'd reached her horse and had one foot in the stirrup when he finally got his hands on her.

He reached one arm around her waist and hauled her backward. She made no noise, but fought like a cat. Her heels struck out at his shins, but holding her as he was, he could anticipate where she intended to strike at him by how her weight shifted.

"Calm yourself, madam. Calm yourself I say."

He was determined to get a good look at her, but couldn't do so while holding her in the air, so he lowered her to the ground without easing his hold. He could only turn her so far without risking her escape and it seemed as if no matter how he tried, she was equally determined not to be seen. The icy cloud of her breath was always moving away from him.

"Damn, but you're fast for a woman. Fast for a man, even."

Compliments usually got a lady's attention, but not this one. She remained silent.

"Tell me," he pulled her back against him and spoke gently through the thick mass of curls that covered her ear. "Why should The Reaper give a whit about the Balliol boy?"

She shivered in his arms and he wondered just how far she would have had to travel in the cold night air before she reached her destination. Not far, most likely, if she was willing to take the boy from the house without so much as a blanket to keep him warm.

"He doesna," she whispered. "Just go back the way ye came. Go."

She ceased fighting him, for the moment. It could have been due to the warmth between them, but he doubted it. She was too vigorous to give up so soon. But then that need to see her face would not leave him. It was ridiculous, of course, but he could not help but recall that other Scottish lass with a head covered in generous red curls, with a brogue to her whisper so similar to this one's. The details of that first woman were fading after more than two years, but he remembered enough to know she was a good deal smaller and shorter than the woman in his arms. He had a silly hope, however, that if he could see this hellion's face, it might help him remember the other one.

With his left hand, he reached around and got hold of her right wrist before easing his arm from around her. She could spin out of his hold and try to get free, but only if she turned toward him first. And turn she did. As she did so, he snatched up her other wrist and she was caught, facing him. All she would share with him, though, was the top of her head, or rather, her hood.

Well, if she wished to play a waiting game, he would oblige her. It should only take but another moment for her to realize he meant to win.

CHAPTER TWENTY

Blair had never fought so hard in her life. Only the one she fought with was not the Englishman, but herself. She so wished to take a gander at the large man's face, but to do so would expose her own. Even though he would have no reason to recognize her now, she couldn't risk him doing so later, knowing she was the woman who'd tried to help his hostage escape. If she could keep her hair covered and her face averted, she could make her way through a crowd without drawing notice. But once someone saw the beauty mark next to her right eye, they never forgot.

Her own little mob, the people she led, were careful never to mention the mark. They knew only that along with Jarvill and Coll, she was one of The Reaper's close companions, and as such, her identity warranted protection. It was the least they could do for the man who fed and protected them, the man that had given them hope.

But to have the Englishman see her mark and then go about asking folk about it would only lead to her downfall.

If her father heard tell. . .

That could never be allowed to happen. This man must never see her face, and so she could never see his. And rightly so. What purpose would it serve to know the face of the man when he was surely about to flee from Scotland as the last one had?

Standing in her boots was doing nothing to keep her warm, however, so it was past time for leaving. She took a hesitant step forward and the man tensed. Then she took another and pushed herself against him as if in need of his warmth, which was true but not her purpose. And just like a man, he released one of her wrists so that he might wrap an arm about her. Another minute passed and he relaxed.

"Come, now," he said against her head. "Return to the house with me. We can have a chat over hot tea, and then you can be on your way. What say you?"

His deep voice rumbled through her very bones. It was nearly her undoing. If it weren't for that man in France—Ash—she wouldn't have been affected in the least. But Ash had possessed such a dark voice. In fact. . .

She started.

It was not possible that she was wrapped in the arms of the only Englishman that terrified her. To even imagine the men were one and the same would make it less likely for her to get away from this one. And get away, she would.

"Come," he said again and pulled back from her.

It was just enough room. She brought up her knee with unrepentant force. He yanked on her wrist, pulling her to one side as he turned his body in the opposite direction, but it could not save him. At least, not all of him.

It could have been surprise as much as pain that made him release her. Two steps and a leap put her on the horse's back. After she was well out of his reach, she dared a glance back and found the man standing, but bent, with his hands on his knees. Standing was a fine thing. An Englishman freezing to death at the hands of The Reaper, while doing much to further the legend's infamy, would make her impossible for the authorities in England to ignore.

She slowed her horse and could not resist one last taunt.

"Go home. Go home and remove yer hands from all things Scottish, aye?"

His head snapped up and even though she was turning away, she feared his glare was far too familiar.

I only imagined it, she thought, while her clever mount wove through the trees for which she had no attention. The other one, the man who haunted her dreams and stole her sleep, would have no business in Scotland, surely.

Unless. Her heart tripped at the thought of it. *Unless he came looking for me.*

~ ~ ~

"So, yer alive. I knew it."

Blair turned away from Shakespeare's perch and faced the oldest of her two brothers in the darkness. She'd left the door open so the moonlight might help her locate the bird. Now Martin stood in the doorway blocking most of that light.

"Hello, Martin."

She'd barely finished whispering his name before he slammed into her. His embrace was enough to set her back a good three feet.

"Oh, Blair! How could you do it? How could you let me believe ye were dead?" He gave her a good squeeze to show her how he felt, then loosened his hold a bit without letting her go. She was grateful she didn't have to look him in the eye while they spoke.

He was right. It was cruel to deal him such a blow when his kidnappers had left him so weak, but she'd had no choice, not if she wanted him to go home and leave her behind.

"I canna explain just th' now. Ye'll just have to trust me, that it broke my heart to do it."

How many times had she dreamed of the chance to tell her brother those words?

"I blamed meself." His voice was harsh in her ear. "If I hadna gone to France. . ."

"Wheesht! The blame is mine for deceiving ye. Forgive me. Forgive me and trust me."

"Ah, mavournin'. Da will be—"

She pulled back and looked into her brother's wet eyes. "I have no da, Marty. And yer da has no daughter. Ye must continue to act as though it's true. For it is."

Martin shook his head. "But you doona understand, Blair. Da's taken a hard blow. The Englishmon has taken wee Finn for a hostage—"

"I know, brother. Wasn't I just in the blackheart's house trying to steal our Finn away? But he wouldna come."

Martin shrugged. "Da says the mon's cast a spell on him."

Blair sighed. Allen Balliol was a superstitious fool.

"He's an eegit," she said. "Finn but believes he's given his word, that to escape would be dishonorable. He doesna understand that sometimes fighting back is the only honorable thing."

With the reminder of how she herself had just been fighting with the Englishman, she realized Martin would know the blackheart's name. She was nearly too afraid to ask, to have her worst fear realized, but she would not spend a sleepless night worrying. It was best to know for certain.

"Speaking of the devil," she said, "do ye ken the Englishman's name?"

Her brother nodded. "Name's Earnest Merriweather, an earl, no less. Nothin' pleasant about the man. And dangerous, to be sure. Ye're lucky to have gotten away before he caught ye."

She nodded, but bit down on her tongue. Truth be told, she was torn, both disappointed and relieved that Ash had not come to Scotland. Her heart had leapt at the thought he might have sought her out, but even if he had, he might still believe she was his enemy. Also, if the likes of Ashmoore had taken up the manor house and control of the area, the threat of The Highland Reaper could not frighten the man away.

She only hoped this Merriweather fellow wasn't similar to Ash in more than form alone.

Martin gave her a pleading smile and squeezed her arms. "Are ye certain ye won't come inside? To see ye would cheer Da to no end."

"Why?" she asked gently. "His daughter is dead."

She pulled Martin close again and wrapped her arms about him to get warm and to hide from his searching eyes. It was time to say goodbye, and she worried she could not do it while facing him.

"Since I was the one to tell him the sad news, I can tell ye he mourned ye, Blair. Truly he did. He e'en placed a memorial for ye."

Now that surprised her. She pulled back to see if Martin was telling the truth. Even in the shadows, she could see him blush. He was hiding something.

"Oh? Where is this memorial, brother? Where might I read my name in stone?"

Martin ducked and shuffled a foot in the straw. "Under the birches, ye know the ones. But 'tis not stone. 'Tis a nice wood cross."

"A nice wood cross. Fer me soul. The soul he no doubt believes is makin' itself comfortable in Hell."

If Martin had defended her, if he'd sworn upon his life that Blair had never become a camp whore as their father had predicted, the old man would have never believed him, for to do so would be to admit he'd been wrong—and Allen Balliol was never wrong.

The old anger rose and warmed her a'plenty, so she stepped away from Martin and went for the bird that was four times the size it had been when she'd left home. Finn had done a fine job caring for it.

"What are ye about, sister? The owl's not well. Finn always played with him every night and every morn, so

Shakespeare must sense something is amiss. If Finn isna brought home soon, he'll return to an empty perch."

She placed the hood on Shakespeare and collected his jesses. For the first time since she'd entered the mews, the owl squeaked.

"There now, Shakespeare. Yer mum's home. All will be right."

Shakespeare squeaked again.

"Aye, my wee birdie. Ye'll be coming with me." She nudged the owl's belly with her gloved fist and he hopped onto it out of habit. "And Martin, our wee brother will keep my secret and so must ye."

Her brother moved to her side and petted the bird. Tears fell down his face unchecked. Two years ago, he hadn't been so tall.

"Aye, I'll keep yer secret," he said, "until you say otherwise. But where will ye go on this cold dark night, mavournin'?"

She hoped Martin didn't notice her hesitation before she was forced to break his heart yet again. "Back to The Reaper," she said. "He protects me." *He keeps me warm* was what she implied.

CHAPTER TWENTY-ONE

Clouds of pink and orange created a beautiful garden from which the sun rose and yawned in greeting, which, for some reason, put Ash in a decidedly foul mood. He pulled the curtains shut on the obnoxiously cheerful day and determined to sleep until the weather better reflected his state of mind.

Tolly appeared with breakfast in any case. Ash pulled a pillow onto his head and ignored the man.

"I was asked to inform ye, me laird, that Finn will no longer be needin' a mews for his owl, since the wee Shakespeare has disappeared."

Ash removed the pillow. "No doubt a larger owl made a meal of him."

"No doubt, sir."

"And the lad?"

"Sir?"

"How is Finn taking the news?"

"Rather well, I think, considering. It hasn't put him off his breakfast at any rate."

Ash pulled the pillow back into place and mumbled into it. "Good. I am not up to being a nursemaid today."

"Very well, me laird," he heard the man say as he left the room.

When the sky proved cloudless at midday, Ash closed the curtains again and ordered a bath, then had a sulk and a soak until both his body and his mind were well pruned.

Until the sun was down, his only companion was his owl ring. He had removed it from its small drawstring sack, placed the sack on the bed, and propped the little fellow on the velvet so it faced him while he brooded. Though he willed it to open its miniscule beak and impart some wisdom, it remained as silent as the grave, as if it, too, had promised to never speak again of Scotia.

But Ash itched to speak of her. And he itched in general from bathing far too long.

He rolled up his right sleeve and stared at the scar on his forearm. The wound seemed so fresh since his encounter with yet another Scotswoman, it would not have surprised him to find blood oozing from the thin white line where his broken blade had imbedded itself. The scar was over two years old, but tonight it felt angry.

He rubbed a hand over it, then rolled down his sleeve and tried to put it out of his mind. He made his way to the window and peered out at the dark woods to the north. Immediately, the shadows before him were forgotten in favor of a memory—memory of the woman who'd given him that bothersome scar.

He tried, and failed, to conjure Scotia's face. She had fled from him in France. He'd left his friends to fend for themselves and began his hunt for a fearless redhead with a beauty mark near her right eye. Either none had remembered her, or a nation of Franks chose to take sides against him. He suspected the latter.

For weeks he'd stomped around the Continent until a letter from Harcourt caught up to him. Northwick needed Ash by his side if he was going to fully recover from his ordeal. And Ash had needed his friend much more than he'd needed his prey. So he'd gone home.

But after two years, Northwick was himself again, and in love, of all things. And rather than sit by while the legend of the Four Kings withered and died, Ash had left town. However, after the encounter in the woods last night, and the new disquiet in his soul, Ash's mind had been dancing around a preposterous question.

Had his destination of Scotland been coincidence or not?

He thought back to the lottery, that night when his name was drawn, but Northwick had hidden the tile and claimed it was his own lot that had been pulled from the small barrel. That deception was no longer significant, so he thought back a few moments earlier, to when Landtree had donated his cursed Scottish property to the loser.

Ash remembered his gut clenching, his heart jumping when the name of her country dredged up such strong emotion. Now he wondered if his longing for her somehow lifted his name to the top of the barrel. Did he will himself to Scotland by way of the lottery?

Ash's name being drawn had set so many pieces in motion. Had a different lot been chosen, North would have never met Livvy. The grinning, love-struck pair would never have driven Ash from London. Ash would never have demanded the Scottish property in order to have a destination. And he would have never encountered that woman last night—a woman who'd dragged a heart-breaking memory from the mud of his soul and made him. . .*want* again.

But was it the woman he wanted, or absolution?

Of course he had regrets. He would readily apologize for believing she was allied with the men who had kidnapped Northwick. He wanted to beg her forgiveness for not tying her securely to a tree and keeping her from ever viewing the carnage that was Givet Faux. If he'd managed it, the big Scotsman would have never planted that doubt in Ash's mind.

Scotia would have never been forced to kill that woman in defense of herself and her brother. But most important of all, she would never have heard Ash accuse her of duplicity nor have been convinced he wanted her dead.

And she would never have fled.

Ash's friends would prefer he blame all his faults on Battle Fever, would have him believe that the red haze was too thick to allow any of them to think clearly. And yet, none of them had questioned her.

Of course Northwick hadn't been in on the fighting, but after the Scot had taken the woman out of the keep, his too-thin friend had been carried away with rage to match Ash's own. North had attacked the still-bleeding form of the Frenchman with all the strength he could find, until he, too, was splattered with as much blood as the rest of them.

And the following morning, North had granted Scotia's boon without question. He'd let her go.

Ash felt fresh anger fill his lungs and a truth startled him.

God help him, he was angry with North!

Perhaps Ash had never allowed himself to be angry with the man earlier because until recently, North had been in a questionable state of mind. Perhaps now that his friend was recovered and, in truth, happier than he'd ever been, Ash's anger could cause the man no harm.

"Damn you, Northwick!" Ash shouted. "Why the bloody hell did you let her go?"

The words died away with no one to answer them, but Ash felt better in any case.

Better, but still wanting.

A wide-eyed footman appeared at the door. Ash waved the young man away.

Heaven help him, how could one strange Scotswoman stir up so much? Worse yet, he'd placed himself in the heart of an entire country full of them! And the only one he wanted would never step foot on Scottish soil again.

He'd packed his bags and half a household. . .and delivered himself to the doorsteps of his own Hell.

Lucky for him, however, the road to Hell led out again.

But before he left, he'd put this Reaper fellow out of business. He'd do as he'd planned, get the property and its people back to prosperity and away from the devastation the previous owners brought about. Of course, Northwick hadn't been among the vultures; he'd only owned the property for a few weeks before Ash had demanded the deed from him.

Soon, there would be no more need of a Robin Hood figure to sustain the crofters of Brigadunn. And if all went well, The Reaper would see justice of some sort. Ash hated to punish a man for helping his fellow Scots survive against greedy and inept landlords, but The Reaper had known what would happen if he were caught. He'd assumed that risk.

Laws were what raised men above the beasts. If there were no law, the world would be a madhouse, as France had been. At Givet Faux, Ash had taken it upon himself to be judge and executioner. And one day, he too would answer a higher law.

The similarity between himself and this Highland Reaper caught him by surprise.

Ash considered, for the hundredth time that day, the woman The Reaper had sent to steal Finn from him. They even had a similar taste in women!

Tolly appeared at the doorway and gave a bow.

"You bellowed something, yer lordship?" the old man asked innocently.

Ash could hardly take the man to task. After all, he had bellowed.

After a moment's thought, he said, "Bring me the eldest son of Allen Balliol."

Finn's young gasp came from the hallway.

"Come to me, Finn," he called.

The lad marched through the door with his quivering chin held high.

"Sit down. I'm told Shakespeare. . .is no longer with us. My sympathies."

Finn looked at the velvet covered chair, then glanced down at his clothes.

"You won't damage the chair, lad. Sit."

He'd have to see about getting the boy some decent attire so he didn't feel so out of sorts in Ash's household. Since Balliol hadn't tip-toed around the stately furnishings, the only thing that might give the boy pause would be the people who now inhabited the house, and all dressed a damn sight better than the supposedly royal Balliol's. But perhaps the rags were the result of a lack of females in the lad's household.

Poor Finn.

When Ash had returned from his near-maiming, he'd barked at the lad to get to bed, then taken his foul mood to his rooms. What had completely slipped his mind was the fact that Finn had attempted to stop him from pursuing the woman. The poor boy probably hadn't slept all night for fear of what his punishment might be. Then Ash had made the lad wait all day before speaking to him.

"Finn Balliol," he said as he walked to the mantle and took the seat opposite the lad. "You are to be commended for keeping your word last night."

"Pardon?" The lad's grip on the chair's arms relaxed not a whit.

"That woman was clearly determined to rescue you from my dastardly clutches and yet you fought her off. I merely thought you should know your actions did not go unnoticed."

Finn was speechless. Ash bit his lip to keep from laughing.

"Actually, *none* of your actions went unnoticed."

While Ash carefully laced his fingers and laid them across his lap, Finn swallowed, then swallowed again.

"I wonder, who is this woman that you would risk all to help her get away?"

The boy took a deep breath and folded his arms. Then he looked Ash in the eye, but said nothing.

"I wonder who are you, to this Hecuba, that she would risk all to come to your rescue?"

Finn's eyes began to swim just before he looked off into the distance.

So, he knew the woman.

"Will you give me her name?"

The boy shook his head only once and salty tears began to pour.

"You will not be punished for trying to help her, Finn. There is no dishonor in coming to a lady's aid."

The boy nodded absently, far too distracted to properly appreciate Ash's generosity.

"What is it, son?"

Finn shook his head. "May I be excused then, yer lairdship?"

"*Sir* will do," Ash reminded.

"May I be excused, sir?"

"Your brother will be here forthwith. Do you wish to see him?"

The boy's eyes flew wide and he shook his head most fervently.

"Obviously, you do not. Well, your brother will feel differently."

The tears flowed afresh and, though irritated, Ash could not resist giving the lad some relief.

"Well, I shall let him have a peek at you, but you're not to speak to each other, is that clear?"

Finn nodded, his small head quickly bobbing up and down, the flow of his tears ceased immediately.

"Can you read? Write?"

"Aye, sir."

"Then you will hie yourself off to my library and I shall find a book for you about this Hecuba woman." Ash stood and urged the boy out of the room.

"Aye, but she was no woman, sir." Finn seemed to forget his troubles before the tears had a chance to dry on his cheeks. "She was a queen, and woe betide those who killed her boy."

Ash took up his coat. "And who taught you Greek history, Finn? That sister of yours?"

"Aye, sir. She told me the tale just before. . .just before she went away."

Perhaps the sister's death was still weighing heavy on the boy's heart. Hopefully that was all that had brought him to tears and not some current worry. But on the way to the library, Ash couldn't help but ask why Finn didn't want to speak to his brother.

"I. . . I dinna want to be tempted, aye?"

They paused at the library door and Ash turned the boy to face him. "Tempted to do what, may I ask?"

The lad's boys flew wide, but he recovered quickly.

"Tempted to run away," he said, then smiled as if he was pleased with his own quick thinking.

Ash opened the library door and ushered his hostage inside, and for the life of him, he could not imagine what the boy was keeping from them all.

CHAPTER TWENTY-TWO

"Mary Dowds is gone," Coll announced as he entered the tent. "That's three this week and the blighter hasna done much more than feed a few crofters and promise better times to come."

Blair gave a nod, but hid her reaction, knowing Coll was testing her. He'd stood beside her since she'd first donned the guise of The Highland Reaper, but he was forever waiting for her to break. It would only be natural, he'd said, if she suddenly tired of the fight and decided to go home. What he'd really meant was, "Surely a woman canna hold out long."

So each morning, when she emerged from her wee room in their shared cottage, Coll would raise a brow in surprise before bidding her a good morn.

As their following grew, as more and more Scots came to depend on her protection, she'd expected that surprise to fade, but it hadn't. And since their numbers were lessening every day, she could feel Coll watching her, waiting for some signal to jump to his feet and hold the door for her as she fled.

But he would never understand. Even if he left, and there was none in The Vale but her, she'd not go home. She'd leave her beloved country before she'd beg her father to take her back.

Mary had been one of the first to put herself and her children under The Reaper's protection. It wasn't as if Blair felt Mary owed her some sort of loyalty, for she knew well how Mary missed her husband, but Blair would miss the woman's five children terribly. They were a clever bunch that seemed to understand the difference between superstition and truth, but who knew how long they would remember what they'd learned? Blair would simply hope the older ones would keep passing their educations along.

"That's ten children in but seven days," Coll pointed out.

She realized Coll might not be prodding as she'd thought. He'd become as attached to the bairns as she was, since Coll looked upon all their young wards as his own. Unfortunately, he looked upon their mothers with the same eye. What the man sorely needed was a clever wife who could keep his attention.

"Aye," she said. "Ten more mouths for the Anglishmon to feed. Thirteen, including their mothers. He'll be changing his tune in a month's time, I'll wager."

Coll sat on the cot and began unlacing one of his boots.

"I'll not take that wager, thought I believe ye may be wrong, Blair. And what then? If ye lose them all, what do ye then?" He pulled off the boot and gave it a shake. A pebble popped out and rolled under the cot. "Will ye go away, as ye've said ye must? What if the bastard turns greedy in a year and takes it all away again? How many will die before another Reaper rises up to save them? A hundred this time?"

Coll stomp his foot back into his boot. His angry fingers worked the laces back into place.

"Collier McGill!" She could hide her frustration no longer. "Bite yer tongue and swallow yer teeth." She put her fists to her hips. "They're my people and I'll not be leaving them to the English wolf wearing the skin of a sheep. Do you truly believe I'd be so easily swayed? Ye're forever thinking I'll slink away in the night and I'm through with yer lack of faith in me just because I'm a woman."

He stood and brought his nose close to hers, his pose a mirror of her own. "Ye think I suppose ye'll bolt because yer a woman? Hah! It has naught to do with what ye have, or haven't, beneath yer skirts, Blair Balliol."

"Then what is it? How could you think I'd abandoned ye all?"

Coll took a deep breath but his frown remained. "Ye're always sayin' we're a family, and that all in The Vale is yer clan. But we ken what ye've done to yer real clan, aye? Ye allow the family of yer blood to mourn and miss ye. What will keep ye from doing the same to the family of yer heart?"

She shook her head while she waited for his words to make sense.

"Ye're wrong," she whispered. "It was my father who chose to mourn me as soon as I left home. My brothers. . .well, my brothers know the truth now."

Coll scoffed. "An accident you never intended."

"No matter."

"Yer wrong, Blair. It matters. It matters that ye keep the truth from yer father. He's a good man. Ye canna deny that at least."

"A good man? Aye, sure. A good man; a poor father."

"Hah! Then ye both have forgiveness to beg. A tit fer a tat."

Blair felt tears rise behind her eyes and was grateful for the dim light.

"What would ye have me do?" she asked. For fear of others overhearing, she lowered her voice to a harsh whisper. It was all the restraint she had left. "Show meself? Do I tell him all, that I'm The Highland Reaper? Or do I let him believe as the others do, that I share The Reaper's bed? Do I beg him to call me daughter only to have him believe he was right—that I'd end as a whore? Better for him to believe I'm dead and gone."

Eventually, Coll's shoulders dropped and he nodded. He lowered himself onto the cot once more. With the matter finally settled between them, at least for the moment, it seemed they had little else to discuss. The tent was suddenly too small for two, so she looked about for her cloak, intending to take a stroll.

He spoke again. "Since my first ride with The Highland Reaper, I've known the days of glory were numbered, that there would be an end to it, one way or another. But I always supposed it would end with The Reaper leaving, not the valefolk."

Blair smiled, glad for the chance to erase the awkwardness between them. "Are ye afraid for the people, or afraid of so many women returnin' to their husband's beds?"

Coll cut her a look that said she'd hit close to the mark, even though his lips curved up in a smirk.

"Or is there a particular lass ye prefer would never go home again?"

He came to his feet and stretched. "And what of ye, Blair Balliol? Have ye gone soft on the man who holds young Finn hostage? What happened that night that ye've yet to tell us? Why are ye suddenly warm on the idea of his success? What might he have said that makes ye allow the bastard to remain on Scottish soil, eh?"

She shook her head. "T'isn't so. I swear it. But it's been two years for Mary and some of the others as well. Ye canna blame them for wanting to go home. And I'll be damned if I'm going to hold them in the vale against their wishes." She raised her chin. "But letting them go has nothing whatever to do with the Englishman. He'll go, and soon. Dinna doubt it."

The risk of allowing another greedy landlord sink his talons into the land and her people was too great. Better to shoo the man away, and fast, as they had the previous lord, Landtree.

Coll sighed, then reached for her, wrapped his arms around her shoulders and set his chin on her head. "Auch, lassie. I fear for me own happiness is all, for I have been happy in the vale with all those bairns needin' a man to look up to. Forgive me for bein' sae selfish. I just dinna like it when things change, aye?"

She gave an unladylike snort. "And yet ye change beds often enough."

Coll laughed and pushed her away. "Auch, nay." He winked. "Never often enough."

He left the tent and Blair collapsed on the cot, her knees a bit too shaky for a stroll. If she was to run off this large Englishman, it would take more than a simple harassing to convince him to go. She would have to frighten him to the bone, frighten him enough to sacrifice his pride and flee. And to do it, she would need to go to Brigadunn yet again. Close work was required. But getting close would mean coming far too near Allen Balliol, and the thought brought a shiver up her spine.

Allen Balliol had said she was dead. Allen Balliol believed she was dead in truth. And if there was one thing Allen Balliol would not permit, it was for someone to make a liar of him.

Blair wrapped her arms around herself and thought of Mary Dowds. . .and wished there was some place on this earth she could run home to.

CHAPTER TWENTY-THREE

"Oh, there ye are, me laird." Tolly pointed out the obvious and entered Ash's study the next morning with a salver in one hand and an envelope in the other. At the last moment, he slapped the latter onto the former and held them out—almost within reach.

Ash sat forward and glared at the man, but it was no use. The Scotsman was far too cheerful and oblivious to be running the household staff of the most dangerous gentleman of the ton. He'd never last. One of these days, Ashmoore would find a dungeon in which to toss the old duff and let him contemplate the errors of his ways. It might take years, and thus Ash would no longer be on hand to accept his plethora of apologies.

He took the letter and Tolly walked away without so much as a bow. Then he turned back.

"Oh, and didn't I forget something else, then?"

"Pray tell," Ash drawled.

"That Martin Balliol's here, awaiting yer pleasure." The man turned to leave again.

"Oh, Tolly. Would you not care to know what I'd like done with the young man?"

"Aye, but of course, me laird. Of course. Forgive an old fool."

Ash was mollified by the fact Tolly recognized his mistake. He'd never correct it, of course, but at least he recognized it.

"Send Martin to the kitchens where Sarah can make him a meal. I'll call for him in a while, after I've finished my business here."

Tolly looked around the room as if searching for some hint of what that business was, then he shrugged his shoulders and left. Ash only hoped the man remembered his instructions by the time he found Martin.

Ash opened the letter from Northwick. The man must have written it only days after Ash had left London for it to have arrived so quickly. Why couldn't his friend just go off and enjoy his honeymoon like every other bridegroom and leave Ash in peace? The last thing he wanted to dwell on— indeed the primary reason he'd left London in the first place—was the acrid smell of love in the air. He'd done his part to bring North and Livvy together, for a more suited pair he'd never seen, but that didn't mean he wanted to sit 'round and watch them giving each other moon-eyes.

And he wasn't about to go shopping the marriage mart for some miss who might be a good match for the devil's spawn. Good lord what kind of a woman would that be? And just because his friend was happily wed to a suitable woman, did not mean Ash wanted the same fate. Although he had to admit he'd have been tempted by Livvy himself if North would not have fallen for the woman first, and if he were in any way worthy of a woman like her. But thank heavens he was not. Livvy had been suitable, yes, but not typical, and it was the latter trait he admired the most.

But Ash was more interested in being suitable for a certain Scotswoman. . .

He quickly shook the notion from his head. He'd never be suited to a stodgy, suitable life, let alone a suitable woman. Besides, the only woman he found himself drawn to was Scotia, and she might as well be a phantom considering his chances of ever finding her again. And every other female in Britain would pale when compared to a willful Scottish lass with an ancient Viking blade strapped to her thigh. . .

Her image wavered in his mind's eye. The cloak, her plaid skirts tied into pantaloons. That hair. Wolfkiller held tight in a firm hand. The beauty mark near her eye. . .

He leaned forward as if he might see those eyes more clearly if he did so. Darkness surrounded her. A horse suddenly beneath her. She was just too far away to see details. Then her voice came to him.

"Go home. Go home and remove yer hands from all things Scottish, aye?"

Ash shook the combined images away. It was simply a symptom of his own jumbled thoughts. He wanted Scotia, not The Reaper's woman. But since it was unlikely to see either of them again, it would be better to remove his *mind* from all things Scottish, at least.

He turned his attention to his friend's letter. He was not quite finished with being angry at the man, but by the time he finished reading the thank you note from North, followed by a beautifully written letter of gratitude from Livvy, he was mollified. The missive contained little else but for a warning that Stanley was a bit restless and might one day soon show up on his doorstep.

Ash decided that to answer the letter would be to encourage North, and possibly Stanley, so he forbore.

As it happened, Finn was a capable reader and eventually became so engrossed in his books that he hadn't noticed Ash leave the entire library to him. It was for the best, as the boy was not hovering about while Ash fidgeted in his seat, waiting for his devious plans to unfold in the kitchens.

~ ~ ~

Tolly reappeared.

"Beggin' yer pardon, yer lairdship, but now Constable Wotherspoon is here to see ye."

A blessed distraction.

Ash nodded. "I'll see him here."

Ash wasn't surprised the constable had come to call. In fact, he was a bit more surprised the man hadn't called upon him sooner. As a courtesy, Ash had sent a message to the man the day he'd arrived, informing him Brigadunn had changed hands and as the current owner, he intended to stay in the area until the property was in order. As he was a Peer of the Realm, Ash expected the man to come quickly to offer any assistance Ash might need, as an answering courtesy, but there was every chance the Scottish and English customs of courtesy might not run down the same roads.

Ash rose to his feet when the man entered the room, prepared to return the man's bow. Since the constable only tipped his head to the side, Ash gestured to a chair and resumed his seat.

"Constable Wotherspoon."

"Laird Ashmoore." The man ignored the chair and, as if all manners could now be ignored, he placed his hat back atop his head.

Ash tried not to stare at the green thing sitting high on his guest's wide head. Tufts of hair stood out above both ears as if they were intended to keep the hat from slipping down to its rightful position. When it was time to leave, Ash planned to watch closely. Would the fellow have to walk awkwardly to keep his hat from tipping off onto the floor?

In addition to the silly hat, one of the constable's ears drooped a good three inches lower than the other—something Ash had never seen on another man. And his nose consisted of three rather red bulbs in the center of his face. At least he was reasonably certain it was a nose as the middle bulb was much larger than the others.

If it weren't for the fierce emotion in the man's eyes, Ash would have suspected someone had been jesting when they'd made the man a constable.

The emotion, if Ash wasn't mistaken, was pure hate. And failure to take this man seriously would be unwise.

"To what do I owe the pleasure?" Ash said, leaning back in his chair. His fingers wrapped around the leather cushioned arm and toyed with the handle of the blade hidden beneath it.

A shuffle of feet just outside the door tempted his attention away from the officer of the law, but he resisted. No doubt the man had brought any number of men along with him to obey his orders. Ash wondered if Everhardt would be among them.

His guest's eyes narrowed as if he were deriving some private pleasure from his own poor manners.

"It has come to my attention that ye have a criminal in your possession. As the law in this district, I've come to take the lad off yer hands."

Ash smiled his most deadly smile. Most men found an excuse to leave the room when they saw it. The constable returned it with one of his own.

Yes, this man was going to be a problem.

Ash resisted the urge to rub his hands together.

When the small stirrings in the hallway turned into a scuffle with Finn's voice added to the mix, Ash forced himself to keep his seat. If the bastards harmed the lad, they would pay dearly.

He slowly inclined his head toward the door. When dealing with a dangerous animal, one should always move slowly.

"I regret you have been misinformed, Constable. I harbor no criminals here. The lad staying here chooses to be here. The son of a business acquaintance, as I'm sure you already know. He is no prisoner, nor has he committed any crime. But of course you'll wish to ask him yourself."

The man sneered, then moved to the door. "Bring him inside."

Ash suppressed the urge to beat them all to a pulp and toss them out on their arses for daring to search the house for the lad. But he would savor that beating another day, he was certain.

Four men shuffled inside. Two of them held Finn's arms. The lad continued to struggle until Ash caught his eye. A slight shake of his head had the boy standing straight and behaving immediately.

"Ye'll look at me, laddy." The foul man grabbed Finn's chin and jerked his head to the side. When Finn glared at him, the man's free hand twitched, as if he were restraining his own habit to strike children.

Ash did some restraining of his own.

"Tell me," the man barked, "why ye're being held here, against yer will, Finn Balliol. And if ye lie to me, I'll know it."

Finn laughed. "Aye, I'm being held against my will, but it be only these blokes doing the holdin'." He nodded to the men holding his arms.

The constable waved an impatient hand and the boy was released.

"Ye and yer family stole his lairdship's animals, and ye are a prisoner here until the stock is returned, isn't that so?"

Finn turned to Ash. "Is he calling me father and brother thieves, sir?"

Ash gave a sober nod, though he was hard-pressed not to smile. He couldn't have been prouder if Finn was his own son. But he felt it prudent to intervene before the constable tricked the lad into insulting him.

"I'm sure our good constable was jesting, Finn. For everyone knows it was The Highland Reaper who took my stock." He stood and let his size do a little of his talking for him. "Did you have more questions for the lad? No? Well, then, Finn, you may be about your business. Feel free to keep a footman nearby, in case you need. . .aid."

With tongue in cheek, Ash watched as the young man bowed first to him, then to the constable, then walked calmly out the door.

Ash resumed his seat. "Anything else?"

"Aye, there is," said the constable, then he waited for Ash's full attention before he would go on. "Might I ask how long ye've been returned from the Continent?"

"Two years," Ash answered. "Give or take."

"Interesting." The man gave a meaningful look to each of his men, then turned back to Ash. "That be all fer now, milord." And without the manners of a ten year old lad, he quit the room.

The last of the constable's men paused at the door, gave Ash a wink, then hurried away. Ash was grateful Everhardt was an astute fellow who would have already recognized his temporary employer was a dangerous man. It looked as if it might be a long while before the soldier would be free to give Ash an update, but Everhardt's safety came first.

He only hoped Everhardt remembered that.

CHAPTER TWENTY-FOUR

To further punish Allen Balliol, Ash assigned the task of replacing his herds to Martin. It was clear the younger man needed to play a more honorable role in his life. For all the good it did Balliol, his eldest seemed little more than a medal the father wore upon his chest and bragged about when given the chance. The fact that medal might be a farce seemed only to bother the son and not the father. Martin was ashamed of something, Ash was certain. He only hoped honorable work would help the young man leave his shame in the past.

As he himself was trying to do.

As soon as Martin had gone, Ash called for Sarah. He invited her to sit in the chair facing his desk, then took his seat again.

"How went your visit with the young man?" he asked, then noted her intense blush. "I trust you did not find it too unpleasant an assignment."

"No, my lord. Martin. . . I mean to say Mr. Balliol is not at all like Finn."

Ash considered the girl more closely. Why had he never before noticed the ragged edges of her sleeves, how the dress was ready to burst at the seams of her shoulders? If it weren't for her generous apron, she'd be quite indecent.

Good God, but she'd been entertaining Martin Balliol dressed that way!

"Before you report what you've learned, Miss Sarah, I would know if the young man acted in any manner inappropriate while in your company."

Her eyes opened wide. "No, sir. He would never—but perhaps I don't know what you mean."

Ash shook his head quickly. "Never mind. Let us move on. I'm going to arrange for some suitable clothing for you, since you'll be eating at my table. I'm afraid it will be local stuff for now. Once we return to London, I'll arrange for a finer wardrobe for you, as befitting your station."

"Pardon, my lord. But what station would that be?"

What station indeed?

"Forgive me for a moment," he said and escaped the room, his heart pounding as hard as his boots upon the floor. Once in the hallway, he turned and leaned on a table against the wall. When he lifted his head, he found his reflection staring back at him from a large oval mirror.

Bloody hell! What in the world had come over him? Since when was it wise for blood-thirsty killers like himself to become the benefactors of children? Was Brigadunn to become an orphanage? The child had an aunt to care for her, and even though the woman was a common Frenchwoman, there was nothing common about her skills. Sarah would do well to learn all she could from her.

And just when had he become concerned over the station of others? That they live the life they were born to live? But the answer was obvious.

Livvy.

North's wife. She'd been forced to hide from Society when Society was in dire need of her wit and wisdom. And together with their other two brothers in arms, Harcourt and Stanley, Ash and Northwick had seen to her rescue and returned her to that Society. Of course, it hadn't been easy, what with Livvy determined to save the entire female population of London and risk her neck in the doing.

An incredible woman. A rare woman. But a woman who had found a hole in the armor around his heart, had reached in and proven to him he was a bit more mortal than he thought he was.

But mortal meant vulnerable, and he refused to be that. He looked into his own eyes and rationalized his interference in Sarah's life was merely what any gentleman would do in his situation, and since his current role was that of a gentleman and not assassin, he would do well to maintain that role.

After a brief consultation with her aunt, Ash returned to the library.

"Sarah," he said as he resumed his seat behind the desk.

"Yes, my lord?"

"Your father was a baron."

"Yes, my lord." Tears sprung to her eyes.

"You are a lady by birth."

She answered with a nod and wrapped her arms around her stomach. He pressed on, even knowing he was causing her upset. He hoped what he said next would remedy that.

"I see no reason why you should not resume your rightful station. Of course, the choice is yours, but if you agree, I would arrange to become your guardian—and adoptive uncle, if you will. You would be presented to society as my niece."

Her mouth opened but she said nothing. Of course he wasn't expecting her to jump to her feet in celebration—

Actually, that was exactly what he'd expected.

"Of course you can take your time to consider it. I realize you may not wish to have your name associated with mine, considering my reputation. . .in certain circles."

Sarah nodded as if she understood exactly to what he referred. It was best that she did.

"I know you care for your aunt very much, but you should know I've already discussed it with her. We've agreed that the choice is yours."

She nodded again, looking no less upset, but her arms slowly relaxed and her hands eventually made it back to her lap. The silence became uncomfortable, but she made no comment, gave him no indication of what her ultimate decision might be.

"Now. Onto other matters. If I haven't caused you to forget the conversation, I should like to know what you learned from Mr. Balliol."

She grew pensive.

"The Highland Reaper? What did you learn about The Reaper?"

"Oh, yes! Martin said the man's been causing mischief for a pair of years, but he's never taken an entire herd before. Martin's embarrassed they were taken on his father's watch, I think. He asked about Finn and said his father is sick with worry."

"I'm concerned only with The Reaper at this point, Sarah. If you don't mind." He'd be damned if he'd bring a cantankerous elder into his orphanage.

"Oh, forgive me. Of course." She concentrated for a moment before going on. "The trouble has gotten worse over time. Men have disappeared from time to time. Women and children have fled from the glen. Some men came home from the war to empty houses. Females are scarce throughout the county. But when folks are hungry, they'll wake in the night to find food at their door.

"As for the man, his throat was cut, in battle apparently, but he survived. Martin's father says The Reaper can't be killed. But because of the injury, he cannot speak. There are two men who do the talking for him. He whispers, you see, but only to them."

"And did you learn what this mute villain looks like?"

"No one knows his face. He always wears a black cloak and hood. Not a tall man, but he has the shoulders of a bull."

"Did Martin have an idea where he might be hiding himself?"

"Yes, my lord. He and his men live in The Witch's Vale, where the mist never leaves nor does anyone who dares enter. I must confess, I laughed at Martin, that is to say, Mr. Balliol. It sounded like a story to frighten small children. But he insisted it is all true."

"Anything more?" He tried to sound patient but it was all he could do to stay seated. He had the general location of the villain's lair. His instincts screamed at him to act. But there was also a certain woman involved, a woman who had already managed to evade him once. If he didn't plan the hunt carefully, she might get away again.

"Martin said that many have gone looking for the man, to ask for help, but the way is laid with traps and misdirection. The secret to finding The Reaper is a riddle, but it makes no sense. And once in the vale, you'll never be allowed to leave. Martin thinks The Reaper kills those who find his lair. He believes it's why he's called The Reaper."

Ash raised his hand to stop her. "I don't suppose he told you the riddle?"

She grinned and nodded. *"Tic, Toc. A map before. A quarter less, or three quarters more.* You see? It makes no sense."

"Yes. I see." He repeated the riddle in his mind lest he forget it. "Anything else?"

Sarah considered, then shook her head.

Ash nodded and stood so the young lady could leave the room. She headed not for the door, however, but for his person. He obligingly leaned down so the lass could place a kiss on his cheek.

"Thank you, Lord Ashmoore." She seemed to be looking for something in his eyes, then smiled when she seemed to find it. Whatever it was, Ash hadn't a clue. At the door, she turned back. "Mr. Balliol would tell me nothing else, my lord. But I am certain he could have. I daresay he knows something important. Would you like me to try to discover his secret?"

"Not at all, Sarah dear. You've done an excellent job. I know all I need to know." And that included the certainty that allowing Martin and young Sarah to spend more time together would be a mistake. The girl was already blushing when she said his name, and her tight dress had likely given the young man the wrong impression of her age.

Good God! What had he done? He'd barely made an offer to act as her guardian and already he was acting the protective father.

It had been an impetuous idea. And although he would not take back the offer, even if he could, he completely expected to rue it.

He slipped his hand into his waist pocket and fingered the little ring, as he had done so often after returning from France. He only did so when he was troubled. For the first year or more, it had given him comfort. Now, it stirred up the mixed images of two women, both wrapped in cloaks. But the strongest image was of the she-devil on horseback, taunting him from a distance, her hair a mass of dark curls in the blue of the moonlight.

Was it The Reaper's cloak she wore?

Was she his wife? Or his leman?

And how could Ash so easily allow the second woman to sully the memory of the first?

He tried to picture Scotia again. That face leaning over him, swaying before his drunken vision, watching her play with his fingers, sliding the ring on one of them. Urging him to close his eyes, annoyed when he was unable to kiss her back. Oh, yes. He'd remembered, eventually.

"Dinna lose it, ye drunk bastard."

He mumbled the same, now, to himself, but referring to her memory.

"Dinna lose it, ye drunk bastard."

"I beg yer pardon, sir?" Tolly stood before him.

Ash shook off the maudlin thoughts and sat again, took out a parchment and dipped his pen. It seemed it might be a wise idea to encourage the level-headed Stanley after all. It seemed the mere recollection of Scotia might keep him from seeing things clearly. Stanley by his side sounded just the ticket.

"I wish to send an urgent letter to the son of the Duke of Rochester, in London. I need you to locate a rider. Someone you can trust to keep his mission to himself." He fixed his butler with a meaningful stare. "Do you understand my meaning, Tolly?"

"Aye, sir. I do. It means if The Reaper gets wind of the letter, it'll be my arse out in the cold with my head sittin' next to it."

Ash laughed. "You're not nearly as simple as you like to pretend."

The man winked. "Not by half, yer lairdship. Not by half."

CHAPTER TWENTY-FIVE

Blair paced in her room, grateful to be back in The Witch's Vale, in a warm safe place with enough room above her head to stand straight. Pacing helped her think. The smell of supper was a bit distracting, however, so she gave up the struggle with her thoughts and went out to sup with the others.

Jarvill and Coll hadn't waited for her before digging into the first hot meal they'd had since taking the Englishman's herds. Now that the animals had been sold off and no longer required guarding, they'd been able to strike their camp and come home.

The vale had been home for two years, but that night, even with her beloved owl perched in the shed on the side of the cottage, it no longer felt like a safe haven. Of course she should have never gone after Shakespeare, but the thing might have suffered injury had she sent Jarvill for him, as she'd sent him to collect some of her own things from time to time. She wondered if her family had ever noticed anything missing.

A week gone by, when she'd laid eyes on the familiar buildings and burst into tears, she should have turned away. Standing in the mews had been both exquisite and painful. Seeing Martin and holding him to her was torture as well, but a hundred fold. Of course she wished she could have gone about her business without them believing her dead, but even if she dared face her father's renouncement, she had other reasons. The most important of which was that many more needy souls would trust a mysterious Scotsman to lead them than the bossy miss who lived down the glen.

And so many had needed The Reaper. They'd been grateful for a leader who could tell them everything would be right again, that their children needn't starve before their eyes, that there was hope. And if she could convince the English to stop coming, they could all go home like Mary Dowds.

All but her, of course.

Her belly begged her to eat, so she ate, all the while staring at the fourth plate, the portion allotted for The Reaper. Jarvill and Coll would arm wrestle for it after they'd finished their own. There was food a' plenty in the vale, even in winter, so another helping was unfair to no one. And Bonnie and Esme, the ladies who cooked and cleaned for The Reaper and his band of three, would expect four dirty plates waiting for them in the morning.

Blair couldn't help but wonder how long it would be before Bonnie or Esme, or both, were seduced into returning to Brigadunn.

Brigadunn. The manor house was named for the ancient brown bridge that once connected one side of the river to the other. But the water had changed course long ago and the bridge merely spanned a trail of boulders with grass and wildflowers growing between them. A pretty sight in springtime. A sight she hadn't seen in daylight since before the war in France, a sight she would never see again without risking her father's notice, even after the current English bully was gone. But by heavens, the rest of them would see it again, and soon.

"We canna dally about," she told her friends. "We've got to frighten this one away, and now. There was a stubborn look in his eyes that I didna care for. And he's the size of an ox on hind legs. It will take the three of us to subdue him."

She took a bite of mutton, but had a hard time swallowing. The thought of facing that man again twisted her stomach, but it was best to have done with it. Truth be told, her mind had played tricks on her since that night when the current owner of Brigadunn had held her close to him. For some reason, her mind wanted the man to be Ash. She needed to keep reminding herself the new Englishman wasn't tall enough to be Ash. But another glimpse of him— just a glimpse, mind—was a wish she tried to keep tucked away in the corner of her heart.

Coll looked up from his meal. "When do we go?" he enunciated around his stew. Then he bent his head back for a bite, as if speaking *without* food in his mouth was poor manners.

Jarvill stood and moved his plate off the table to make room for the wrestle.

"Tomorrow night," she said without meeting either man's eyes, then forced herself to eat again, keeping an arm wrapped about her bowl to protect it from wayward wrestling arms.

"But we've only just come home," Jarvill complained. "Can yer brother not stomach fine food for another few days?"

"'Tis *my* stomach I'm worrit about, Jarvill. This man does things to it."

"Like the man in France, ye mean?" He pushed The Reaper's portion over to Coll. There would be no wrestling tonight.

Blair removed her protective arm and sat a little straighter. "'Tis similar, but not the same. This one could never be as dangerous as the other."

Jarvill snorted. "Dangerous with a blade? Or with yer heart?"

Coll frowned as he had not been privy to her earlier discussion with Jarvill, about the effect Ash had once had upon her, but she shook her head, telling Coll not to expect an explanation. Then she turned to her right and told Jarvill the truth.

"Both," she said. "It would kill me, I think, to see that first man again. I'd shiver and shake until I was but a puddle in me boots. This is why I must stay away from England, and England must stay away from me. Handsome or no."

"Perhaps," said Coll, as he dug into his second helping, "we should see if the parade of English. . ." He filled his mouth. "If the parade might stop if one of them died of an accident. And there's always poison, o'course."

CHAPTER TWENTY-SIX

It had been a week since his unfortunate encounter with The Reaper's assassin—for how could Ash think of her as anything else? With one bold, unladylike action, she'd nearly assassinated the entire Ashmoore line of successors. After his nether region had recovered, he'd been able to acknowledge that it was a fine tactic on her part, but now that she'd revealed her skills, by Jove, he would not be caught off guard the next time they met!

And they would meet again. He would make damned good and certain of it. It had become even more important to him than catching The Reaper. He'd simply convinced himself that catching the woman was essential to catching the villain. She'd make a fine bit of bait, after all.

He sat astride his horse trying to keep his mind on the number of animals entering the pens and away from disturbing memories that made him wince and fidget in the saddle, but he'd failed so many times already, he was forced to rely on Martin's count to be correct.

A hundred head stolen.

A hundred head replaced.

But as he watched a black and white spotted calf catch up to its solid black brother, Ash realized he was replacing his stolen cattle with *his stolen cattle!*

He took a deep breath to cool the heat rising in his neck. No sense in tipping his hand until he knew if Martin was aware of the trick.

Ash waved an arm.

Martin loped over to him. "Yer lairdship?"

Nothing nervous about the young man. In fact, Martin Balliol looked quite pleased with himself. His big smile hid nothing. This bit of responsibility had even improved his posture.

Ash hated to dash his fine mood, but this was one young Scot to whom he refused to play nursemaid.

"Martin," he said casually, "do you suppose you could send a message to The Highland Reaper?"

A dark scowl dropped immediately into place on the lad's brow before he looked away. After a deep breath, Martin looked back.

"Leave it to me, sir. What message would ye care to send?"

Ash couldn't be more pleased to find that at least one Scot in the glen might be on his side in this silly war.

"Inform the criminal that although my missing cattle seem to have been returned to me, young Finn will remain my hostage until the purchase price has been returned. And for heaven's sake, send the spotted calf back to the drover. It will do neither of us any good if others realize we possess animals that supposedly are in the hands of The Damnable Reaper."

Martin's scowl grew fierce as he looked over the cattle now milling about in the massive corral. Ash raised an arm and pointed at the spotted calf. Martin gave a smart nod in understanding. He looked so disgusted Ash thought an encouraging word was in order.

"Do not look upon this as any sort of failure, Mr. Balliol. I told you to duplicate the original order of animals, and damn me if you could have come any closer."

Martin sighed and nodded. His grimace eased into a begrudging smile.

"Will there be anything else, yer lairdship?"

Ash was tempted to send a warning to The Reaper's woman, but he'd be damned if he was going to admit what had happened the last time he'd seen her.

"No. Nothing more." He turned his horse, but Martin reached for the bridle to stop him from moving away.

"I should thank ye, sir," he said, looking Ash in the eye. "Finn looks none the worse for wear. . .*from what I've seen*."

Understanding dawned, but Ash could not betray Finn's trust. It wasn't for Ash to tell Martin that it was his younger brother's idea not to speak with him.

Ash merely nodded.

"The drover sent a bottle of brandy for ye, laird. I've sent it up to the manor."

Ash nodded again, then nudged his horse forward. Martin stepped back.

A little responsibility, away from his father, had gone a long way, it seemed.

~ ~ ~

Later, after Finn and the rest had gone to bed and left the house to settle, Ash sat in his study and stared at the African chair. It had arrived that afternoon with a letter from Northwick insisting that he might feel more at home with a stick of familiar furniture about. Of course it was a lark. The chair—a bit of wood and leather—had always been the least comfortable chair in his friend's library. When the Four Kings would gather there, the seat went to the last man standing—the punishment for a game of musical chairs. It was a fact, if Ash was the last to sit, he'd more often than not prefer to stand before submitting himself to the uncomfortable contraption.

Northwick had finally found an excuse to exorcise it from his house. Ash would have to remember to return the favor before leaving Scotland at the end of summer. It was a pity to leave such a sentimental thing where it couldn't possibly be appreciated.

Discomfort, while sitting, led his thoughts back to the woman who'd left him for dead in the woods on a cold winter/spring night. As her knee had come for him, he'd at least been able to turn a bit. Had he taken the blow head on, he'd never been able to crawl back to the house. Finn might have found him in the morning, frozen like a garden statue tipped on its side.

Had he not turned. . .

Phantom pains shot through him and he jumped to his feet. He needed distraction, and the brandy from the drover would have to do.

He pulled the cork and let the heady flavor surround him as he poured the entire contents into a crystal decanter Tolly had left for just that purpose. As the aroma hung like a cloud around him, he remembered a similar cloud that clung to Harcourt, Stanley, and himself while they'd tried to drink themselves dead with grief and guilt. For months, they'd searched for North, knowing full well the province where the kidnappers were holding him but unable to find him. They'd had no choice but to give up and go home after they'd searched every blade of grass, every hovel, then they'd searched it all a second time. They'd done everything but start digging, to look beneath the very sod.

But leaving one of them behind was not something they could have accomplished sober. So they'd drank.

Even now, the memory of his hopelessness urged him to set the stopper aside and pour himself a stout glass of the liquor. The little ball rang like a bell as he tossed it onto the tray and hefted the now heavy decanter.

One finger. Then two. Remembering that the entire household was abed, he poured four. And even as he set the bottle aside and stopped the opening with the little ball of winking glass, he knew he drank tonight not to forget, but to remember.

To remember a slightly gentler lass, a woman called Scotia.

He removed his coat, tossed it over the back of a comfortable couch, and took his drink to the African chair where he sat carefully. He raised the glass in a silent toast to his best friend, acknowledging the fact that North had known the perfect thing to send to bring a smile to lips that seldom smiled.

He'd fled from his friends, but he did miss them a little. Not enough to invite them to join him, of course. It was not unlike the way he would miss the ring if it weren't in his pocket. It was part of him. They were part of him. No matter how far he traveled, they would be with him. If putting Hadrian's Wall between them wasn't distance enough to provide a respite, nothing else would do the trick.

He set aside the half-full glass for a moment to remove his cravat. Then he unhooked some buttons and allowed some air against his skin, wondering if it was the Frenchwoman or the Scottish staff who kept the house so hot.

He pushed away the possibility that it might be the thoughts of Scotia that warmed him. But the thoughts pushed back. As he took up his glass again, he summoned her image. A beauty mark. A full black cloak. Her hair when she'd tossed her hood back, to impress upon him the fact he was her only hope. Her muddied hem. The cold square of her fireplace.

With his free hand, Ash fingered the ring through his vest pocket. Touching it gave him comfort. Looking at the little owl did the opposite, so it remained in his pocket.

Scotia. Come to me.

He straightened, brought the glass to his mouth, and poured the whole of it down his throat. Only after he'd swallowed the last of it did he find a bitter taste on the back of his tongue that had nothing whatsoever to do with brandy.

Alarm sang in his brain. He jumped to his feet and reached for the bottle he'd emptied into the decanter. He smelled the opening, but with the aftertaste still in his mouth, it was impossible to tell where the slightly acrid smell was coming from! His mind reeled. Was it his own panic that made the room spin? Or was it the poison?

He stuck his fingers into the back of his throat and gagged himself, but his stomach would not turn! He tried over and over, knowing it was his only chance, to get as much of the poison out as possible, but his body would not cooperate!

The floor shifted.

Poison! Hardly a noble death. He'd much prefer to die with a weapon in his hand. But who was his foe? The Reaper would be coming for him after all, but who had been the accomplice. Tolly? Martin? One of the footmen? With Scots in his household, he should have been more on his guard!

Then he thought of Finn. Sarah. The Frenchwoman. Those he trusted. Which of them would find him in the morning?

He lurched for the decanter and knocked it from the tray. It fell to the floor beside him. Not all of it spilled.

He reached for the empty bottle but it was beyond his reach. As his fingers stretched toward it, the dark glass seemed to stretch farther away. He commanded his body to move, to crawl, until the hard glass was within his grasp. Then he crawled back.

With all his miniscule might, he lifted the bottle over his head and brought it down upon the decanter. Glass and the tainted brandy flew everywhere, but none of it would find its way into another mouth, another belly.

With the house turning into a storm-ravaged ship beneath him, Ash's stomach finally turned. But he knew it was too late.

CHAPTER TWENTY-SEVEN

Blair waited in the barn.

Her heart was rocking so hard beneath her ribs she was worried the sound would wake the household. But they'd had little choice, she tried to convince herself. They'd needed to do something drastic. This Englishman would not tuck tail and run as the others had.

"For the good of the people," she murmured. She wouldn't have risked such danger just because the man reminded her of Ash. But even as her whisper fell silently among the straw, she knew it was a lie. May God forgive her, she was a coward. Frightened of a memory. Frightened of anyone who might stir that memory.

Of course this English lord could never compare to Ash. She'd had only a fleeting look at him in the darkness with the lighted windows of the manor behind him. She wouldn't be surprised to find he was a lanky chap with blond hair and that her imagination had taken control of her eyesight. But there had been some look about him that promised he would never be intimidated by the likes of a country phantom.

The call of a nightingale—her signal to open the barn door.

She pushed it wide and stood back as Jarvill and Coll carried their victim through it. Her stomach dropped when she realized the Englishman was wrapped in a sheet, but she closed and bolted the door before she dared make so much as a squeak.

Coll dropped his end of the load and walked to the wall where the light of a single candle glowed from within a closed lantern. He opened it an inch, then took up his end of the wrapped body once more and helped Jarvill place it on the chair she'd prepared in the center of the floor. The body was limp as a wet flag.

He'd drank too much. They'd killed him!

Blair was going to be ill. No matter that he was a Peer of the Realm, he'd been a man—a gentle enough man who'd kindly invited her to return to the manor and talk things over, a man who she'd nearly maimed in her bid to escape. If they'd known he would drink so heavily, they'd have put a great deal less Belladonna in his brandy.

God forgive them!

Jarvill began tying the man's torso to the chair. Coll knelt to do the same with his feet.

"Why tie him to the chair if he's already dead?" she whispered.

"Why indeed," Jarvill answered, "unless he's not dead after all? We had to wrap him in a sheet to carry him. If the barn were another fifty steps away from the manor, we'd have not been up to the task, aye? He's a monster, is this one. I understand now why you claimed he'd not flee like the rest."

He wasn't dead? He wasn't dead!

It wasn't just her soul she was relieved for. She felt the same way about her enemy as she did for a large animal. It would have been a true pity to put him down when he'd done little to deserve it. He'd taken her brother as a hostage, but Finn had been well cared for—better cared for than under their father's roof. How could she begrudge the man for that?

Coll strained to move a heavy leg.

Ash had been a monster as well. Heaven help her, did England produce so many that size?

Jarvill pealed back the sheet so he could bind the man's hands, and he was right to do so. A man like Ash might be able to burst his bonds; they'd be smart to use every inch of rope possible. The collar of his shirt got caught and was peeled back as well, but she wasn't about to ask Jarvill to fix it. She didn't want her friend to think her some bawdy maid to notice such a thing. But she did notice.

She also noticed how the white fabric stuck to the body beneath.

"Why is he wet?" she whispered again.

Coll snorted. "Had to dip his head in the horse trough. He'd tossed up his accounts on the rug. Slept right through it, aye? But he smells better."

She took a step back, not wanting a whiff of sick. There were few animals in the barn, not enough to make it warm, but she tugged off her cloak and handed it to Coll to play the part of The Reaper. She had too many things she wished to say to this man and not the patience to relay it through one of her friends. The sooner they were away, the sooner she could get warm.

She shivered, but it was more out of pity for how cold their prisoner must be than for herself. But the longer she gazed at that half-bare chest, even in shadows, the warmer she got.

"Wake him," she told Jarvill.

She stayed a good ten feet back. Coll came to stand beside her with his hands on his hips, his hood pulled forward. Standing behind the chair, Jarvill tipped it back on its hind legs and shook it. The man's head wobbled a bit, then settled again when the chair rested back on all its legs.

"There's a fine chance the man willna wake, if the cold water didna stir him," said Jarvill. He walked around to face the unresponsive man, grabbed the man by the hair to lift his face, then slapped him none too gently. "Wake, yer lairdship."

The man growled. A few breaths later, he snored. Jarvill released his hair and the man's chin dropped back to his chest.

Blair huffed. She wasn't going to be getting warm any time soon, it seemed.

"Here," Coll said. He retrieved a stool from the wall and sat down, then slapped his knee. "Come. Sit. This cloak can cover us both."

"Shhh!" She shook her head at him. "No speaking while you're wearing the cloak. Remember it."

Coll nodded, then lifted the dark fabric like bird's wings. Since she'd removed her attention from the prisoner's chest, the cold air had begun seeping into her bones, so she accepted her friend's invitation and sat on his knee. The dark wings wrapped around her and her chills were gone in no time at all.

Jarvill sank down into the straw piled in the corner, wrapped his plaid in a cozy cocoon, and lowered his head. And with nothing to worry over while they waited for their sleeping giant to rouse, Blair allowed her thoughts to roam where they would.

Ash.

Did he ever think of her? And if so, did he think of kissing her? Or did he still believe she'd been the enemy? Did he rue the night he could have executed her in the stables near Givet Faux? But instead of heartache washing over her and bringing tears to her eyes, as it usually did, it only disgusted her. She'd barely known the man and yet she'd been hurt more by his cruel assumption than by the prospect of her own execution.

She could only hope that she'd outgrown whatever defect had inspired such nonsense. It gave her hope when the memory only tugged at her a bit. Never again would she allow a man to leave her distraught and hopeless. She was The Highland Reaper—the one sought by others when they were similarly afflicted.

She was the cure.

Blair sighed and wondered if the man would wake before sunrise. If not, they would have to maneuver his bulk onto a horse and take him to The Vale with them.

Finally, the man's head moved. Then it bobbed. A moment later, the chin rose from the chest and the man stared straight ahead. At her.

He shook his head as if trying to shake off the effects of the drug.

Wake, ye bloody bastard.

It was time. She dared not wait until he had complete control of himself.

She nudged Coll's arms and he opened them slowly. Then she stood and walked toward the Englishman, veering away at the last moment to walk around him. She began to hum. Finally, she put words to the tune.

"Fee. Fie. Foe. Fum. I smell the blood of an Anglishmon. Be he live, or be he dead. . ." She paused to run a finger along the man's neck. "I'll grind his bones to make me bread." Then she laughed and hummed her way back to Coll, who had risen from the stool.

"Poison," the Englishman muttered, turning his head from side to side.

Blair wondered if he was still not sober enough to remember her dramatics.

"No. Not poison," she said. "but it could have been. Remember that, yer lairdship. It could have been. And the next time it will be. If ye fail to leave us in peace."

He laughed. It steadied his head.

"I *came* to bring you peace, woman."

It was her turn to laugh. "Ye can either go home to England or go home to yer maker. But ye will make yer choice now, or it will be made for ye."

For a moment, they simply stared at each other. She wanted a good look at his face, but she dared not allow him to see her mark. There was no telling just how much he would remember in the morning.

"Shall I have the lad taste my food?" he queried.

Blair refused to react, but instead bent her head toward Coll who pretended to whisper in her ear.

She nodded and turned back to the prisoner. "One less Balliol whining over the crown of Scotland, says The Reaper."

The man's head turned as if noticing Coll for the first time—the black cloaked figure he'd likely been itching to catch. He looked back and forth between them, then shook his head.

She shivered.

"She's cold, man. Give her your coat." The man's head wobbled. "Coward."

Jarvill took his plaid from his shoulders and brought it to her. She rolled her eyes, but took it just the same. Then she realized she could use the material to hide her face so she could get a better look at the man they'd nearly killed.

"Bring the light," she whispered to her friend. "I would see his face."

Jarvill hesitated, but did as she bid.

With the wool draped over her head like a hood, she turned toward the Englishman, glad she'd be able to stop imagining a resemblance to the man who haunted her dreams even when she wasn't asleep.

Blair dared not get too close waited for Jarvill to bring the light. The prisoner waited silently, but the tilt of his head told her he was aware of every movement. His shoulders stiffened and he pulled at his restraints when her friend walked up behind him. She was relieved to see him alert, even though it meant he would be harder to handle.

She nodded at Jarvill, who lifted the lantern at the same time he took a handful of the man's hair and pulled back.

Dark, hauntingly handsome features rose into the warm light. He winced from the brightness, then blinked while his eyes adjusted. She winced as well—not from the glaring light, but from the pain in her chest as she realized this was no apparition brought on by her imagination.

"Ash." Her lips formed the name, but no sound escaped her.

He squinted at her, then closed the eye closest to the lantern and looked again. The strain must have been too much, for both his eyes rolled back in his head, then closed and remained closed. Jarvill released his hair and looked for her reaction. She was quick to compose herself and Jarvill relaxed. . .at least until Ash spoke again, his eyes still shut.

"Release me, Scotia, my love. And I'll give you back your ring."

Blair sighed. Her heart melted at the endearment. After all this time, he still thought of her as Scotland. With little thought for witnesses, she moved forward, reached out a hand and held it against his cheek. It was flesh and bone beneath her hand, not some ghost conjured to soothe her. With her other hand she pushed the plaid back from her face, willing him to see her as clearly as she saw him, willing him to be pleased.

And he was pleased.

"Ah, Scotia. You seem so real to me," he said. "Kiss me quickly, before you disappear."

"What the devil?!"

Coll's curse came from just behind her, but she could not resist tasting those lips while she could. Some insanity ruled her—likely that same defect which had turned her into such a fool in France. She'd resolved never to let it happen again, and yet nothing could stop her from taking what she wanted, if only for a moment.

Hopefully, Ash would remember her as only a dream come to warn him away, as she'd intended.

His taste brought back a whirlwind of memories, not all of them unpleasant. He had enough wits about him to kiss her back. She could have wept when he did so, the pressure of his lips against hers was pure absolution and she returned it with all her heart.

Coll put a hand on her shoulder but she gently shook him off as she ended the kiss. She could not help hovering

210 L.L. Muir

close to Ash's face, drinking in the sight of him. She'd
nearly forgotten those eyes. Dear lord, how could she have
forgotten those eyes?

Jarvill took a step back, shaking his head as he went.

"Scotia," Ash whispered. "Forgive me."

She paused staring at his lips while she tried to
understand what he was apologizing for. France?
Suspecting her? Letting her go? Kissing her? She wished
he'd specify his regret, but she'd be damned if she'd ask.

She could feel the weight of unseen armor being
lowered onto her shoulders; a barrier between her and the
man for whom far too many tears had been shed already.
She'd had years to learn how to protect her heart. She might
have kissed him, tasted him, but he could not hurt her
again.

"Leave Scotland, sir, and all yer sins will be forgiven
ye," she said with a smile.

"Scotia." He leaned forward and pressed his lips
against hers, only this time, he pressed much harder. It was
her turn to feel drugged. That invisible armor shuddered
beneath his assault. She could almost believe she was back
in the woods with him where he'd pressed her up against a
tree. It was a frustration to be sure, not being able to pull off
his ropes and wrap herself around him, but she settled for a
feel of his hair between her fingers. Her own mane created
a curtain around them and she drank her fill of him,
breathed his scent into her lungs, then reluctantly, ever so
reluctantly, pulled away.

He breathed out with an exaggerated sigh. "How can I
leave when you taste like that?"

The barn door burst open and two footmen entered
with pistols raised.

Jarvill tossed the lantern at their feet and turned to her.
"Go!"

While the armed men were distracted by the spreading
fire, Coll ran to the opposite end of the barn and held open
the small door, the arm beneath his black cape beckoning to

her. Blair turned to follow, but her skirts were caught. When she failed to pull them free, she looked behind to see what held her, only to find Ash's hand fisted around a wad of the dark fabric, a rope dangling from his wrist.

She turned back to her friends. "I'm caught!" she cried. "Leave me!"

Jarvill stepped back inside.

"No! I order ye to go, do ye hear? Both of ye, go!"

A pistol fired and a ball struck the wood just above the open door. She was grateful neither of the men had been hit, but even more grateful it got them moving.

Ash's men stomped out the last of the flames and with them, any light. She put all her strength into wrenching her skirts free, but Ash held fast. A moment later, another man's hands wrap themselves firmly around her arm.

"Tie her up," Ash growled. "She's slippery."

CHAPTER TWENTY-EIGHT

A heavy rain announced the first day of spring. Ash stood at the parlor window and watched the torrents cut tiny rivers into the drive as if the heavens were attempting to wash away all his sins with one good bath. But since such absolution was impossible, there was no point to getting wet.

Besides, he couldn't quite bring himself to stray very far from the prisoner now locked in his larder. Neither could he bring himself to take her into the village to have her placed behind a descent set of bars. The rain you see. Deucedly inconvenient. And no signs of letting up.

Pity, that. He smiled.

But even if he was angry over being poisoned, he'd rather forgive Scotia and let her free before he'd involve the constable. It was likely real justice was rarely served by the bastard, and Ash would never willingly place a possible innocent in the man's keeping.

Scottish law deemed landowners to be their own authority and as long as Scotia remained on his land, he could meet out his own justice. And damn him, but the possibilities had not only chased away his headache, but had him all but whistling the afternoon away. There was every possibility his staff assumed the poison had addled his brain considering how he'd danced around the manor all day, trying his best to keep away from the kitchens and the prisoner residing in the larder. But he needed a sound plan in mind before he dared speak with her again. She was capable of making the very earth move beneath his feet if he were to stare too long at her lips, let alone get a taste of them. He needed a plan that would succeed whether or not he found himself in a puddle on the floor. A plan that could not fail.

A plan to remove this Reaper fellow from her life.

He forced his smile away in order to concentrate, but the only thing that came to mind was the damnable larder door!

Not another room in the house was suitable for housing such a clever creature. There were too many windows in the manor by half. What he needed was a medieval tower with only arrow slits to allow in a bit of light and air. In fact, keeping her prisoner in a tower sounded like such a perfect solution to his problems he considered asking Tolly if there were any such properties nearby. But then again, his first Scottish property wasn't working out so well. Taking on another would be foolhardy.

But a tower. . .

It would be punishment enough, he thought. Instead of seeing her jailed, she would simply be locked in a tower for the rest of her days. And he could be her warden, see her every day, and never need to forgive her.

He shifted his weight and sensed something hard beneath his boot. A small crystal shard, from the broken decanter, no doubt, had imbedded itself into the bottom of his boot. He carefully removed it and tossed it into the fire. If there were the slightest trace of the drug upon it, it was dangerous.

If he hadn't ultimately been able to empty his stomach, her concoction would have been the death of him. Of course she'd argued that it wasn't her fault that he drank enough for four men. And that had been the end of their argument. Or rather the beginning of the end. He didn't know why it always happened that every conversation concluded with his lips on hers. Perhaps he was simply putting her in her place, reminding her he would always have the upper hand.

Or was she reminding him of the contrary?

Damn it if he didn't catch himself headed for the kitchen for the fiftieth time that morning. He stopped at the edge of the carpet—as if it were some gang plank—and considered. What was his excuse this time?

He snorted and continued through the house. He was lord here. He needed no excuses to come and go where he pleased.

Thank heavens the drug had worn off before daybreak so Everhardt was able to slip away before being seen. He'd locked Scotia in the larder and waited to make certain Ash could see straight as well as think straight before he'd returned to his place in the village. Clever old Tolly had sent for him, though Ash had never once confided in the old man that he'd stationed one of his men in town. He'd have to interrogate the fellow later in the day and see if he could get a straight answer from him. Tolly was an odd old Scot who'd softened considerably after Ash had taken in the Balliol lad. Perhaps it was Finn who had inspired the softening.

Ash entered the kitchen and found it deserted, then he found the door to the larder standing wide.

No! His heart burst in his chest. He could not contain a roar of frustration that echoed in the high ceiling and mocked his pain.

How could he have lost her yet again? First, in France before he'd been able to think clearly, then that night she'd come to rescue Finn. Of course at that time, he hadn't realized who she was. His heart had tried to tell him, but he hadn't listened.

All day, he'd been so terribly pleased to finally have her under his thumb. The devil take him for leaving her side for even a moment! By God, as soon as he got his hands on her again, he was going to buy every bloody tower in Scotland until he found one suitable to contain her.

The voices of women, speaking French, neared the outer entrance and he turned toward the sound. The door swung open and Sarah stepped inside, blinking rapidly as her eyes adjusted to the dim interior. When she finally noticed Ash, she stopped quickly and curtsied. Considering the worried look on the young lady's face, Ash schooled his features before he frightened her to death. If his face revealed everything he was feeling, she surely would have turned and run back outside.

As Sarah bobbed, however, a regal mane of red curls was revealed behind her. Scotia stepped around the girl so the Frenchwoman could also enter. Only then did Ash notice the rope securing Sarah to his prisoner.

He dared not look at the latter, lest she read too much in his expression. He was afraid she read him far too easily as it was.

"Fantine, I would imagine Sarah to be far too light an anchor for such a prisoner. Is there a reason you could not tether the woman to yourself?"

The Frenchwoman blushed for possibly the first time since they'd known each other.

Sarah giggled. "The pair of them weren't able to fit in the loo together, my lord. And you did say she was to be tied securely when the need arose."

Ash cleared his throat for a variety of reasons.

"Did it occur to you to give her a longer lead and a bit of privacy?"

The Frenchwoman snorted. "It occurred to us," she conceded, "but zen it also occurred to us that she might take her time to untie her end of it, *non?*" She looked pointedly at Sarah, who was making quick work of her own knot. "But perhaps you should not trust us to sink of such sings, monsieur. Perhaps we should leave her in your most capable hands and return to cooking your dinner."

She brushed her hands together as if washing her hands of any further responsibility for his prisoner and walked away. Sarah giggled once more and followed. He finally looked at Scotia and caught her giving the girl a wink and a wide smile.

Her smile dropped when she looked back at him.

"The sunshine won't last long," she pointed out.

He inclined his head. "Then it is most fortunate your needs coincided with its appearance. Shall we?" He gestured toward the larder door.

"We?" She swallowed forcibly, then licked her lips.

He refrained from doing the same, but only barely. He glanced at the dark recesses of her makeshift cell. Imagined following her inside and closing the door behind him.

His breath quickened, as did his heart. Thank heavens no one else could hear it.

She swallowed again, then walked into the larder as if she were walking to the executioner's block. It was the hardest thing he'd done all day, but he closed the door behind her, slipped a heavy padlock into place, then dropped the key into his pocket as he strode from the room.

~ ~ ~

Intent on putting some distance between himself and his prisoner, so he might think clearly, he nearly passed the library without noticing Finn. It was the boy's sniff that drew his attention. A second sniff drew his curiosity. He hurried into the room and over to the chair where the lad sat sideways with his legs pulled up to his chest.

"Are you ill, Finn? Are you cold?" He reached to touch the small forehead, to check for a fever, but the boy knocked his hand away.

"No. Go away," he choked before running his expensive new sleeve under his nose.

Ash forbore a scolding and produced a handkerchief instead.

Finn took it and tossed it over the back of his chair, then wiped his nose on his sleeve again.

Ash sighed and walked to the African chair. He'd clearly done something wrong for which he needed some sort of punishment. The chair would at least be a start. Caring for a child was hardly an inherent talent of his, and he'd likely botched the job something fierce. Perhaps the lad was still mourning over Shakespeare, though he'd hardly been bereft until now. There was every chance that sitting in the library, surrounded by the works of that other Shakespeare, had finally summoned up some emotion.

"I am sorry about Shakespeare," Ash offered.

The child turned hateful eyes in his direction.

"Are ye going to let her go?" he demanded.

Ash straightened. This was about the woman? Did the lad believe she'd been abused somehow? Aside from being held captive in a dark larder, of course. Then Ash remembered that the lad had defended her from the start.

"Have you decided to tell me her name?"

Finn pulled his lips between his teeth and shook his head, loosening tears to splash across his cheeks.

It was too bad of him to try to use a child against her, but he would welcome any weapon he might use to keep her away from her Reaper. They were at war, after all. She was a prisoner of war. It would be foolish to let her leave since she'd just go back to fighting against him.

"Perhaps," he began, stomping his conscience under foot. "Perhaps, I should take a ride into the village and ask if anyone knows of a young woman with a beauty mark near her right eye. A beauty mark in the shape of a tear, turned on its head."

The boy bolted off his chair and flew at Ash. He simply braced himself and let the child do his worst. As it turned out, the child hadn't considered hurting him but took hold of his lapels and pulled him forward until their noses nearly touched.

"Ye must promise me ye'll do no such thing. I'll have your word in honor, sir. I'll have it or I willna let go."

"Word *of* honor," Ash corrected, trying not to laugh at the little show of force.

The boy released him and sighed. "Thank ye, sir." Then the lad's arms came around his neck and he nearly choked Ash with gratitude.

When he was finally able to straighten, Ash opened his mouth to point out that he hadn't given his word but had merely been correcting Finn's choice of phrase, but he couldn't bring himself to do it.

When the lad stepped back, the storm cloud had returned to his small face.

"If ye'll not release. . .her. . .then will ye release me? Sir?" Finn didn't look very hopeful so it was a bit easier to deny him this time.

"I cannot," he said simply.

"But you must," Finn whined.

Ash shook his head. "What has one thing to do with another, lad? Help me to understand."

Finn shook his head and headed for the door. "I canna," he whispered to himself, but Ash heard it.

CHAPTER TWENTY-NINE

Ash found Tolly in the study. The man was standing with his head pressed against the window so he went to see what had snared the butler's attention. Amusingly enough, the old man's eyes were closed, his mouth hanging open, and his gentle snore creating a circle of fog on the glass. It was a neat trick, sleeping on one's feet.

Ash walked to the doorway and pretended to be passing by.

"Tolly?"

The butler straightened immediately and used his sleeve to wipe the fog from the glass before turning from the window.

"Yes, my lord?"

"I need you to keep on your toes. If young Master Balliol heads for the kitchens, I want him stopped."

Tolly frowned. "As you say, me laird."

"If he gets a chance to speak to my prisoner. . ."

"It's my arse, sir. Yes, I understand, sir."

Ash wondered if he'd find the man sleeping on an angle next, blocking the way to the kitchens. He couldn't resist sticking his head back into the study. Tolly was trying to shake himself awake. It was the least Ash could do to help along those lines.

"And Tolly?" he barked.

The old man jumped. "Yes, me laird?"

"You have a strange red circle on your forehead. Were you aware?"

Tolly's hand rose to cover the spot where his head had been pressed against the glass. It was, in fact, quite red. "I will have it examined, sir."

"See that you do," Ash said. "You never know but it is a symptom of something or other."

Tolly bowed, his hand still on his forehead. "Right you are, sir."

And with nothing else to do, he found himself whistling on the way to the kitchens again.

The reason for the whistling, of course, was the same reason for yet another trip to the larder. Hell, the reasons for his humor, both good and bad, would likely be found sitting upon a bag of wheat in the darkness. And as angry as he'd been with her for fleeing from him two years before, he still found himself thinking of her as the village beauty and he, an enamored young man with a fist full of flowers.

But she wasn't. And he wasn't. He must remember that. He must let her go and make a life for herself, but damn him if he'd send her off to make that life with The Reaper. And he'd let her go only when he was damned good and ready.

It seemed each time he was determined to have a long conversation with Scotia, his attention was turned away—as if she were a witch distracting him from ever getting 'round to asking her about her witchery.

But not this time.

He stopped at the kitchen door, his hand poised yet frozen in the air. He had a fleeting thought that perhaps it was he who was not prepared for this conversation. Perhaps it was he who chose to steer away from the subject the last time he'd come to confront her.

No. I'm ready for the truth, no matter what that truth may be.

His hand fell to the door and he pushed it open. When it swung shut behind him, there was no echo left of his whistling, no smile left to his lips. He pulled the key from his pocket and unlocked the larder, then pulled the door wide.

"Come," he said and stood back to allow Scotia to pass without the need for brushing against him. It was going to be a difficult conversation without his senses turning him into a bumbling schoolboy.

She did not hesitate and stepped into the light. She, too, wore no smile, as if she realized they'd reached some crossroads. She looked about the kitchen and seemed alarmed to find no one else about.

"We've yet to be poisoned, if that is what worries you," he said.

"Of course not. The Reaper no doubt believes I've been appointed as the new Royal Taster."

Ash nodded. She was likely right. If she ever slipped his grasp again, they would have to worry in earnest.

He indicated a stool and once she was perched upon it, he sat on the edge of a table opposite. He crossed his arms. She folded her hands. With not a red hair out of place one might think she was sitting for her portrait to be painted if not for her less than picturesque surroundings.

"I'd like to hear your name," he said.

She smiled. "My name is Scotia, apparently."

He sighed his disappointment in spite of the fact he hadn't truly expected her to give up her secrets for the asking.

"You have my ring?" She looked at his suit pockets expectantly.

He held out his arms out to his sides, his palms up in invitation. "A ring for a name, perhaps?"

Of course he hadn't indicated which ring she might get for it. In all honesty, he didn't know whether or not he could part with the little trinket.

"Keep it," she said. Then her eyes skimmed his pockets again. She all but licked her lips.

He turned his head away for a moment to keep from looking at those lips. "I'm going to ask you a question now. I've waited two years to hear the answer."

She swallowed audibly, then raised her chin and waited.

"How did you know Northwick was being held in the fortress? And your brother, of course."

She stiffened and glanced at the back door. He pushed himself to his feet and had a firm hold on both her wrists before she could rise.

"It was cowardly of me not to ask you before we entered Givet Faux. We might have avoided our misunderstanding. Forgive me." He lightened his hold, but kept her wrists in the circle of his fingers. Gentle restraints, but restraints all the same.

She shook her head. "I suppose the truth can do no harm now, can it? Northwick was rescued, after all. Try to remember that." She looked up into his eyes.

Ash sighed. "Of course I remember it. I remember it every day."

She smiled faintly.

He smiled in return, then raised his brows and waited.

After a deep breath, she began. "There was only one thing of which I was guilty, yer lairdship."

He released one wrist, pulled his stool closer, and sat. "Tell me."

CHAPTER THIRTY

Blair forced herself to stop glancing at the door to freedom, although she enjoyed the power she held over the man. She could make him nervous or allow him to relax depending on where she chose to rest her eyes. But after a while, she gave up toying with him when she realized she wished the truth to be known as desperately as he wished to know it.

She started with the day she'd realized that he and his friends were probably looking for the same men. He admitted he'd noticed her the day they'd arrived in Reims. For all her stealth, he'd noticed every move she'd made.

Her recounting brought them quickly to the day they'd gone to Givet Faux, but neither of them mentioned his climbing the steps and shaking his head, to let her know her brother had not been inside. Nor did she need to tell him how devastated she'd been, which was the reason she'd hung back and noticed the man leaving the fortress. Finally, she told him how she'd seen that man leave a note on their table at the auberge. When she told him what the message had said, his breath caught. Then she reminded him of the note he'd found attached to his finger with an owl ring.

"My only crime was burning the message. If we hadn't found Mm... If we hadn't found my brother and

Northwick at Givet Faux, I would have told ye about it. Ye still would have been able to ransom yer friend."

"But ransoming North wouldn't have saved your brother."

She hung her head and nodded. "Yes. It was a risk, and I'm sorry for it. But I dared do naught else."

"Was that your reason for fleeing? Because you didn't wish to tell me I'd been tricked?"

She shook her head. "By then, it didn't matter if ye knew. My brother was going to live. That was all that mattered at the time."

Ash dropped his head. "So you believed I was capable of killing you. I understand."

She laughed. "I was hardly in my right mind. Anything could have reduced me to tears. I wish I could excuse myself because ye frightened me, but the truth was, I frightened myself. I was afflicted with a strange obsession with ye. Perhaps that obsession kept me from worrying about my brother. Perhaps. . ." She shrugged. "I was not myself. I canna understand the whole of it, aye?"

She looked up to find him staring at her in wonder.

"Then you weren't afraid of me?"

She shrugged again and stared at her own fingers. "I tried to explain it to someone, recently. I was more afraid of the affect ye had on me."

She waited, then looked up to find him smiling. She should have kept the last to herself.

"I had considered another possibility, that I had, perhaps, frightened you away. . .with my. . .attentions."

She caught her breath, then laughed lightly. "I suppose I was testing that possibility last eve, when I kissed ye in the barn, don't ye suppose?"

"You kissed me in the barn? Last night? I thought I'd imagined it." And by the look on his face, he was imagining it again.

"Does this mean ye believe me?"

He studied her for a moment. "What is your name, woman? I cannot go on calling you Scotland, for pity's sake."

"I dinna ken why. I rather like it," she whispered.

"I wish you had not fled that day," he whispered back.

She gave her head a vigorous shake. Her hair bounced around her and a strand caught in her lips. But before she could free it, his fingers were there, dragging along her mouth, pulling the hair aside. It took her a moment to remember what she'd been about to say.

"I had no choice but to flee. I needed my brother to return home without me. I can never go home in truth. And he would never have left me in France, if he'd believed I was alive."

Fantine bustled into the kitchen and paid the pair of them no mind at all.

Ash frowned at the Frenchwoman, but still, she ignored him. Blair had to bite her lip to keep from laughing at a man who thought everyone should live and breathe according to his moods.

"Fantine," he barked.

The woman disappeared into the larder and came out with half a bag of flour, a cloud of white billowing at her heels.

"Monsieur," she said as she dropped her load on the table at Blair's back.

"Fantine," he said again.

"Monsieur?" Still, the woman didn't look at him.

"You may not have noticed, but we are attempting to converse here." He gestured to himself and then to Blair, nodding pointedly. "Whatever you're about can surely wait until tomorrow."

The cook gave nary a pause in her fussing about. "Non," she said as she slammed a pan on the table.

"I beg your pardon?" He frowned as if he really hadn't understood the word.

"*Non, monsieur*. You like your bread when you break your fast, not zose silly Scottish scones. I start zee dough when zee sun is gone. I made zee fire bright. Zee heat raises zee dough. No good for conversations. You and *mademoiselle* will converse elsewhere."

Ash folded his arms and glowered. "You are trying to keep me from putting her back in the larder," he said, accusingly.

"*Non, monsieur. Mais vous*. . .But you will do as you will, *n'est ce pas?*"

Suddenly Blair understood and she was touched. Small prickles began behind her nose and tears filled her eyes. "She's making the fire for me," she confessed. "As she did last eve."

Ash turned his attention away from the Frenchwoman. "You suffered? There were not enough blankets for you?"

Fantine stopped fussing and put her flour-covered hands on her hips. "*Mademoiselle* is afraid of zee dark, *monsieur.*"

He snorted. "She most certainly is not."

"She most certainly is," Blair said quietly. She wasn't proud of the fact. In truth, it was a mite embarrassing to be The Highland Reaper and to always need either company or a candle.

His brow furrowed.

She smiled at his obvious concern. "It is true, my lord. Ever since Givet Faux. I realize it sounds silly—"

He jumped to his feet. "Fantine! Mademoiselle will not be left in the dark." He scooped Blair up into his arms and while frowning into her eyes, continued speaking to the other woman. "Clean up your things. When you've finished, send two footmen to my room with a dozen candles."

Blair's heart stopped abruptly, like it had walked into a solid wall, or the solid wall of chest against which she was pressed.

"Your room, *monsieur?*" Fantine didn't move.

"My room," he said.

Blair began to struggle. He squeezed her firmly until she stopped.

"I'd rather be locked in the dark," she spit, "than have half of Scotland believe I spent the night in yer room, ye daft bastard."

"Language," he said, then tisked. After a long moment, he sighed and put her on her feet. "Just what do you propose I do with you?" He raised a finger. "Other than let you go."

"You could put me back in the larder, but give me a candle."

He shook his head. "You could burn my house down around my ears."

"You could lock me in a bedroom," she suggested.

"With a window? With a candle? Then you would burn my house down around my ears, *and* escape."

Their noses were nearly touching. Their breathing fell into the same rhythm, but she couldn't seem to do anything about it while her mind searched for any alternative to the dark little room. No matter how strong she supposed her invisible armor might be in the light of day, it was nowhere to be found in the darkness.

"Ye could put Fántine in with me, without a candle. If I'm not alone, the darkness is nay so bad." She bit her bottom lip in anticipation. There was little he could argue over.

His left brow rose, and with it, the corner of his mouth. She was certain it meant trouble.

CHAPTER THIRTY-ONE

An hour later, Ash was seated on the floor having a late picnic across the threshold to the larder. His enchantress sat just inside the small, dimly lit room while he sat just outside it. Two full candelabras burned on the table behind him. A single fat candle sat on a plate on the floor, next to a wedge of pale cheese. With both his presence and the candles, she shouldn't be at all frightened—not even for her reputation.

She pointed at the plate. "They're of a color. The cheese needs but a wick and we could burn it as well."

"Yes," he said. "So different, yet so similar."

She tilted her head to one side and a mass of curls hung nearly to the floor. He resisted the urge to run his hand through it, as he would a waterfall. The point of his efforts was to chase away her nightmares, not become one.

"I've the impression ye're not speaking of the cheese and the candle," she said.

He smiled. "I was thinking about The Reaper."

She grinned. "Would he be the cheese or the candle?"

He pretended to give it serious consideration before answering. "The cheese."

"Hah! Because he feeds people?"

He shook his head and tried to maintain a sober expression. "No. Because *I'm* more. . .illuminating." Then he laughed.

Her smile was replaced by a look of surprise. "Ye? Ye were speaking of yerself and The Reaper? So different, and yet so similar?"

"To be honest, it is not the first I've entertained the idea." He brushed crumbs from his hands, then gestured toward the remaining food and raised a brow.

She shook her head. "I've had my fill, and thank ye."

For lack of something better to do with his hands, he cleared away the picnic. When he returned, he set the fat candle on the floor beside him, then folded the tablecloth and set it aside as well. It would make a fine pillow later, not that he'd be sleeping. If his Scotia needed to sleep with the door open, he would remain in the doorway, alert and ready for anyone who thought to either come or go.

There was every expectation The Reaper would attempt her rescue, but he had enough men stationed around the manor to warn him well before the blackheart stepped foot inside. And if she intended to sneak past him in the night, he intended to catch her, literally, in the act.

The chance of getting his arms around her made him almost wish she would try.

With the barrier of the picnic removed from between them, she scooted back another foot and onto the pallet made up for her the night before.

"So," she said, fidgeting nervously with her finger. "Tell me what ye believe to have in common with my Reaper."

Inwardly, he winced. Outwardly, he'd not give her the satisfaction of seeing how the little word—*my*—had pained him. He turned sideways and scooted into the middle of the doorway so he could lean his back against the wide frame. If she would be comfortable, so would he.

"First," he said, "I will tell you what we do *not* have in common."

She grinned.

He addressed the candle. "He breaks the law. As far as Scottish tradition is concerned, I am the law here."

"Therefore he breaks ye?"

He tossed her a frown. "You know precisely what I mean."

"Fine. Is there more, then?"

"Of course," he said, though he was making it up as he went. What else did he even know about the blighter? Surely there was more of a difference between them than just their height.

"Go on." She sounded to be on the very verge of laughter.

"I'm rather tall," he mumbled.

She scoffed. "But surely ye've heard. My Reaper is not a short man."

"No, but certainly shorter."

She laughed. "I concede. He is shorter, but so are all but a hundred other men, surely."

Ash nodded. "And he's. . .well, quiet."

She giggled.

He wanted to turn and crawl up to his room. How the devil had he come to such a silly undertaking?

"I think you'd best move on to your similar qualities. You can revise the first list afterward."

He nodded, though he hardly wished to go on. He'd either end with praising his enemy or vaunting himself. Neither action would help his cause, but perhaps he could drag the blackheart down into the mud beside him.

"We've the both of us killed many men," he said seriously.

"Have ye?" Her brow creased. "Are ye certain The Reaper has ever killed anyone?"

"The man has fought in battle. Of course he's killed before."

She looked off into the shadows and nodded. He was pleased if she was seeing his enemy in a less than romantic light and decided to press on.

"We have frightful tempers," he said.

Her head snapped around. She was smiling again, damn her.

"Nay. Actually, he doesna. So that's another trait to add to the first list. Ye've a temper and he has none."

"Fine." Ash took a breath, realizing he was about to lose the temper he never remembered having been a problem before meeting her. "You must admit that we both care about the people of Brigadunn. We both are attempting to help the people and the land recover from past atrocities. I am simply doing so legally."

"Oh, aye. And if The Reaper had gold spilling from his pockets, no doubt he could do the same."

"But do you not see?" He turned to face her, feet and all, and absently noticed he was well inside the larder when he did so. "Brigadunn has need of only one of us."

He wondered if she'd understand his inference, that she needed only one of them, and that The Reaper was not the best choice for either Brigadunn or herself.

She looked at his feet, then at the door, no doubt measuring his proximity to her pallet as well.

He scooted back two inches.

She sighed and looked into his eyes. "It is simple enough. Yes, ye're here—now. But for how long? Just until ye realize that ye cannot make much of a profit from Brigadunn and still be fair with her people? Or will ye send a manager to cheat us all in yer stead? Shall we just do our best, hope we can fatten our children before times grow hard again, until someone else wins us in a game of cards?"

He reached out and took one of her hands firmly in both of his, then looked back at her with the same intensity.

"I did not win you in a game of cards."

"No. Ye lost a lottery. All the glen kens it."

She'd said it as if it were the worst of sins. Something that could not be forgiven.

"You've been misinformed, Scotia. I *stole* you from Northwick." And with that, he pulled firmly on her hand until she lifted off the pallet and onto his lap. He crossed his shins and she sat in the wide circle made by his legs. Her legs hung over his right knee. His hands encircled her waist while she clasped her hands before her and tucked her head beneath his chin. He'd intended to kiss her, but he could wait a while longer.

The risk of her escape prevented him from letting his guard down completely, of course, so he pulled a length of plaid from her pallet, pulled it around both of them, then twisted the ends around one hand and held tight.

"Tell me about the darkness, sweeting."

A few minutes passed and he was coming to accept she did not wish to share her troubles with him when she finally spoke.

"Ghosts," she said.

He could hear the tears in her voice and lifted her chin to find silent drops collecting beneath it, wetting his fingers.

"Ghosts come to me, in the darkness. Waking or sleeping, it makes no matter. They come."

"Ghosts?" He tried not to sound skeptical. "Who are they?"

"The men I killed at Antwerp."

"In battle?"

"Aye. In battle. A battle in which I had no right to be. If I'd not slipped inside the ranks, those men might have lived. They remind me of it. Just their faces before me. The rattle of death."

"But sweeting," he said carefully. "In Charleville, you were sleeping in the dark, with no fire. Barely a candle in the hallways—"

"That was before Givet Faux. After all that happened there, something changed. Now the ghost of that woman comes with the others."

"The woman? *I* killed the woman, Scotia. Her blood is on my hands."

She smiled at him. "A sweet thing to say, all in all, but Wolfkiller did the job I sent it to do. It was well-seated," she swallowed awkwardly, "well-seated before ye let fly yer blade. I can still feel the snap of yer sword when it broke against mine. I feel it often. And I'm glad I sent Wolfkiller with Martin. I never care to touch it again.

"I had hoped, with all my work as. . .at The Reaper's side, I might have earned some forgiveness. But still the faces come. When it's dark."

Ash freed his hand from the plaid and pulled her tight, hoping for a bit of redemption himself by holding her as she wept, as he'd failed to hold her long ago, when she'd fallen apart with no one to catch the pieces.

"Forgive me, love. Forgive me for not tying you to a tree, or locking you up in some safe place to keep you from following us into Givet Faux that day. It was unforgiveable, but forgive me anyway?"

She smiled up at him then, placed a hand along his cheek, and gave him a brief kiss.

"Ye silly man. Of course I forgive ye. But had ye tied me up, or locked me up, I could not have been so forgivin'. Ye understood back then. Ye knew. And ye were a little afraid of me, I think."

Ash nodded. "Yes. You terrified me. I was terrified you'd be hurt. I was just too much a coward to do anything about it." He smoothed her hair away from her face and pecked at her lips with his own. "But I'm not that coward anymore. And I will do anything necessary to keep you from being hurt. Even if I have to board up all the windows and lock the entire house with only you and me inside."

She laughed, albeit nervously.

"That reminds me," he said. "Do you know of any old tower keeps nearby? Something I might purchase for a reasonable price?"

"A tower keep? What are ye needin'?"

He shrugged, deciding that some silliness was better left unspoken.

CHAPTER THIRTY-TWO

From a haze of blue dawn, the sun rose and woke the birds. Ash held deathly still, to prolong the spell and pray that for once the sun would reconsider.

There was only the slightest change to the woman's breathing, but it was enough to tell him she was awake, though she pretended not to be. Was she, too, wishing the night could have lasted a bit longer? Or was she hoping for a chance to escape him?

His arm pulled her closer. And there they lay, pretending nothing was unusual about nestling close on the larder floor, until Tolly came puffing into the little room, a parchment flapping in his hand.

Stiffly, they rose until they were sitting side by side. Ash took one of her hands and laced their fingers together before he reached for the paper.

Tolly placed both his hands on his knees and struggled to catch his breath. It was either long past time for the man to retire, or he was playing Ash for a fool. But either way, he would not risk running the man into his grave. As soon as The Reaper was removed from power, or removed from the area, and the constable replaced, Ash would bend his attentions to Tolly's future. Until then, he would supply the man with a runner. Perhaps Finn was just the boy for the job.

Ash stood and helped Scotia to her feet, then opened the note.

   "To the Right Honorable Earl of Ashmoore," he read aloud.
      "Dear Sir,
      I am escaping you.
      Sometimes defiance is the honorable choice.
      Finnian Balliol

"Damn! I knew he was upset, but—"

Scotia snatched the message from his hand and read it again. "What do ye mean, he was upset? What upset him?"

"He asked if I was going to release you. I told him I could not. So he insisted I had to release *him*, as if he believed it was unfair for me to hold you both."

The woman moaned and crumpled the paper in her hand.

"He wasn't thinking about fairness," she complained. "He was worried about Shakespeare."

"I don't understand. The line about defiance being the honorable choice? I don't recall—"

"Not the writer, the blasted bird. The *owl*."

"His dead owl?"

"Shakespeare's not dead," she said. "But he would be soon enough if ye didn't let one of us go."

His mind stumbled across the clues that had been strewn in his path, clues he should have seen long ago, the ring he'd been carrying in his bloody pocket for two years!

He grabbed her shoulders. "You're Blair Balliol. Martin was the unconscious young man with the swollen face!"

"And my wee brother has gone off to find the Witch's Vale to feed Shakespeare. Only he doesna ken the secret to getting there safely. He'll end with walking off a cliff in the mist. There are markers leading the way, but they are of a purpose, misleading. We have to catch him before he gets too far. And before it gets dark!"

The pounding of the door knocker reached all the way to the kitchens. Tolly stumbled away to answer it.

"Perhaps someone already found Finn and is returning him." Ash began pulling her after the old man.

She resisted. "No! No one can see me. Do ye not understand?"

He stopped and noted the desperation in her eyes. "Is this about your father?"

She shrugged. Her mouth moved, but she found no words.

Then understanding dawned and an invisible fist found his middle. He forced himself to say it. "Or is it about your Reaper?"

She stared at him for a moment as if his soul were laid bare for her, which it most likely was. Whatever she saw there finally made her look away.

"Both," she said quietly.

He considered locking her back in the larder, ensuring there was a crack or two to allow light inside, but no more. There was no one to tell him that he couldn't. And it was a fact he could not stand to let her go, no matter how she felt about the villain.

"My kingdom for a secluded tower," he mumbled.

She glanced at the larder and took a step back. "Ye have no reason to keep me," she said. "Ye've got yer answers. All of them. Let me go."

His mind sought a valid reason to deny her. His vision caught on a bottle of cooking sherry standing lonely on a shelf, and his reason presented itself along with the first step in an inspired strategy.

"If I allow you to leave, there will be nothing to keep your Reaper from poisoning us all. And I have no intention of leaving Scotland until my task is done here. I'll have to keep you until the property is put to rights, and the tenants can prosper. Your lover will have to make do without you for a good while, I'm afraid."

Meaness swirled inside his soul. . .and it felt good.

Tolly burst through the hallway door, then closed it and leaned back against the wood as if he were being chased.

"Yer lairdship. Beg pardon," he huffed. "The Constable is here. He's brought a wee army, I'm afraid."

"An inconvenient time, Tolly. Send him away." Ash had chess moves to plan.

"Weel, when I say he's *here,* I actually mean—"

There was a bang on the door at the old man's back.

". . .here."

"*Lord Ashmoore!*" The constable's voice was muffled by the wood. "*I demand an audience, sir.*"

The door began to slide open. Tolly pushed back and it snapped shut. Without releasing his prisoner's arm, Ash moved quickly to add his own weight to the door. What could he do? No doubt the constable would complicate things if he were to catch even a glimpse of that beauty mark, let alone her wild tresses.

And why was the constable so determined to see inside the kitchen, unless someone told the man Ash was hiding someone there? If he managed to lock her in the larder, the lawman would not rest until he looked inside.

"What I need is Stanley," he admitted aloud, but since his highly influential friend wasn't about, he was simply going to have to let his precious captive free.

"Well, what good is a friend who fails to appear the very moment you need him, I ask you?"

Ash turned to find his white-haired friend dusting off his clothes just inside the kitchen's yard door. It took Ash but a heartbeat to recover. He'd been so close to allowing Scotia to flee, it had sickened him.

"Stan. Good to see you," he whispered, although the constable was making far too loud a fuss to be able to hear much conversation through the door. "Pity you will not be home to receive my letter."

Stan raised a white square. "I have it here. Your man and I crossed paths after I was well inside Scotland. Excellent reading."

"Glad to amuse, my friend. I'm afraid I must patronize the constable for a moment. We cannot allow him to see her face." He nodded at the woman. "Fetch her that cloak by the door, if you would not mind." Ash gave the woman's fingers a squeeze. "Scotia," he said pointedly. "You no doubt recognize His Grace."

If Stan was surprised, he hid it well behind a charming smile as he wrapped the cloak around her and helped tuck her hair beneath the hood. Later, Ash would warn his friend from using that smile in her presence again.

"If you play nicely," Ash explained to her quietly, "the constable will never get a good look at you. Do you understand?"

She nodded.

He turned to his butler. "Tolly, I need you to faint. Just where you are, if you please. Right up against the door."

"Gladly, sir." The butler melted to the floor and Ash could not say for certain that the faint hadn't been real.

"Hold on to her," he told Stanley. "Back by the door now. You've just arrived and she's ill."

"Excellent," Stan said, flashing her one last smile as they took their places. Then she dropped her head against him, damn her.

Just then, the yard door burst open behind the pair, and four men pushed their way inside. They fanned out around the cavernous room, pistols at the ready.

"Don't just stand there," Ash told the two nearest intruders. "Help me move my butler out of the way. The constable cannot get in."

The men tucked away their weapons and did as they were told.

Ash pointed at one of the long tables. "Put him there."

A heartbeat after Tolly's body was lifted away, the hallway door flew open and bounced against the wall. The constable stormed through the opening and half a dozen men followed. One of them was holding his leader's ridiculous hat.

"What are ye hiding, Laird Ashmoore, eh?" The constable held his hands like claws as if he was prepared to pounce on Ash and begin ripping him to pieces. His disturbing nose was curled up on one side.

Ash ignored the man and pointed to an armed bloke standing next to Stanley. "Fetch the Frenchwoman from her gardens. She's as good as any doctor."

The man hesitated, then reached for the door.

"Here now," barked the constable. "What are ye about? Ye'll take no orders from him. I'm in charge, here."

Stanley cleared his throat behind his hand, no doubt to mask a laugh. The constable failed to notice. Ash would have been offended if the man weren't so ignorant of his own ignorance.

The armed man looked uncertainly at Ash, who nodded. "Go."

The man spun on his heel and fled.

Seven armed men left. The odds were more favorable. Especially since one of the constable's men was Everhardt. But no one's blood would be shed unless necessary.

"I apologize, Constable," Ash offered without a hint of regret. "My butler suffers a bad heart. I'm afraid your visit is ill-timed. Again."

"I doona believe it in the least." The man wandered over to Tolly and poked him in the belly with a pointed finger.

To the butler's credit, he didn't flinch so much as an eyebrow.

Ash took off his coat and folded it, then tucked it under Tolly's head. Sarah appeared in the doorway and he sent her to fetch Tolly a blanket.

"And who is this?" The Constable tilted his head at Stanley who gave the man a haughty glare.

"Forgive me," Ash said to his friend. "This is the constable. Constable Wotherspoon, this is His Grace, Viscount Forsgreen, the future Duke of Rochester."

Stan ignored the man and addressed Ash. "Not so far in the future, I'm afraid."

"That bad?"

"I'm afraid so."

Ash sincerely hoped Stan was exaggerating for the constable's benefit. "As soon as Fantine has a look at Tolly, I'll have her see you to your rooms. If you'd like to take the lady to the drawing room, she can at least rest comfortably while she waits."

Stan nodded and headed for the hallway door through which the constable had entered. The latter stepped in front of him.

Stanley stopped and glared. "Ashmoore? Your constable seems confused."

Ash laughed. "I'm afraid it is not the first time, my friend. Here, Constable," he said to the ill-mannered oaf in a patronizing tone. "Why do you not make yourself useful and take your men outside in the rare sunshine. I will join you as soon as we have finished turning my home into a hospital."

The man turned a rather satisfying shade of purple.

"I doona believe it in the least," he spat at Stanley this time. "If ye're who ye say ye are, why would you sneak into the kitchens instead of using the front door, eh?"

Stanley sighed, as if resigning himself to the odious fact that he would need to actually speak to a commoner. It was rather frightening to see how easily the attitude came to him.

"Constable," he said, his mouth framing the word awkwardly. "I would have preferred the front door, but my lady was rather in a hurry to exit the carriage, and your horses blocked the drive. Your men blocked the doorway.

And damned if we were going to stand about in the mud while you ran about playing law man."

The smaller man snorted. "I suppose ye can produce this carriage, milord?"

Stan smiled. "You needn't look far. *Constable*. It's just outside there." He stepped aside and pointed to the yard door, all the while supporting Miss Balliol. "It will be the one with the *ducal* crest. I'm certain Ashmoore's servants will be happy to help if you fail to locate it."

Stan's tone was no help to the man's color.

"Are you feeling well, Constable?" Ash looked around the room. "I can have my Frenchwoman look you over if you like, but you'll have to wait your turn." Then he dropped all pretenses and narrowed his eyes at the bastard. "Or you can state your business and remove yourself from my property once and for all."

Constable smiled. "I've three cells waiting in town. Someone will be sleeping behind those bars tonight, I warrant. I've only to decide which of ye it will be."

Ash exchanged a smirk with Stan.

The constable harrumphed. "It seems ye're holding a prisoner—"

"Not this nonsense again," Ash said dramatically for the sake of a room full of witnesses. "The boy is no longer here. And he was never a prisoner."

"A woman, this time. And ye've got her locked up—"

"In the larder, I suppose?" Ash laughed.

The man stomped around the kitchen and found the door to the larder standing open. He lifted the padlock and pointed at it.

"Ye always keep so serious a lock on your pantry?"

Ash smirked. "And you do not?"

The bastard threw the lock across the room where it thumped ineffectually against a broom.

"Where is she?" he snarled. "I'm told she's The Reaper's whore."

Stan gasped loudly. Ash suspected he'd done it to cover the same reaction from the woman in his arms.

The constable pressed on, far too emotional now to watch his tongue. Perhaps they'd have the truth from the man after all.

"And if ye're not holding her hostage as you did the boy, then she'd be here for another reason, would she no'? A man like The Reaper would hardly take kindly to sharing, so it stands to reason—"

"If you tarry just a moment, Your Grace," Ash winked at Stanley, "he is about to reveal his theory that I am The Highland Reaper—a Robin Hood-type character who has been absconding with cattle and people alike for the past two years. Since we returned from France, in fact. Apparently I have had an imposter standing in my stead in the House of Lords all this while."

Stanley laughed along.

"It would explain why ye've been keeping the woman here." Constable turned to the cloaked form. "Remove yer hood," he ordered.

Stanley urged Scotia, or rather, Blair Balliol to lean against the wall, then stepped between her and the little man. Ash closed in on his other side, ignoring the tension that rippled through the armed men at their backs.

"I am afraid that is slander, Constable," Ash growled. "And we have a room full of witnesses."

Stanley leaned in. "And if you touch so much as the hem on my lady's mantle, I'll personally drag you from here to Newgate and hand-pick your cellmates. Do I make myself clear?"

Constable laughed in their faces, his breath a putrid cloud of old mutton and strong spirits.

"Anything the English lord wants, the English lord gets," he snarled. "And now we ken why." He turned away and looked around the room at his men. "Uppity friends to bend and wash the blood from 'is hands, sweep away the entrails of any man who crosses 'im." He swung back to face Ash and lowered his voice. "If yer not the bloody Reaper, yer as good as. Ye belong in my jail, and on to the gibbet. And I'll escort ye to both, see if I don't. . .on me way to Newgate, of course."

He backed away and spit at Stanley's feet.

"Keep the whore close, milords. If I she takes a step beyond Brigadunn, she's mine."

CHAPTER THIRTY-THREE

Blair shook beneath her cloak as she waited for the sound of the constable's men to fade. Whether it was fear of the man or fear for her brother that caused her to quiver, she knew not.

Ash's calm voice broke the silence when he told Sarah to send for Martin.

"*Send* for him," he clarified. "Do not go fetch the man yourself."

He sent Fantine to shut the heavy curtains in the drawing room, then addressed his butler who was still laid out on the table. The poor man had slept through most of the ordeal.

"Tolly!" Ash barked.

The man jumped and his legs fell off the table. He caught himself before he could hit the floor and break into a dozen pieces.

"Yer lairdship?" Tolly blinked rapidly.

"Fine job, Tolly. When Martin arrives, send him to the drawing room, if you please."

Stanley pulled her hand to his forearm and turned to escort her from the room.

"Just a moment," Ash said. "I will take her from here."

Stan's brows shot up. "It is like that is it?"

Ash frowned and shook his head. "No. It is not like that. Fleeing is the woman's forte, and I have no intention of allowing it at the moment."

Blair blushed as if her forte were something to be ashamed of. Then, to punish the man for making her feel that shame, she turned to the handsome friend, still holding his arm. "Yer Grace, it is a pleasure to see ye again."

Stan looked at Ash, then back at her. "The pleasure is mine, Lady Scotia."

"I'm afraid I do not miss those days in France, but I am glad I could help ye find yer friend, Northwick. Do you remember?"

The man stepped back, breaking her hold on him, but offering a deep bow. "Indeed I do. I am forever in your debt."

Ash snorted. Rather ungentlemanly, that. "Your debt is precisely what she is after, old boy," he warned.

Blair ignored him and pressed on. "Could ye take me for a short ride in yer carriage, sir? My young brother has run off, ye see, and he's headed for danger. Even Lord Ashmoore canna deny it."

The viscount looked at Ash and waited.

"Oh, for heaven's sake." Ash took her by the arm and dragged her away. Once they were all inside the drawing room with the doors closed, he released her. "Enjoy a little freedom while you have it, my lady."

She dropped her mouth open and pretended surprise. "What are you saying? The puppy is allowed to run amok through the *entire* room? Aren't ye worried I'll befoul the carpet?"

Stanley laughed. Ash scowled. She couldn't have been more pleased.

"Are you going to introduce me properly?" asked Stanley after he'd caught his breath.

"No," Ash said and crossed his arms.

"I see," said his friend. "I'm not to touch her, smile at her, or know her name. Is that correct?"

"Shut up, Stanley," Ash growled.

She tried not to react when Fantine came in and drew the curtains shut, leaving her dependent upon candlelight in spite of the bright morning. Of course she had no need to worry; Ash would never leave her alone, especially with lit candles. Though, at the moment, she felt desperate enough to burn his house down around his ears if it meant she'd be able to find Finn before he came to harm.

After the Frenchwoman left, Ash dragged a chair in front of the doors, sat in it, and crossed his arms again. Blair removed her hood as she walked to the far end of the room and turned. She hung her tongue out her mouth and panted like a puppy.

Stanley dropped his smile. Ashmoore dropped his frown. The pair of them were suddenly far too interested in her mouth.

"Oh, for heaven's sake," she said, then marched to a chair and dropped herself in it.

They sat in silence for ten minutes. When Martin arrived, Ash allowed him inside the room, then resumed his seat. Her brother took one look at her, swallowed, then bowed to Ashmoore.

"Ye sent for me, yer lairdship?"

For a moment, Ash simply looked her brother over as if he were seeing him for the first time. Blair realized if her brother's face hadn't been so badly swollen in France, events might have played out a bit different when Ashmoore arrived at Brigadunn. That night when she'd come for Finn, if Ash had known who she was. . .

Blair shook her head to keep her thoughts from straying any farther. The worry was Finn and Finn only.

Ash cleared his throat. "I suppose I need not introduce you to your sister." He turned to his friend. "Stanley, you know this young man better than I, since you helped put him on a ship at Zeebrugge."

While Stan and Martin got reacquainted, Ash looked on, obviously a little shaken. Or perhaps it had been his pride that was shaken after standing so near the truth without seeing it. Martin was shocked to see Stanley once again, then even more shocked to learn Ashmoore had been in on his rescue.

Blair blinked back the moisture in her eyes as her brother expressed his heartfelt gratitude to both men. Her tears dried of their own accord when Martin promptly forgave the lords for lying to him about his sister's death— as if she weren't right there in the room with them. Eventually, Martin looked around the room, then at her. "Where is Finn?"

"Since you hardly look surprised to see your sister," Ash said, "you must have known she was alive. Do you also know she—"

"Yes. I know," Martin interrupted.

Blair rolled her eyes. They were obviously referring to her relationship to The Reaper, and she was in no mood to defend herself.

Ash gave her a smug look. "You will be relieved to learn, Martin, she is the reason Finn did not wish to speak to you. He did not trust himself to keep her secret, I suspect."

"Where is he?" Martin pressed.

"He's gone to the Vale," Blair said. She got to her feet, grateful they'd gotten past their posturing and were ready to speak of the matter at hand. "He doesn't know the way, Martin. He'll be lost on the mountain, or walk into a trap. We have to go after him."

Ash stood too. "*She's* not going anywhere."

Martin gave him a hard look. "Baiting The Reaper canna be more important than finding Finn."

"I do not give a damn about the blasted Reaper!" Ash exclaimed, then turned aside with a frown as if he regretted the disclosure.

Then why does he keep me?

Martin shook his head, confused. "Why can she not go with me, now, to find the lad?"

Her heart lightened when it seemed as if Ash had no good reason to give. But then his brow lifted.

"The property is being watched," he said. "The constable is set on getting his hands on her. She must stay here where she and her beauty mark will be out of sight."

Blair wished it wasn't true, but she could not help but argue. "I'll be out of sight in the Vale, my lord. Just allow me to return to The Reaper. The Constable will never find me there. I'll locate Finn and take him along."

Martin stiffened. "Go ahead and keep her," he snapped. "Another day away from the devil's bed is another day away from the devil."

"Martin!" she cried and stumbled back as if an arrow had pierced her very heart. Of course she was to blame for his assumptions, but she hoped his sense of familial loyalty would override them.

"My feeling as well, Balliol." Ash turned to his friend. "Do not fail me, Stanley."

"Do I ever?"

A moment later, she was left in the room with a broken heart, a pair of candelabras, and a grinning Englishman who'd taken Ashmoore's seat in front of the doors. The only warning she'd been able to give them before the doors slammed shut, was for them never to trust the markers. Her brother had known the rhyme, Ash had insisted they could decipher it, and for a moment she'd allowed her pride to overshadow Finn's danger. By the time she'd recovered her wits, it was too late. They were gone.

Stanley sighed. "So, Miss Balliol, is it? If you will but find a comfortable seat and settle yourself, I will tell you an astonishing tale of a lady who, until recently, hid behind the *nom de plume*, The Scarlet *Plumiere*." He leaned forward and his grin widened. "Then you can tell me how you came to be The Highland Reaper. What do you say?"

~ ~ ~

It took an hour to do it, but eventually Blair secured the viscount's promise to keep her secret. Only after reminding him a dozen times that he owed Northwick's life to her, did he relent. She wondered if that mightn't have been the case had the Earl of Northwick not recovered fully and found happiness with his new bride. If he were writhing in a hospital somewhere, she doubted his friends would have been so grateful to her. But obviously, happiness was worth a heavy price.

And no matter what happened from then on, she would have no need to fear Stanley would betray her. Of course, he tried to exact an additional price for his silence—a promise she would not try to escape—but she insisted she'd already done enough to earn his loyalty, in this matter at least. To ease his mind a bit, she told how Northwick himself had also granted her a boon when he'd allowed her to slip away quietly.

After baring her secrets and her soul to the handsome man—and in spite of the fact he sympathized with her plight—he still refused to allow her to leave. He appreciated the fact that she'd saved over a hundred women and children from starvation who'd been at the mercy of his less scrupled contemporaries, but still, he remained resolute.

He was moved nigh to tears when she described the school they'd established in the Vale, how she sought to teach the children to show respect for the superstitions of their parents and grandparents, but they shouldn't be afraid to search for the truth. She told of the cavern they'd turned into their church and the priest they'd convinced to join them, how many of their fathers and husbands knew where they'd gone and were grateful they'd been cared for. Some men, who weren't able to care for themselves, were able to join them.

How they still needed a leader to give them hope, that one day they might all go home. But they still needed their beloved Reaper.

And still he would not let her go.

"You remind me of someone, you know," he said.

Blair sighed. She took the change in subject to mean that he was finished with her begging.

"Let me guess," she said. "I remind ye of this *Plumiere* woman."

He laughed and got to his feet, then took up one of the candelabras. His shadow flew along the curtains when he turned and motioned for her to precede him out the doors. "Of course you do. But I was thinking of someone else entirely," he said. "Ashmoore."

It was her turn to laugh. "Ye see me as a large brooding monster who suspects innocent women to be bedding down with the devil? Or as a cold-blooded kidnapper and torturer of soldiers?"

The viscount paused and considered. "I'll own," he finally said, "that even I was a bit suspicious when you fled from us in France as you did. But I thought it most likely Ashmoore's. . .*ardor* had frightened you away. Thereafter, he carried that blasted ring about with such preoccupation, we assumed he was besotted with you.

"Since he left soon after you fled, he never did see Martin's face after the swelling faded. What a fool he must feel to find the truth has been tending his land?"

As the viscount led her up the stairs, she confessed about the ransom demand she'd burned.

"Oh, I say, that was deucedly clever of you. And if there is anything Ashmoore appreciates, it is a clever mind."

"Well, I'm not clever enough to have won ye to my side," she said grudgingly.

He laughed and led her inside a bedchamber. Having never been warned of Ash's lack of trust where she and candles were concerned, he brought the candelabra along. Before she could think to protest, he'd locked himself inside with her and pocketed the key.

He checked the drawers and wardrobe, for possible weapons most likely. After a quick look out the windows, he seemed satisfied. The candles he left on the dressing table and returned to the door. She was relieved, of course. She had no intention of staying the night locked in a room with a bed and a strange man. It would be no different than what Ash had proposed the night before.

Stanley bid her good afternoon, but then turned back with a frown.

"We are a brotherhood, you see," he explained. "The Four Kings, they call us, as a matter of information. I would sacrifice my own mother before I'd betray Ash or the others." His grin returned. "Well, perhaps not my mother—she's rather a dear thing—but you get the idea. Surely you and your companions have a similar trust?"

Reluctantly, she nodded.

"We are a lucky few, I think, to know such devotion."

Again, she nodded.

"Although it is early, I suggest you try to rest. Ashmoore never fails to get his man, or woman, or young person. And remember you risk too much if you leave this place."

She lifted a hand to keep him from turning away. "Ye said I reminded ye of Lord Ashmoore?"

"You do."

"How so?"

He raised a brow. "If you consider, you'll see you both are attempting to help the same people. It is only your methods that differ."

The sentiment was much like Ash's comment, that he and The Reaper were similar. And even though both men saw things much simpler than they truly were, she smiled and nodded. Stan had been so kind. She only wished she could ease his mind by promising she'd see him in the morning.

But she didn't like to lie when she could help it.

CHAPTER THIRTY-FOUR

Stanley, Viscount Forsgreen, soon to be a duke for pity's sake, sat atop an impatient horse just in sight of Brigadunn Manor and waited for his "responsibility" to escape from the room inside which she'd been locked for the night.

To keep her guessing throughout the day, he'd popped up at her door two or three times per hour with one query or another. *What would you find appealing for dinner? Care for some tea? What do you know of this constable fellow? What is this I hear of you poisoning Ashmoore?* And after wearing himself thin on the stairs, he decided it was time for them both to have a rest, and he'd bid her goodnight one final time.

He'd nearly laughed aloud at the regret on her face as he'd pulled the door shut behind him. Likely she felt a heavy guilt for her intentions to escape at the first opportunity. He was offended she believed he might be so gullible. After all, as The Reaper, she was a notorious thief. And notorious thieves could hardly reach notoriety if they couldn't break themselves out of a simple bedchamber only twenty feet off the ground.

It wasn't as if he truly wished her to escape; he only hoped she would keep herself so occupied with trying that Ash would have time to track down the boy and return home before she succeeded. And to this end, he'd put a few obstacles in her way, the first of which was a man below her window. Then second, he'd had all horses removed from the stables.

Stan imagined her cursing when she caught her first glimpse of the fellow on the ground, and he chuckled.

Of course she might choose to take his advice and rest while she could. After all, he'd been waiting half an hour and she had yet to look out the window. But, no. She'd been out sorts with worry for her brother, but tried to hide it behind the plea to let her return to the people who needed her. If it hadn't been a fellow King counting on him, he might have just let her go. Hell, he might have escorted her up the mountain himself. But he didn't have the luxury of acting the hero tonight.

The sunlight on the manor mellowed to a golden orange then disappeared altogether when storm clouds rose in the west. If she waited until dark, she'd have better odds at slipping past the constable, but she'd also have better odds of getting hurt trying to get out her window, especially if it rained.

He pulled his hood forward again to cover his white hair. His horse exhaled beneath him, finally accepting they might not be going anywhere.

A breeze rustled through the leaves above his head, and with nothing more to distract him, he once again marveled that Ash had missed all the clues he'd included in his letter to Stan. With all the details his friend had gleaned concerning the famous Highland Reaper, Ash must have been mightily distracted to have overlooked his own notes. Otherwise, he might have deduced, early on, the woman was the villain he sought.

For instance, The Reaper had three people in his inner circle, comrades who spoke for him and passed on his orders. None but they had ever heard the man speak. And all four of them were never seen at one time, in one place.

Some claimed the man was tall. Some said he was short and broad, like a bull. Therefore different people were wearing the disguise. It was obvious.

This business about him being hard to kill—merely rumor meant to engender fear.

People disappeared, but no bodies were found. An army of undead at his beck and call? None had actually seen this army. And any Scotsman, or Scotswoman, with a well-trained pair of collies could collect a hundred head and disappear over a hill in a matter of minutes. An army? No. An army of quiet, well-trained *dogs?* Perhaps.

The voice? The Reaper never wished to be heard. Why? Because he had the voice of a woman. If asked, perhaps some of these witnesses might have noticed The Reaper's rather delicate hands.

Ash had chosen to believe Miss Balliol to be the villain's mistress. Not an altogether foolish assumption. But once he'd learned she was the same mysterious Scotswoman who'd fought with them inside Givet Faux, how could Ash assume the woman would take orders from a mere cattle thief?

Of course Stan had realized, upon reading the name of Martin Balliol, that the woman might very well be the elusive Scotia. But poor Ash had never heard the young prisoner's name, nor seen his face after the swelling began to ease. He'd been long gone, chasing after the sister. Then, after leaving the Continent, the Four Kings had agreed never to discuss the experience again. Giving up on finding North, even though it was Napoleon's attempted escape that demanded it, had been the greatest shame of their lives, but Ashmoore's especially. Even the mention of the country disturbed his friend until a few months ago, when they'd finally pulled Northwick aside and confessed.

If Ash had heard the name of Scotia's brother before ever coming to Scotland, Stan might not be hiding just inside the wood line, subject to his own vow of silence, unable to cure Ashmoore of his blindness where Miss

Balliol was concerned. But now it was the least he could do—even if it meant sitting a horse all night in the newly arrived, misty rain.

A mist not dense enough to obstruct his view of her window, thankfully.

His outriders were stationed at other points around the house in case she picked the lock and escaped by another route. His ears strained for a distant whistle, since it looked as if she was not so foolish as to climb down a wet wall.

His horse sighed again. If he weren't wearing a fine pair of boots, he'd dismount and stand beside the over-dramatic beast—

The light in the woman's window disappeared, leaving a dark square in its stead. A long moment passed and he wondered if she might actually do the reasonable thing and sleep.

The shutters opened outward. The man on the ground gave no indication he'd heard anything and continued his slow scan of the yard.

Stan expected a string of bed sheets to emerge and was not disappointed when the now caped woman leaned out the window with the very things held in one arm. But she did not drop them. There was a flash of silver, like a bird escaping from the room, sailing out and up, then catching on a small chimney, the makeshift rope of white following like the thick tail of a kite. When she pulled, however, her silver anchor slipped from her target and tumbled off the roof. The clever woman snatched up the slack before it could fall against a window below her.

It was the candelabra. He'd all but handed her the means of escape.

The next section of the house turned at a right angle just beyond her window, so the chimney stack was an easy target. He might have considered the same plan if he'd been in her position. And, like her, he would have kept trying.

After five attempts without the metal catching on so much as a nail, he began to feel sorry for her, imagining her frustration.

Poor thing. And stubborn.

A sixth try. The metal caught!

She tugged. It held!

She tugged again. It slid away.

Her arms must be flagging, he thought. Then he wondered how long it might take her to realize her plan was flawed. For pity's sake, why didn't she simply tie the sheets to the bedframe and lower herself to the ground since the man stationed there was pretending to be far more interested in defending the house than in preventing anyone escaping it. If she were quiet, she might easily sneak around the corner without believing he'd notice.

He couldn't bear to watch, and yet he could not look away.

A wagon came into view as it entered the drive from the far side of the house. Along the sides of the box sat half a dozen chattering maids. A young man in livery drove the single, swaybacked plow horse Stan had allowed to remain at the manor in order to take the day staff home. With so few residents to care for, he'd been informed, the night staff would suffice until morning.

His eyes came back to the exercise in futility at the window. The woman leaned on the windowsill, resting her arms, but she didn't rest for long. After a brief stretch, she took careful aim and threw, leaning far out the window to allow more slack.

Stanley found himself rooting for the candelabra to catch, straining along with her, holding his breath as she carefully pulled back. Biting his lip as he willed the damnable silver to hold on!

And then it did.

He nearly jumped out of the saddle with excitement, but caught himself before he made much noise. The woman looked utterly stunned. In fact, she stood there so long he wondered if perhaps she'd forgotten what she'd planned to do next.

Perhaps she might swing over to the adjacent window, climb inside, and walk through the house as if she'd been given leave to do so. She might sneak out the back door to the stable, steal a bit of man's clothing, pile her hair in a cap and take a horse for a late bit of exercise—only there would be no horse for the taking. And his outriders would be there to stop her.

Northwick's woman, Livvy, had done something similar. She'd forced her maid to order her a carriage, then tied that maid to a chair so she couldn't tattle before Livvy slipped away from the house.

Of course Miss Balliol wouldn't have any sway with the staff. She wasn't the lady of the manner. The closest thing she had to a lady's maid was Sarah. . .

Sarah who had become romantically involved with Miss Balliol's brother. . .

Sarah who was very close to the size of the woman standing at the window, wondering what to do next.

Stanley closed his eyes for a heartbeat, just long enough to wish Ashmoore had smarter friends. Behind those closed eyes, he saw the horror on Ash's face when he discovered Stanley had indeed failed him.

~ ~ ~

Stanley caught up to the wagon just as it was building up speed for a small hill. The passengers were deathly sober. The only sound came from the squeak of the wheels, the creak of the wood, and the hooves of the old nag.

He pulled up level with the nag and reached for the leads. The young man in livery looked terribly disappointed, but Stan couldn't tell if it was due to being discovered so soon, or because he was going to have a devil of a time getting the wagon to crest the hill.

Stan turned a silent but fierce frown on the boy, then shared it with the maids. The five maids. Five quite unrepentant maids who were likely, at that moment, reveling in the fact their countrywoman had just bested an Englishman.

He couldn't help wiping the smirks from their faces.

"You do realize," he said, "that the constable and his men are lying in wait for her. You may as well have delivered her to the man in chains.

He should have been more pleased that his words had horrified each and every one of them, but he was too horrified himself to enjoy the moment.

CHAPTER THIRTY-FIVE

Ash and Martin dismounted beneath an outcropping of stone and made their way, for a while at least, on foot. The path was narrow and precarious and Ash would have had a difficult time trusting any beast to carry him when one side of the trail dropped sharply away to a promontory forty feet below.

Neither he nor Martin would say it aloud, but they were lost, and hopelessly so. The devil of it was, they shouldn't be lost at all.

They'd paused at the foot of the mountain and looked directly at the elusive Witch's Vale. They'd watched the mist roll across the face of the cliffs. They'd seen exactly the route they should take to get there, and they'd followed that route.

And they'd ended up on another mountain entirely, staring across a chasm at those damnable, mist-covered cliffs.

If he didn't know better, he would deduce the moniker of *Witch's Vale* was derived from the fact that actual witches had put some spell on the place to keep men like him away. But he *did* know better. He was nearly certain he knew better.

In the event young Finn had travelled the same route, they bellowed his name from time to time, for Martin was confident Finn did not know the secret to finding the hide-out of the infamous Reaper. What lad of ten could have kept such a secret from his older brother who had, in essence, been his closest friend since he'd returned from France?

Ash hadn't disavowed Martin of his belief, though he might have; Finn had successfully kept his sister's secret, even after she'd been locked in the larder of the same household. The lad had never given up her name and had managed to avoid his brother. A brave and clever lad if ever there was one.

Brave and clever.

Finn would have found a way to the Vale. They needed only be as clever as he.

Their path suddenly ended. Whatever ground had once continued for the next twenty feet had toppled away.

"We must start again," Ash said. "And before night falls in an hour."

They were halfway down the mountain, hoping they didn't end up on the wrong side of it, when Ash noticed a strange shadow in a stretch of rocks. It so intrigued him, he dismounted for a closer look. He bent over the spot, and the shadow disappeared.

He straightened immediately, then glanced at Martin to see if the young man was paying any attention.

"What is that?" Martin asked, pointing to the spot where the shadow had been. But it had disappeared. Martin pointed at nothing.

A chill slowly snaked its way up Ash's spine. He could not suppress a shiver as it raked him over.

"What is it you see?"

Martin frowned at him. "What do you mean?" He got off his horse and joined Ash in the rocks, then pointed again. "That's odd. It's gone."

They both remounted and looked at the spot again. Right where they expected it to be, there was a distinct arrow made of small rocks, sitting like a chameleon atop a sea of small rocks. It was the shadow that gave it away. Once they dismounted and leaned over the spot, there was no longer a shadow to see.

Fiendish and inspired—and it pointed away from the vale. In fact, it pointed a clear pathway over the cliff! Was it a lie? Was The Reaper's hideout not in the Vale at all?

She'd mentioned markers. This had to be one of them. And they were not to be trusted. If they'd been surrounded by mist themselves, they might have followed that deadly path!

One thing was certain. If they didn't make a decision soon, they'd have to spend the night where they stood, in the rocks. Either that, or they'd end up back at Brigadunn without Finn, and he refused to fail her.

"Martin," he said, "let me hear that riddle again."

~ ~ ~

Blair was not one to whine about the rain, nor for lack of a horse. But with Finn in danger, she couldn't help grumbling over Stanley's clever move.

"Remove all the horses? Was he mad?"

It was a good thing Tolly had thought to have the carthorse spared, or even the day help would have been pent up at Brigadunn manor for the night.

"Blasted man. Not trusting. . ."

She wrinkled her nose. Just because he was wise not to trust her didn't mean she had to respect him for it.

"See if I ever address him as *Yer Grace* again."

She struck out for the top of a high hill, certain she could find a clearer path to Mary Dowd's croft. There, she would find dry clothes and send word for Jarvill and Coll to come fetch her. No doubt Cameron Dowds would welcome a few coins for his trouble and Blair could have a chance to speak with Mary, to make certain the woman harbored no guilt over leaving the Vale. Of course, Blair's feelings had been hurt when Mary had not bid her farewell, but she understood. The Reaper was a protector, sure. But he remained a shadowy figure, even among his own. Few in the Vale had reason to deal directly with him, and it was likely Mary would never have come to the Reaper's own cottage to seek out Blair, even had she wished to.

Blair could only guess what Mary and the rest supposed about her sharing a bed with their leader. But when she imagined sinning with a man, it was not Jarvill or Coll who came to mind, or even the phantom of a mysterious man in a cape—it was Ash.

She summoned a memory of that morning, when she'd awakened next to him in the larder. She on her pallet, he just behind her on the bare wood floor. His fingers had twitched, then relaxed. His breathing sped, but he made no move to rise. After a moment, his hand pressed against her, pulling her closer to his chest, no longer pretending to sleep.

She'd said nothing, her silence an agreement of sorts, to allow the moment to go on.

If only Tolly hadn't come.

If only Finn hadn't run off.

Might Ash have turned her? Kissed her? What sweet things might he have said?

Without her attention on the wet and rock-strewn path before her, she stumbled and cried out, but caught herself before her ankle could twist. Nearly at the top of the rise now, she paused to look behind her. No one emerged from the trees below. There was no sound of horse or cart in the distance.

She turned and finished her climb. Cresting the hill, she stopped short. Not ten feet away, a half-circle of men awaited her. In the center stood the constable, his horrible hat dripping water only inches from his nose.

She lunged to her right, then shot to her left and back down the hill. After three steps, a man was there to block her way.

It was Everhardt! Ash's man—the one who had fought with her at Givet Faux!

He gave her a subtle shake of his head. "Forgive me," he whispered. "They would have caught you in any case. And he knows about the beauty mark, knows who you are." Others ran to join them. "I've got her," he announced over her shoulder. "Do not give me away." he whispered near her ear.

Stunned, she offered no resistance when he took her by the elbow and led her back over the crest. He gave her arm an extra squeeze. "I told her you have her young brother. She won't give us any trouble."

She stifled her gasp.

Finn? The constable had Finn?

After the initial panic eased, she was relieved the lad wasn't half way to The Witch's Vale and the dangers along the way. She had quick feet and with a little luck, she could likely get away from the lot of them, but there was something about Everhardt that made her pause. Had he been trying to warn her? Had he known it would be better for Finn if she came along? Or had it been the other way around—would Finn be harmed if she was to get away?

Whatever the truth might be, she decided to simply trust the man in light of her past experience with him. Everhardt wouldn't lead her into danger, even though he seemed to be working for the enemy at the moment. Knowing Ash, even as little as she did, he'd planted the man among Wotherspoon's ranks before he'd ever arrived at Brigadunn.

"The Reaper's Whore." The constable spat at her feet. "I gave ye fair warnin'. Ye should have stayed with yer lover at the manor."

Even before Cornelius Wotherspoon had become constable of her town, Blair had avoided the man. Her father had grown up with him and warned her and her brothers to never trust the man. Therefore, they didn't. Of course Father had attributed the man's dislike to a jealousy over their royal name, but he blamed many a misunderstanding on the same. Blair believed they'd been at odds since they were boys. Perhaps a lucky punch, a bloody nose, or an embarrassment of some sort.

But now the man had turned his nastiness on her Englishman and she could not help but rise to his defense.

"Come now, constable," she said cheerfully. "Ye make it sound as if Ashmoore is The Highland Reaper."

"Do I?" The constable grinned.

Of course that was exactly what he wished his men to believe. So she thought it best to lead the mob away from such thoughts before Ashmoore ended up in a noose for being his own enemy.

"If my lover, The Reaper, resides at the manor," she paused and grinned herself, "what makes ye suppose it isn't Tolly?"

Any retort Wotherspoon might make was drown out by the raucous laughter of his men. Everyone knew Tolly.

She sought to add wood to the fire. "Perhaps that is why the man is so tired all the time—stealing sheep at night, but ever so slowly."

Their now-merry band tromped through a birch forest for a few minutes before they came upon the horses. Everhardt helped her mount since her hands were tied together, then he climbed up behind her. For a moment, they were ignored while the others gained their own animals.

"I'll keep yer secret," she whispered, "if ye'll keep mine."

"And what secret is that, milady?"

"Doona tell Ash and Stanley I walked right up to the constable and as good as announced myself. I'd hate to have them say it."

"To say what?"

"I told ye so."

CHAPTER THIRTY-SIX

Sarah was inconsolable.

She'd all but thrown herself across Ash's desk when she heard he'd returned. It was the middle of the night. His boots were full of rain. But he would not be surprised to find even more water on his desk from the flood of tears and. . .other fluids. . .escaping the girl's face—that was, if she ever removed herself.

Fantine arrived in her nightclothes and pushed her way through the bodies crowding the doorway to his study.

"Thank you, mademoiselle, for coming straight away," he told her. "Sarah, here, seems unable to accept my forgiveness. Perhaps you can convince her—in another room, of course."

"Of course, monsieur." The Frenchwoman took a firm hold of the girl's shoulders and hefted her to her feet, something none of them would have dared to do for the simple fear of getting themselves wet.

As the wailing faded down the hall, Ash peered closely at those waiting for an audience. All appeared equally as repentant as Sarah, and all just as guilty.

He addressed the mob at large while leveling them with his darkest look.

"Since you cannot possibly fit in this room all at once, I shall simply express my disappointment in the lot of you.

You allowed a single woman to destroy what trust we had built here at Brigadunn and in so doing, you share responsibility for her fate. As soon as the sun is up. . ." He let the anticipation simmer a bit. No doubt they all feared a sacking. "As soon as the sun is up, we shall start again. But this time, my trust will be hard won. Do I make myself clear?"

Ten heads nodded in the doorway. Countless others nodded in the hall. He was tired, disgusted, and in no mood to have their various sins recounted, since Stanley had found Martin and him on the road and already told him the gist.

"I suggest you get some sleep," Ash added. "In a few hours, we shall have a woman and a child to find. Now, go."

All bodies cleared out but one.

Stanley sat in the African chair, his head bowed, his hands braced on the arms as if he expect the lash to strike his back at any moment.

"Come, now, Stanley. You cannot believe I included you in all this. You never lent her your mob cap and apron. Nor did you help her into that cart. You are the victim here."

Stan shook his head. "Truth be told, it surely feels as if I did."

"Yes. She has a way of turning us all inside out. Brandy?" Ash poured two glasses, then took a sniff of the bottle before replacing the stopper.

Stan raised a brow.

"I'm afraid it has become a habit, old sock. Have you forgotten this innocent lass who slipped your net is the same woman who poisoned me recently?"

"Ah. I supposed I had." Finally, the man smiled, if only a little.

"Of all the women in the world, you cannot consider yourself unworthy simply because Scotia escaped you. It is hardly a small club."

Stan took his drink and raised it. "To catching her."

Ash shook his head. "To being free of her."

His heart lurched to a stop.

He'd said the words in jest, but was it possible he truly felt that way? Or was he simply trying to prepare himself for the inevitable, when he realized his Scotia truly belonged to another.

It took a second brandy to get his heart started again.

~ ~ ~

Thunder crashed, and Ash woke on the couch to find Tolly hovering with a glowing candelabra. He didn't remember lying down. And since the brandy was still with him, he couldn't have slept long.

"The constable has her," Tolly announced as soon as Ash was upright. "And he has our lad, yer lairship." He stepped back and gestured toward the door. "Yer man is here."

Everhardt stepped through the door and frowned at Stanley, who was draped sideways across the African chair as if he'd been sacrificed upon it.

"Stanley, wake up," Ash growled. His friend had imbibed no more than himself, so the man should rouse easily enough.

The viscount had to roll off the arms of the contraption in order to dismount it, then he took another chair before his eyes were completely open. "Carry on," he mumbled.

Everhardt shook his head in disapproval.

Ash frowned. "We are not drunk, Everhardt, so you can stow that glare."

The man looked neither convinced nor repentant for his quick judgment, but considering his wet clothes, he'd likely been up all night, so Ash excused him and pointed to an empty chair. "Sit. Tolly will fetch you some food while we talk."

Everhardt shrugged off his damp jacket and did as he was bid. "It's true, my lord. I've been sent to tell you, secretly, that the constable has your. . .woman. They have the lad as well." He lowered his voice. "Someone from the manor must have let slip about her beauty mark; the constable knew she was Finn's sister before we caught up with her. The boy was used to gain her cooperation, of course."

Ash voiced his next concern. "She recognized you?"

"Yes, but she said nothing. He's locked her in a cell. No one is to touch her."

Ash nodded, relieved. If they believed her to be a whore, they might have treated her like one.

"Wotherspoon has directed me to ingratiate myself to you, convince you my services can be purchased, that I can spy for you."

Ash raised a hand in a bid for a moment of silence, admitting he may in fact have had too tall a brandy. His mind was caught in a storm not unlike the one currently trying to destroy the manor.

Finn was *not* freezing to death on the edge of a cliff—a possibility that nearly drove him insane. Scotia had *not* returned to the arms of The Reaper. At least not yet. But both were in the constable's keeping. The very dangerous, easily angered, highly insulted buffoon had her. But surely, if the man were using her as bait, she was safe enough.

If she were behind bars, she was safe from herself at least. And what was more, Ash could collect both Balliols from the same location. But first, he needed to know what Cornelius Wotherspoon had in store—or rather, what he wished Ash to believe.

He lowered his hand, ready for more.

"Why you?" he asked. "Why not one of the others, someone he has known longer."

Everhardt shrugged. "Because I am also English, I suppose."

Ash's head began to shake before he'd even finished his thought. "No. Something is amiss. You are not to return to him. I hate to give the man much credit, but I think he knows I sent you to him for the same purpose. He is taunting me. I will not put you within his reach again."

Everhardt nodded. "I will tell you, some bloke was lamenting the farthest he had ever been from Scotland was Charleville and the River Meuse. I let slip that I had been there as well. We talked about the Place Ducal for a piece, then I realized the constable was giving me a wicked eye. His manner toward me changed. Then, after the woman was brought to him, he acted as if we were chums. When he suggested I spy here, he acted as if the idea had suddenly struck him, but I believe he'd been considering it for a while, sir."

Ash's stomach felt as if it were suddenly filling with cold ashes, and those ashes were working their way up his throat.

"Charleville?" Stanley sat forward. "What does the constable know of Charleville? And so close to Givet Faux?"

Ash nodded. "The constable is sending me a message, but I'll be damned if I know what that message is." He turned to Everhardt. "After you are rested and fed, of course, how long would it take for you to get to Charleville and back again?"

"Too long, I'm afraid, my lord. Miss Balliol and her brother are to be tried in four days. Or rather, three days, once the sun is up."

~ ~ ~

Tolly sent footmen about the glen to invite any who dared, to join the Earl of Ashmoore and take up arms against the constable. No mention was made of Blair Balliol's capture, in deference to the secret she kept from her father, but Ash hoped many a Scot would come to the aid of young Finn.

The rains remained heavy throughout the day and by mid-afternoon, it looked as if the sun had already set. Just before five o'clock, shadows appeared in the distance and slowly became a solid army of crofters as they neared the manor. Wet from the mist, bearing plaids of one color or another, and armed with a host of blades, they looked more like a thirteenth century army come to run an Englishman out of their country, not to fight beside one. He only wished Finn and Scotia were there to see it.

He shook away the thought. Scotia would never be returning. And he had to stop thinking of her as Scotia. Scotia was a ghost, from his past. That was all.

As Ash saddled his horse in the stable, Martin's face appeared on the opposite side of the beast. His eyes were wide, but he said nothing, and for the first time, Ash realized how much the young man looked like his brother. Martin had been anxious since he'd been awakened with the news of Finn and Blair. Now he looked ill.

"What is it, Martin?"

Before the other could answer, someone bellowed from the yard.

"Laird Ashmoore!" It sounded like Allen Balliol. *"I demand to see Laird Ashmoore!"*

Martin whimpered.

Ash immediately understood. "Does he know your sister is alive?"

Martin shook his head.

"Do you suppose he would rather hear it from you?"

Martin shook his head again.

Ash sighed and strode outside to face the man who had promised to spill Ash's blood if any harm came to Finn. At the moment, Ash thought himself deserving of any beating Balliol might have in mind.

The man stood with a sword in one hand and a torch held high in the other. He grimaced against the light and moved it aside to better see his enemy as he walked forward. Ash came to a stop with merely five paces between them.

"I understand your need to fight me, Allen Balliol, but I ask you to stay your sword until your. . .family. . .is restored to you."

The older man tossed the sword away from him and sank to his knees in the mud. And still he was as tall as the Scot standing behind him, which hinted at the height he must have enjoyed since his youth. Allen Balliol had, more than likely, been looking down on people all his life regardless of his family name.

But not at that moment.

"Lord Ashmoore," the man began in all humility. "I'm here to declare my fealty to ye fer the rest of me days if ye'll but help rescue me wee bairn from the clutches of that bastard. I'll do anything ye ask of me. Anything at all. But doona let the devil have him."

Ash looked behind him and found Martin staring agape at his father.

"Martin, help your father to his feet," he said.

Balliol's shoulders slumped, but Ash could not allow the man to worry his plea had been ignored. He gestured at the other men gathering in the yard.

"We were just about to pay the constable a visit, Balliol. Perhaps you'll join us." He told a stable lad to saddle another horse.

Balliol gave a single nod and stood before Martin reached his side. He forced his shoulders back, but he stared at the ground. Keeping his youngest from him appeared to have taken all the wind from his sails. The fact such a proud Scot would come and beg an Englishman for help said much about a father's love. But Ash was curious to know if the man felt as strongly about his daughter.

"Martin." He met the young man's eyes. "Now, I think."

At least the young man didn't pretend ignorance. He hung his head for a moment, then took a breath and turned to face his wary father.

"Da."

"Son?"

"I was wrong about Blair. She didna die in France."

The torch drooped in the old man's hand, then recovered.

"She lives, Da. Yer daughter lives, and she's been hiding herself in The Vale with the others."

Ash thought it was a fine thing Martin did to spare his father from further details.

"I. . ." Balliol cleared his rough throat. He teetered, but caught himself, pulling away from his son's extending hands. Then he gulped in a deep breath and let it out slowly. "I have no daughter," he finally said.

The tears streaming down his face, however, belied his words. Allen Balliol loved all his children, it seemed. He simply could not step around his own pride to acknowledge it.

Yes, Blair had known her father well. But at the moment, she was at the whim of a vicious man, and the love of her father might give her a bit of needed strength. The old man only needed a shove. And Ash was more than happy to oblige. It no longer mattered if Blair wished to keep her identity a secret or not. The time for secrets was over.

"No daughter?" Ash queried. "Well, then, it will be no concern to you that Martin and Finn's sister is also being held by the constable." A murmur quickly rolled through the rag-tag army in his yard. He let the news settle before he verbally shoved Balliol again. "Yes. Martin and Finn have a sister. And if it weren't for that sister, Martin wouldn't be with us tonight. He would have died among his kidnappers, along with my dearest friend, the Earl of Northwick. It was *Martin's sister* who discovered their lair. It was *Martin's sister* that insisted on fighting her way through a fortress of villains, to rescue your son. Surely you owe something to *that* woman."

With wide eyes, Martin faced his father. "I swear to ye, father. I didna ken Blair had been there. I thought I'd only dreamed it, so I said nothing. Only when I was half way to home did they tell me she was dead. I thought perhaps it had been her ghost that had been at my side when I was rescued."

Balliol reached up a hand and laid it against his son's face for a moment, but said nothing.

"And you," Ash looked around the faces filling the yard. "Surely you all owe something to the one who has saved your families from starvation. Has The Highland Reaper not done enough for Brigadunn's people to earn a helping hand, to rescue one of his friends?"

Judging from the immediate roar of the crowd, The Reaper had already won the day, damn him. But as it happened, it wasn't the mention of The Reaper that rallied the timeless army, it was the appearance of two more riders.

CHAPTER THIRTY-SEVEN

Cornelius Wotherspoon eased back into his chair and sipped his whisky-laced coffee. It was more whisky than coffee, truth be told, but none need know it. Once he was away from Scotland, he'd sip whiskey all day if he liked. A doctor told him once that it was the whisky that made his nose red and tender betimes, but the doctor was a pious fool. Wotherspoon knew full well all he needed was a finer climate and his body would come 'round.

Over the edge of his cup, he surveyed the new villains decorating his jail. Of the three cells built into the far wall, two were occupied by his childhood rival's offspring—the woman on the far left, the lad on the right. Justice was sometimes a sweet boon, for Blair Balliol was not just The Reaper's Whore. She was the woman he had once wished to kill with his own hands but had been told she was dead.

And now, it was if she was risen just for him. A sweet boon indeed.

The center cell he reserved for his most important guest, the Earl of Ashmoore, whose arrival was surely imminent. The bastard had taken a shine to the Balliol brats for some reason, and Wotherspoon was certain the man would not suffer overlong without his pets. In truth, he was surprised the man had not come the previous night, but apparently the earl did not care enough to get wet.

As The Reaper's whore, it was anyone's guess which man would come for her first. If The Reaper showed his face, Wotherspoon knew just what to do. But he had three days until all the chess pieces needed to be in their places. No need to fash.

In three days, The Reaper must be off the board.

The front door burst open and Wotherspoon spilled his coffee down his chest. He jumped from his seat and flapped his shirt, sucking air through his teeth as he waited for his skin to cool.

The woman laughed, but he ignored her.

"The Reaper! He's come," shouted Geordie, his eyes wide and bulging.

Wotherspoon ground his jaw. "Wheesht! Did I not tell ye to be quiet about it, damn ye? Ye'll wake the dead, let alone the living. And the fewer witnesses, the better. Where is he?"

"Just forced his way into me mam's house, he did. Mam got away, but he's still inside, picking through her larder."

Without a woman to tend him, the bastard was likely peckish, he reasoned. The villain's next stop would likely be the jail, but it was best not to take any chances.

"Take four men from out back and bring the bastard to me. Silent as death, do ye ken? Gag him if needs be. And gag yerself as well if ye canna keep yer wits about ye."

Geordie nodded and left. Wotherspoon turned back to find his prisoners standing at the bars, both their mouths agape.

"Are ye surprised The Reaper got here first? Well, take heart. The English bastard will be along shortly, make no mistake." He smiled at the lad. "Meanwhile young Balliol here can witness firsthand what comes from crossing Cornelius Wotherspoon."

"You'll not punish The Reaper before he's had his trial." The woman had found her tongue. Her breath came fast, but her hands were steady, perhaps due to her tight hold on the bars. Even so, he could smell her fear from across the room. Did she fear for her lover? Or for herself, if her lover were caught and unable to rescue her?

"The Reaper willna have a trial, Princess. Surely, if he's not the Earl of Ashmoore, The Reaper is no more than a phantom, a contrived figure to blame fer all yer misdeeds." He snorted. "A tale to frighten children."

He laughed outright at the confusion on her face, then he turned and perched his arse upon his desk, faced the door, and waited. But his wait was not long.

The door burst open again, only this time it was Pinker. The man was a twin. His brother, Paler, died as a babe. His mother never got 'round to calling him anything else.

"The Reaper's at Hay's mercantile!" Pinker shouted.

The mercantile was hell and gone from Geordie's mum's house. The old woman must have taken her fine time reportin' her intruder, so The Reaper must have gotten clean away before Geordie and the others were sent after him. It might be a fair while before they dared return to the jail to report their failure. That left him five men low.

"Save yer breath to cool yer porridge!" Wotherspoon rolled his eyes. "Fine, then. Take four. . . No, take *two* well-armed men and fetch the blackheart to me. Dinna make a ruckus. I want him brought along quietly, but dead will do."

Pinker nodded but didn't move fast enough for Wotherspoon's liking.

"Move yer feet, damn ye, before the blighter gets away!"

As he shuffled outside, Pinker turned sideways to allow room for Alistair Maughan's great belly to come inside. The latter looked as though he'd left half his plaid at home, for there was far more of the man's body showing than another man could stomach.

"I've seen The Reaper," Alistair said quickly between little puffs of air. "Stealin' weapons from Smithy's forge." Puff. Puff. Puff. "Saw him with me own eyes."

Wotherspoon crossed his arms. "*When* did ye see him?"

Alistair frowned. "Just the now. I ran all the way."

Wotherspoon doubted that Alistair ran at all, but made a guess as to how long it might have taken the man to walk from the Smithy's. Unless The Reaper was racing a horse about the town, he couldna be in so many places in a quarter of an hour.

He smirked. Either Ashmoore or The Reaper was trying to divide his forces. Perhaps they were even working together. But no matter. Their little plan was about to go a bit astray.

"Alistair, stay here. Let no one inside but our own. If ye see The Reaper again, shoot him—as quietly as ye can," he said, then walked out into the busy night.

Including the half-naked Alistair, he was now nine men low. Ten if he counted the English spy. Ashmoore would believe the numbers were now in his favor, but he'd be wrong.

Wotherspoon restrained his hands from rubbing together as he went to collect a new set of pieces for the chess board.

~ ~ ~

The emotions boiling in Blair's blood should have given her the strength to bend the jail bars, but they didn't. And the only thing keeping her from screaming in frustration was her wee brother.

Finn knelt, facing her through the two sets of bars that separated him from her. His little face fit completely in the gap between two of those bars. Too bad his head would not, or she'd tell him to squeeze out and slip away.

"All will be right, Finn," she said for the hundredth time. "Ye'll see. Lord Ashmoore is so cross with me fer leaving him, he'll bring down the walls and the bars with it. No doubt in me mind."

"Is he cross with me as well?" Finn swallowed hard.

Poor mite. He had enough to worry over without fearing Ash.

"Nay. He thought leaving a note, like ye did, was an honorable thing to do. He was proud of ye, but worried for ye at the same time. For we thought ye might end with falling off a cliff in The Vale. I was happy to hear you'd been found, no matter that it was the constable's man who found ye. Yer safe, now. All we need do is wait."

"Then ye doona suppose we'll hang, sister mine?"

She'd had to strain to understand his whisper. Then she laughed, for both their sakes.

"Nay, Finnian. We've done naught wrong. The constable thinks he's a clever sort and is but using us as the cheese for his mouse trap."

Finn giggled. "Laird Ashmoore makes for a mighty large mouse."

Blair laughed again. "Only Ashmoore is verra, verra clever, Finn. In France, he saved our Martin from a horde of men much more evil than our constable. He's more than capable of popping us free."

Mollified, Finn went back to playing with the tie from his boots and Blair rested her back against the bars so the lad might not read her thoughts.

Yes. Ashmoore was capable, and she thanked God that someone was. For it seemed The Reaper was capable of little more than being captured by one man or another. Even the folk in The Vale recognized her inadequacies. The two questions that niggled her now was, *how long had they been wanting to leave?* And, *how long had Coll been right about her?*

He was right; she was weary.

In the time between one breath and the next, a great weight was lifted from her shoulders. And she couldn't wait until The Highland Reaper was no more.

CHAPTER THIRTY-EIGHT

They had far too many Highland Reapers.

The town of Brigadunn was alive with people running about. Half of them were dragging black capes behind them, the other half gave chase. Ash wondered, at what point were the chasers going to realize that in following one cloaked figure, they'd passed another two on the street.

He sat atop his horse, watching the antics from a hillside along with The Reaper's men. Speechless, they watched as one man got hold of a Reaper Decoy, only to jump back as if he'd been burned. The two exchanged slight bows, then the first man waited a moment, giving the decoy a slight head start, before giving chase once again.

"They're all mad," he said aloud.

"Nay," said the man named Coll. "They but do as they were told, to chase down The Reaper. Only none of them wants The Reaper caught."

The man named Jarvill nodded. "There's not a soul in Brigadunn hasna been touched somehow, by. . .a. . .his generosity."

From somewhere below came the echo of a pistol shot.

Ash nudged his horse awake. "All but one, at least," he said, and took a straight path down the hill.

~ ~ ~

The constable's headquarters, including the jail, were in an imposing building located on the same road as an equally imposing church. The edifices sat at opposite ends—a visual lecture for the inhabitants of Brigadunn. *You can't be in both places at the same time. If you're in church, you won't be in the jail. And vice versa.*

Ash and his two unlikely companions left their horses to walk the last block. A miniature village green lent as silly an aspect to the building as did the constable's hat to his appearance. Nevertheless, the space was empty. And Ash realized that only an alley still separated him from his Scotia, or rather, a lass named Blair who belonged to The Highland Reaper.

He spared only a glance at the darkness between the buildings, then hurried past, only to find that his two companions had disappeared.

He turned back to the alley. Coll and Jarvill were standing against the wall, but as Ash moved closer, he realized the pair were standing quite still with hands over their mouths and pistols aimed at their heads. Stanley and Everhardt, clothed in shadows, were barely visible between The Reaper's men and the wall.

Stan grinned. "You didn't think we'd be foolish enough to try to grab *you*, did you?"

Ash waved a hand and the two men were released. Their hackles were up, but they held their tongues.

"Come," Stan ordered, and disappeared.

Ash had no choice but to follow, and as they got farther and farther from the jail, his frustration grew unbearable. Then he realized his friend might well be leading him to where Blair and Finn were being held, and his frustration cooled.

Stan ducked inside a small shop and waved them all inside. The door closed, revealing a wrinkled old woman who gave Ash a wink, then disappeared through a little red door.

Ash attempted patience. "Someone was shot?

Everhardt nodded. "Someone inside the jail."

Stan put a hand up. "It was a man. We heard him moaning."

Ash nodded, relieved. He had allies a' plenty tonight, but the people he could not bear to see harmed were the two men before him and the Balliols. Coll and Jarvill he was not so sure about.

"I am sorry, Ash," Stan said. "You have to go home. Immediately."

"I beg your pardon?" He looked from Stan's nodding head to Everhardt's and back again. "I will go home once I've collected—"

"Not tonight, my friend," Stan said sadly. "This is all a trap, for you. Wotherspoon has far more men that we suspected. He has been hiding them from view. If not for rather loyal friends of The Highland Reaper, we might never have known. I do not know what you have done to this Wotherspoon, or when you did it, but he has plans for you. And until we know what is behind it, you need to remain on home ground."

Ash was already shaking his head.

Stan shrugged. "Look at it this way. You know precisely where she is. She cannot escape. And since her trial is scheduled in three days, you know Wotherspoon must care for her until then. Besides, the town is full of eyes and ears who will watch over her and the boy. If anything suspicious occurs, inside or outside the jail, I am certain we will be informed."

"True! True!" The old woman's voice warbled through the red door.

Everyone laughed but Ash. He pulled Stan aside and tried to speak low so the others wouldn't hear.

"You do not understand. She is in there waiting, hoping. . .*someone*. . .will come for her. Praying she will be rescued from yet another blackheart. And the boy? How can I let him believe, for four days, that I would not come for him?"

Stan gave him a pitying look. Ash worried his friend had not been listening, so he tried again.

"Stanley. Please. Her heart will break. Not because she cares for me, but because she. . .counts on me. You are asking me to break her heart for another *three days.*"

Over Stanley's shoulder, he caught a baleful eye from Jarvill. And if he hadn't known before, he did now. Jarvill was Blair's Balliol's Reaper. And The Reaper didn't care for an English lord to be discussing a woman's heart that supposedly belonged to him.

As they stared at each other, the red door opened. They all turned when the old woman emerged, a covered basket in her hands.

"No worries, young Ashmoore. I will be sure to tell yer lady that yer friends had to drag ye away, that it broke yer heart to go. And the laddie too. They will be happy ye're safe. And The Highland Reaper himself will thank ye, mark me words." She winked once again, and left.

Jarvill glared at the door as if he might follow after the woman and change the message, but instead, he turned and glared at Ash.

Ash glared back. "If you're not the cursed Highland Reaper, then who the hell is?"

Jarvill's brows rose for a moment, then he grinned from ear to ear. After Ash closed the distance between them, however, Jarvill was far too busy sleeping to smile at anyone.

CHAPTER THIRTY-NINE

Ash woke on the floor of the larder. After returning from the village, he'd come as some sort of reparation for Blair and her brother forced to make their beds in jail cells.

The pallet remained, though he'd given no orders for it to be removed once Scotia had escaped. Perhaps Fantine had some sense of intuition that he'd need to visit the space his prisoner had occupied. He'd often wondered if the Frenchwoman was able to read his mind. Perhaps she was also able to read his heart.

He sighed, but he was not yet ready to rise. He resolved to spend only ten minutes more thinking of Scotia. Then he would put all thoughts of her aside for the remainder of the day. Surely, with Stanley's help, he could come up with some task to occupy his mind. But for the moment. . .

Scotia. Come to me.

The plea was not new. He'd invited her memory hundreds of times in the past two years, but this time, he had a clear image of her face, her hair, the sound of her voice.

He remembered the feel of her lying in his arms the morning before, pretending she was not yet awake. Her back to his chest. Her waist rising beneath his hand in time with her breathing. The smell of her hair.

In the night, they'd laughed. Over what, he could not recall. But he remembered distinctly the vibration of her laughter moving from her body into his. He'd absorbed it like a thirsty man bending to drink from a stream. He'd sought to make her laugh over and over again until they'd laughed themselves silly, like children. Worn themselves out as if they'd been running through fields in the sunlight.

He only wished he would not have fallen asleep. He might have had hours upon hours of simply holding her while she breathed.

Lord help him! He was in as serious a state as Northwick had been. A man in love. Of course it couldn't have been so simple an affliction as an obsession. It was obsession that had brought him to Scotland. This was more.

This was dire. This was a catastrophe.

She could not feel anything similar for him if she was willing to risk falling into the constable's hands in order to get to another man.

And why should she give him a second thought?

After all they'd been through together—the horror at Givet Faux, the fact he'd threatened to hang her, the night she'd poisoned him, the long night she'd spent alone in the darkness on that very pallet, fearing her demons—there was little to endear him to her. And worse yet, there was little hope a life together would be so different. It was foolish to wish otherwise.

He was the man who was determined to bring her lover to justice. How could that win her heart? His life was draped with a web of violence. Why would she wish to join it? It was unfair for him to want her to.

Unfair.

He sighed again and got to his feet. When he emerged from the larder, Fantine was concentrating over a bowl. He doubted her concoction warranted that much attention.

"Fantine?"

"*Oui, monsieur?*" She did not look up. Nor did she pretend to be surprised by his sudden appearance.

"You may clear away the pallet," he said and walked out of the kitchen intent on locating Stanley. He watched in fascination when his feet brought him back a moment later. Or perhaps it had been his stomach that led him. He could only think to ask her if she might make him something for breakfast.

"*Oui, monsieur.* And zee pallet? Are you certain?" Still she did not look up.

"Leave it."

"Oui, monsieur."

This time, he was grateful she had such serious mixing to do, for if she would have looked at him then, she might have noticed his blush. And he was blushing, for what other reason could there be for the heat in his face?

There would be no harm, he reasoned, for leaving the pallet where it was for the next two days. After the trial, after he removed her from the constable's grasp, she would be gone from his life. And there would be no need for her memory to haunt his larder. . .

~ ~ ~

Blair imagined the constable meant to show her a long and miserable night when he'd given her a single thin blanket and a bare floor for sleeping. But he obviously had no idea how horrible the night could be when one is waiting for news of a kidnapped brother. At least she'd known where Finn was, tucked safely nearby and not wandering through the mist on a dangerous mountain. That happy thought kept her warm enough.

Neither was Martin much of a worry. Even if he had spent the night searching for Finn, he'd not been alone. Surely between the two men, they could have kept each other from walking off a cliff in spite of the markers.

If she was lucky, they hadn't even noticed the markers.

She set her sights on keeping Finn's spirits up. Each and every time the lad had nodded off to sleep, she'd thank

heaven she could allow her shoulders to droop for a wee
while. She tried not to think too much about Ashmoore or
his lips. If he or the others managed to rescue her, she
would trust her people into his keeping, and she would
leave the glen for good. Her father would never hear of her
again. Ash would never learn she was The Reaper. Her
brothers would have to be content with the knowledge that
she still lived, somewhere.

And if there was one dream she could not indulge in, it
was the fantasy of winning Ashmoore's heart. Even if he
were enamored of more than just her Viking blade and too-
willing lips, what future could she have with him? An
English earl had obligations to marry within their station, or
some nonsense. The only position he might offer her would
be that of his mistress.

Though it might be tempting to accept any opportunity
to belong in his life, she could not accept the occupation her
father had predicted for her if she were to follow an army
about France. But even if she had no father, she could not
do it. She was a good girl. If one discounted a few broken
commandments, of course.

No. That dream was not for her. And she feared she
might not ever wish for the life of a wife and mother if the
husband in question was not Ash. . .

~ ~ ~

For the next three days, there was yet another reason
for Blair to appear cheerful. Fact was, her refusal to fash
and fret frustrated Wotherspoon to no end, which cheered
her all the more. But all that pretending wore on a body,
and when no one was looking, she pressed her hands
against her face and cried as silently as she could.

When darkness fell, she would have welcomed her
ghosts if that same darkness hid her worries. But the spirits
never came. Whether her ghosts avoided her brother just
two cells away, or the snoring of the night guard in the next

room, she couldn't be certain. Or perhaps they'd come to call that night in the larder but found her wrapped in Ash's arms and decided never to return.

She smiled and imagined telling him he was so fearsome a man that even ghosts were frightened of him.

"That smile will be wiped clean off yer face before the day is done, I'll warrant," the constable sneered.

The guard beside him slipped a key into the door and she could feel the grind of metal against metal as the lock turned.

She jumped to her feet and fairly skipped to the opening.

"Good morning, Finn," she sang cheerfully and offered up her wrists for the manacles to be placed on them.

"Morning, sister mine," her brother said sleepily.

Apparently, they weren't to have any breakfast again today. She only hoped her brother wouldn't complain, for nothing cheered Wotherspoon as much as complaining did. The man was already whistling. No need to make him sing.

When the manacles slipped easily from Finn's wrists, another guard brought a length of scratchy rope to use instead. She held Finn's gaze as he was tied. He never flinched. Together, they were led outside and down the middle of the street. She and her brother held their heads high. In other circumstances, her father would have been proud.

The heavens hung low and gray but either held back their rain for some later time, or had wrung themselves dry in the past few days. There was no telling the direction in which the sun might lie, so it would have been difficult to identify the time of day if Blair had not been so recently awakened.

For all the people gathered to watch them go, one would think it was a holiday, albeit a somber one. No one cheered, no vegetables were thrown. Curiosity won out and she dared a look about her, finding that the people had gathered to show their support, not to mock them.

In spite of his bindings, Finn grinned and waved. As
Blair's gaze dragged along the line of people, she realized
every face was familiar. *Every* face! They weren't just the
townspeople—the crowd included the women and children
from The Vale, many with their husbands now beside them.

They've come down the mountain. . . for me.

Her tears blurred the faces, but she smiled back at
them. When she came near to sobbing outright, she turned
her attention back to the road, to what lay before them. She
raised a shoulder and wiped her eyes on her blouse to clear
her vision. Around the bobbing figure of the guard pulling
her chain, she saw the mob gathered before the kirk. The
doors stood wide, the entrance a square of shadow. But all
around the steps stood a hundred people or more. Half way
between her entourage and the kirk stood a scaffold with six
nooses hanging from the topmost beam.

Six? Why six?

She glanced at Finn, but he had not yet noticed. He still
grinned. Still waved.

She looked about the street, to see if others had noticed
as well, and found an army at her back. Those whom they
had already passed had moved into the road and brought up
the rear.

She glanced at the constable, walking at her right side,
and found his face red as a rose, his nose fairly purple. His
odd green hat was pulled low for once, and, tilted forward.
It hid his eyes from most, but not from her. They flashed.
His cheeks rippled from the clenching of his jaw.

She thought it wise not to laugh aloud, for the man was
dangerous. She'd known him for half her life and
remembered he had a bully of a son her age who bullied all
but her. When they'd been ten, the boy had called her
Princess. Likely he'd overheard her own father calling her
the same. . .

Princess.

The constable had called her *Princess* but had been
mocking her—just as the Scot at Givet Faux had done.

She stopped abruptly, her feet unable to function when her mind was working over-hard to summon the memory of the other Scotsman's face. Could it be that the stocky boy with hair the color of young carrots had become the large brute from Givet Faux? That man's hair and beard had been a much darker red. His body had been that of a blacksmith.

What had the boy's name been? Ian? Ivan? *Ivan Wotherspoon!*

"Ivan," she said aloud, ignoring the tug on her wrists. She turned to the constable, who had stopped to frown at her. "I remember your son, Ivan." She swallowed. "Is he here?"

Wotherspoon's frown disappeared as if all emotion had been melted from the man's face like so much hot wax. He stared at her, unblinking. She simply stared back, unable to break whatever spell held them there in the middle of the road.

Finally, his shoulders turned. She assumed he was going to resume walking without answering her question, but then his shoulders turned back toward her, and with them, his outstretched arm. When her body flew to the side, she remembered thinking it strange that she hadn't felt him strike her. By the time she hit the ground, however, her face argued otherwise. After the briefest explosion in her head, she remembered no more.

~ ~ ~

Ashmoore watched the strange exchange between Blair and Wotherspoon and wished they were standing closer to his side of the street so he might hear their words. As he noted the entire crowd leaning their way, he realized he was not alone in that wish. The constable's back was to Ash, so he could not read the man's lips. And Blair hadn't said much at all. She appeared confused, which was a bad sign. He always assumed his Scotia was a step ahead of the rest of them.

Suddenly, the constable recoiled. . .and struck her! Her body flew to the side before he heard the delayed sound—the smack of Wotherspoon's hand!

His own body moved without thought, shedding the tattered cloak he'd worn for disguise as he burst into the street. The roar he'd heard had come from his own mouth, he realized, when he was suddenly out of air. He thought only to get to Wotherspoon, to kill him with his bare hands, to feel the destruction as it happened.

A few steps more.

The crowd moved in around him, and he worried they might impede his progress. There were already women kneeling beside Scotia. He was grateful since he'd be unable to care for her until the offender was dead.

He reached for the man.

The bastard raised a pistol.

It made no difference. A bullet couldn't stop him.

But the pistol pointed away. . .at Scotia's limp body.

Ash stopped and bid the red haze to recede, to let him see clearly.

The bastard's eyes dared him to move.

Distinct clicks. Four of them.

He knew without looking Wotherspoon's henchmen were holding pistols on him, but he would not look away from the rabid dog. The one he would destroy. In time.

Wotherspoon's face was mottled with color. His hat sat low on his brow. He had Ash off his property, and now in his custody, and yet the man did not seem pleased. Something was amiss, but Ash doubted it was anything in his favor. In fact, his senses warned him he was in real danger.

Wotherspoon shook his head and seemed to recover from a haze of his own. He closed his eyes for a moment. Then, after a deep breath, he opened them again.

"Come," he said. "Yer just in time fer yer own trial, Ashmoore." To the pistol bearers, he said, "Bring all but the egg-haired Viscount. Take that one back to the jail. Unless his king comes for 'im, he's not to be released. I shall deal with 'im after."

The constable then tucked his pistol behind him, then resumed his march to the kirk as if nothing at all had happened.

Ash was prodded to follow. He exchanged a quick glance with Stanley. Three armed men were leading his friend off in the opposite direction. It was Stanley whose assignment for the morning was to get Finn Balliol into his carriage and out of the constable's reach. Once that was accomplished, Stanley would attempt to use his royal position to intimidate. Neither of which he could do from inside a cell.

Of course they would find a way to get the lad to safety, and there was every chance Stan's position in British society would hold no sway whatsoever considering the constable's obvious distain. But Ash had a new concern that sent a shiver up his spine like so much sweat dripping backward.

It seemed there was, indeed, a spy at Brigadunn.

Ash looked to his left and found Martin looking at him expectantly. "Find the spy."

Martin nodded smartly, and after a brief glance at his sleeping sister, shouldered his way back into the crowd.

CHAPTER FORTY

Considering the crowd, or rather, the entire village in attendance, there was no choice but to hold the public trial in the church. With the current weather, it would prove unwise to hold it on a hillside. The only other option in the area was Brigadunn Hall, but that would have never been considered. Once on his own land, Ash would be the highest authority. In town, just beyond Ash's property, Wotherspoon ruled in most matters unless the District Sheriff was available. There was no bailiff, and Ash had been led to believe that the sheriff only came around once or twice a year, for Brigadunn was located far from the heart of the largest district in Scotland. And that district included much of the rather difficult-to-navigate Highlands.

With the darkness outside and the dimness of rush lights, the figures depicted in the stained glass windows appeared menacing. The shadows in the recesses of the chancel, behind the lattice, jumped and moved with the candlelight like a collection of unworldly beasts waiting to be unleashed as soon as someone was pronounced guilty.

For the moment, Ash was contained rather effectively on the second pew with two men wedged next to him on both sides. Three of the constable's men sat behind him, and another three on the front row. If he tried to jump over the bench, he'd have to jump high enough to clear the tallest man. So it appeared he was going to be tried after all. At least it was gratifying to know the constable considered it necessary to assign ten men to control him alone.

One guard held on to the rope tied to Finn. Two guards hovered over Blair Balliol's body after they laid her on the front pew. He added the pair to the list he was creating in his mind—the list of people who would pay dearly for laying a hand on his woman. Or rather, The Reaper's.

He turned slightly, to view the crowd behind him, to see where his own men were stationed, but his movement made the ten men around him far too nervous and he was instructed to face forward. He laughed low in his chest. The two men immediately at his sides tried to put a little space between them, but the next men on the bench prevented it.

They repeated this same dance fifty times in the next two hours while they were forced to wait. For what, the constable would not say, only that all parties were not yet accounted for. Ash only hoped there were no officers available to search Brigadunn manor for Everhardt. Wotherspoon had more planned here than just a trial, and the six nooses were a clue. Ash simply could not think which six people those nooses were meant for. If the constable wished to hang himself, Blair, Finn and Everhardt—not that this combination made any sense— then who were the other two? Collier and Jarvill? Was the man so set on bringing The Reaper to justice he would hang every suspect? But why the boy?

And why now? As far as Ash understood, the constable had meddled little in The Reaper's crimes. Martin had hinted the constable might have demanded a portion of The Reaper's booty in exchange for turning a blind eye. Then why hunt The Reaper now? Had the man beneath the hood suddenly ceased paying the price?

The kirk doors opened wide and Wotherspoon looked up with a wide smile. Twenty large men, all dressed uniformly in blue, filed inside the church and down both walls. When they stepped forward, there were two men between each set of pillars.

Next entered a man in barrister robes. The door was closed behind him.

"Welcome, Milord Sheriff." The constable grinned.

The lethargic crowd roused and murmured with excitement. Wotherspoon bowed deeply as the sheriff marched smartly up the left aisle and waved an impatient hand for the constable to get out of his way. He took his place behind a long table and sat.

Ash should have been relieved to have a level-minded man of the law presiding over the trail, but that niggling would not cease. Wotherspoon was far too happy to see the sheriff. He had to know something Ash did not. Perhaps the new authority had already been bribed.

"Summon the first criminal," the sheriff called. Then he waved one of his men to him and they spoke low, ignoring the constable.

"If it please the court," Wotherspoon called to the rafters, "I call Finnian Balliol to face the charge of conspiracy."

A fat man nudged Finn from behind until the boy stepped into the prisoner's box stationed at the head of the aisle to the right.

"A child? You said nothing of a child, constable."

Wotherspoon forced a smile. "When I sent my request, Milord Sheriff, I did not believe I could catch him in time."

The sheriff looked doubtful. "You've charged him with conspiracy? You truly believe this Reaper fellow would conspire with a child?"

"I do," said Wotherspoon. He turned to Finn. "Finn Balliol, when my men and I found you, you admitted you were on yer way to The Witch's Vale, to the home of The Reaper. Do you deny it?"

"Yes. I was trying to feed my owl. Now it's likely dead because of ye."

Someone shouted, "Murderer!" The crowd laughed. The sheriff pounded on his table, demanding attention.

Perhaps it was the constable's determination to see a child hanged, or perhaps it was the fact that Blair had yet to awaken, but Ash could feel the red haze rising. He took a deep breath and pushed it back, bid it to wait. He could not simply tear apart an entire church full of innocent people in order to save one.

The constable turned to the crowd. "It has always been common knowledge The Reaper's lair is in The Witch's Vale. This lad's testimony confirms it well enough I think." He turned to the Sheriff and waited while the other man considered.

"I hope there is more to this trial than deliberating where the villain lays his head, Constable."

Wotherspoon rubbed his hands together and turned an unsettling smile on Finn. "Worry not, Milord Sheriff. The Highland Reaper will be unmasked today, I assure ye. And his accomplices."

It was no surprise when the lad squirmed in his seat and bit his bottom lip. Ash had no doubt the lad feared for his sister and worried he might let slip his tongue and seal her fate.

The sight of the lad fidgeting brought to mind a conversation they'd had recently about how a gentleman, in dire need to relieve himself, should resist dancing about even if his eyes should cross.

Ash frowned and lifted his chin to get Finn's attention. Once the constable moved to one side, the lad noticed him and lifted his brows in silent question.

Ash immediately crossed his eyes, hoping the lad might also remember conversation and understand Ash's prompt. With Stanley no longer available to spirit the lad away, it was important the lad help rescue himself.

Finn suddenly giggled. When Wotherspoon examined him closely, the lad's face pinched as if he were in pain.

"What's this?" the constable demanded.

Finn swallowed hard and sheepishly turned his head to the side as if embarrassed. "Ye gave me no time this morn. Took me away before I was awake, even." He leaned forward as if he were going to whisper. "I'm in dire need of a piss, sir," he said in full voice.

The crowd laughed. Ash was tempted to applaud the little actor; he could not have done a better job of it himself.

"Auch! I doona believe it in the least!" Wotherspoon roared above the chaos.

A woman brought forth a tankard for the sheriff. His shoulders relaxed. "Now, now, Wotherspoon. You canna use such cruel methods on your prisoners in a court of law. Let him get to it. Send a guard along. After all, we'd allow you to do the same, aye?"

The crowd laughed again.

Ash jumped to his feet, as did the ten men surrounding him. Since none were nearly as tall as he, Ash was still able to look Finn in the eye over the top of the three heads in the front row.

"Finn Balliol," his voice boomed, "I'll expect you to remember all you've learned at my house about honor. About doing the honorable thing."

Finn nodded and smiled as he was led toward a door in the transept by a limping, slow-looking man with a kilt so short he was difficult to watch. One of the sheriff's guards, standing at that door, followed them out.

"Back on yer arse, Ashmoore," spat the constable. "Yer turn will come soon enough."

"Look here," said the sheriff. "You'll address him as Lord Ashmoore, Wotherspoon, or you'll address him not at all."

The nasty man smiled to one side of his face and gave the sheriff a shallow bow. "As ye say, Milord Sheriff."

Because he was feeling contrary, Ash decided to remain standing until he was asked nicely, so he folded his arms and waited.

Wotherspoon glanced at someone behind Ash and a pistol cocked.

"That's is quite enough, Constable," said the sheriff. "Your men will holster their weapons for the duration, is that clear? This is a kirk, after all. And your choice, as well." He nodded respectfully at the trio of priests who'd been sitting silently on a row of chairs before altar and sanctuary as if guarding them from the sight of unworthy eyes.

As one, they inclined their heads in appreciation of the sheriff's show of respect.

Ash noticed the blur of red out the corner of his eye and turned to see Blair sitting up in the pew where she'd been laid. She held a hand to her left cheek where the constable's hand had struck and turned to look about the chapel. Her eyes found Ash immediately and it pleased him to note her look of panic easing away. Her brow pinched again, and, after a cursory glance to either side of her, her gaze returned to him.

"Where's Finn?" she shouted over the low murmurs that filled both the chamber and the arched ceiling.

"Where, indeed," snarled Wotherspoon. With a nod, he sent two guards out the side door where Finn and his over-exposed babysitter had fled. The sheriff's man was in all likelihood, chasing after the boy.

A man leaned from two rows behind Blair and spoke to her. Then her attention turned to the transept.

A long moment later, the two guards returned with the babysitter puffing in their wake.

"He's escaped, yer lairdship," said one man to the sheriff.

The constable roared. "I'm nay surprised in the least," he spit in Ash's direction. "Ye put him up to this."

Ash couldn't help but smile, especially when Blair gave him a look of sincere thanks. He would of course tell her the truth sometime in the distant future, that it was

Finn's quick thinking that got him out of the constable's clutches.

Much later.

For now, he'd bask in the fact she supposed he was her hero. The mere taste of it made him determined to make it so in truth.

Unfair or not, he wanted her love. But if that weren't possible, he wanted her happy. And as soon as he knew for certain where her happiness would lie, either with him or with The Reaper, then he would do whatever possible to ensure that happiness.

For the moment, however, they would all be much happier when this farce of a trial was over.

"Move along, Constable." The sheriff drained his tankard, looked ruefully into its depths, then set it aside. "Who do you charge next, and what are the charges?"

"Blair Balliol!" The constable turned an ugly smile on her, then gestured to the prisoner's box.

For a moment, she only sat and stared at the little platform with the rail encircling it on three sides. Ash had to admit, it did look rather out of place in such an elegantly designed church. The scuffed rails made the box look like a beggar come to pray.

Blair stood slowly, then clutched at the guard to her right who bent to aid her. The men surrounding him tensed and he realized he was bent over the front pew as if he meant to fly to her side, which of course, he was prepared to do. If necessary, his guards could be shook off like so many flies.

Hands tugged at his elbows as the men around him summoned enough courage to finally touch him.

"Please, laird," said one. "We'll all suffer if ye should get away, sir."

He turned to frown at the young man still holding his left arm, then replayed his words in his mind. He looked again at Blair. She was walking, with her guard's assistance, to the box. A brief glance his way. A slight shake of the head. A slight tug to one corner of her lips, then it was gone.

Ash stopped himself from grinning like a fool, but only just. He was so relieved. Apparently, young Finn had learned his acting skills from his sister. The constable's attack hadn't taken quite the toll he'd feared, thank heavens.

He felt a bit like Finn at that moment and thought it might be best if he sat down and placed his tongue between his teeth to keep from giving something away. His guards released an audible sigh and he chuckled silently.

She stepped inside the box and leaned delicately on the rail. Her guard stood just outside the rail, poised to come to her aid, no doubt.

"Forgive me, Milord Sheriff," she said and raised a hand to her head. "Constable Wotherspoon's blow has me a wee out of sorts, aye? I canna remember what I might have done to upset the man."

For a moment, the sheriff considered her dispassionately. He made no indication he'd even heard her words. Eventually, he gave a slight nod and turned to the constable. "This is the woman you've told me about?"

"She is, milord. This is The Reaper's Whore."

CHAPTER FORTY-ONE

When the blood ceased pounding in Ash's ears, he was pleased to realize the church had gone eerily silent. None gasped. None laughed. None murmured. The only sound was the stirring of air as a hundred people silently breathed in and out. . .and waited.

"Verra well," said the sheriff. "I've done a bit of investigating on this Reaper fellow, and I've been told he has a woman who rides with him betimes. I trust you have proof this is the woman?"

"I do, milord," said Wotherspoon. "My men and I came upon young Finn Balliol three days hence and he told me—"

"I object, Milord Sheriff," Ash said calmly. "Finn Balliol is not here to question or give testimony."

Wotherspoon's nose curled to one side. "Aye, my lord Ashmoore," he enunciated clearly, "but my men were witnesses, aye? They can tell what they saw and heard. I only thought to keep from wasting the sheriff's time by recounting my own bit of the story. . ."

"Very well," said the sheriff. "Objection noted, but I will hear it. Constable Wotherspoon will then produce his other witnesses for confirmation. Proceed."

"As I was saying," the man said dramatically, "we came upon Finn, all running and out of breath. . .headed toward the Witch's Vale. I asked him why his tail was afire. He said he was headed up the mountain to fetch his wee owl. Now, everyone in town kens of Finn and his owl, Shakespeare. So I asked him why his owl was on the mountain. He said The Reaper took it and he was going to bring the bird back."

In the rush of his rehearsed report, the man had run quite out of breath and paused to catch it again. Then he began again.

"I asked Finn how he knew The Reaper took Shakespeare, for I'm always on the lookout for thieves and the like, aye? Even if it was only a bird what was took."

The crowd chuckled at this, but the fool thought they were laughing at some joke he'd made. When they'd actually been laughing at him.

"And what did the boy say?" The sheriff cocked his head and waited.

"He said his sister told him. That his sister lives *with* The Reaper in The Witch's Vale. And again, it is common knowledge The Reaper often raids with a woman at his side. So if this is The Reaper's companion, she is guilty as The Reaper himself. Over the past two years, I have had nigh a hundred testimonies of The Highland Reaper's thievery. I beg ye, Milord Sheriff, to pronounce sentence on this woman so we might move on to punishing the rest of them."

This was met with a furious outcry from the onlookers which took the constable by surprise so much that he took a step back and bumped up against the sheriff's table.

The Sheriff then pounded on that table until the crowd quieted.

"That is a lie," Ash called out. "The lad would never say such a thing about his own sister. And how convenient he is not here to argue for himself. In fact, are you quite certain, Wotherspoon, that you did not instruct your man to let the boy escape?"

While the sheriff beat upon his table to no avail, Ash realized he'd only drawn attention away from Blair momentarily. There was nothing he could legally do, nothing he could say to get her out of her predicament. There was no one available to testify that Blair was anywhere other than at The Reaper's side; it was common knowledge her father believed for the past two years that she was dead. What other hope was there? That The Reaper would appear at any moment and claim not to know her?

His sudden idea was so dangerous he knew he should take a moment and reconsider, but he was afraid he might do just that.

As he pushed himself to his feet, he had a fleeting impression of Blair and her Reaper riding off toward the misty vale with no trouble chasing them from behind, her head turned back over her shoulder, in her eyes, a look of gratitude.

He shook the image away and found Blair frowning at him from her box. Her brows crushed together in concern and worry. For a moment, he simply took in the sight of her.

He would give anything for her. Anything for her happiness.

"Point of order!" he called out to the sheriff.

Slowly, the crowd gave up their murmurs and the room fell quiet but for whispering.

"Lord Ashmoore?" The sheriff waved the constable to one side so he could see. "Since you seem to think of yourself as the woman's council, I will allow you to speak, but only if you have something in mind other than inciting a mob."

Ash bowed. "I do, my lord."

The sheriff nodded. "Proceed."

Ash was careful to hold the constable's gaze before he spoke the next.

"I believe I can satisfy the constable and convince him to drop the charges against Blair Balliol, but I would need to speak to the pair of you privately."

"I doona believe it in the least, milord." Wotherspoon pointed at Ash. His arm shaking with panic. "'Tis a trick! Dinna let him move from that spot or we'll all wake up in our graves!"

The sheriff shook his head. "I am afraid the constable is right in this."

Ash felt all eyes upon him as he considered his next move. But there was one set of eyes he felt more pointedly than the rest. He resisted looking in her direction for as long as he could stand, but finally, he stopped fighting himself and faced her.

Whatever she read in his eyes, she did not like and began shaking her head. "What are ye about?"

He sent her a wink, then lifted his chin. "I will confess," he told the sheriff, "if you let this woman free and vow there will be no charges made against her."

Wotherspoon's mouth fell, but he recovered himself and hurried to the sheriff's table for a private conversation.

"No!" Blair cried. "What can ye be thinking?!"

"Done!" the constable shouted as he turned. "But do not release her quite yet. The villain's confession must be enough to warrant her release. If he confesses to beating his servants, or some such, it will buy him naught."

"Ash! No!"

Ash ignored Blair outright. He truly would have preferred to have done this in private, but then again, the town would know all soon enough.

He looked squarely at the sheriff and said, "I am The Highland Reaper."

CHAPTER FORTY-TWO

Blair's heart exploded in her chest. She couldn't breathe. She couldn't think. And all she could hear was her own blood coursing through her ears.

Ash had not just confessed to being The Reaper! He had not!

But he had. Dear heavens what had he been thinking? Had he truly believed the bumbling constable could have produced enough proof to hang her? Was the sheriff so daft that a man such as Cornelius Wotherspoon could have convinced him that anyone allied with The Reaper should be hanged?

Of course not. The sheriff seemed an intelligent man concerned with upholding the law. The sort of man who had earned his office. Why then had Ashmoore given the constable his fondest wish? Was he planning something? Did he have a grand escape planned for them all? Did she dare trust?

Absolutely not. Ash was out of his mind, clearly. But why confess to being The Reaper. . .unless he was protecting her? Did he know her secret? Stanley had promised never to tell, and she trusted the future duke to keep his word. And there wasn't a soul in town who would give her away to the Englishman from whom she'd stolen a hundred head.

If she told him now, would he take back his confession? Or would he be more resolved to it?

The Earl of Ashmoore was about to hang, but why? Why confess if not to protect the true Highland Reaper?

Dear lord!

To protect The Highland Reaper—the man he believed she loved.

It was all so ridiculous, she could not help but laugh, giddy with the knowledge that there was no other man for Ash to be jealous of, and that Ash was jealous in the first place. He cared for her after all, and possibly as much as she cared for him, for wouldn't she willingly hang in his stead? She had no idea how to manage it, however, since she could not possibly allow him to know her secret. And if they ended with fighting over the noose, the constable would be happy to hang them both.

She continued to laugh until she had everyone's attention.

"He's lying," she declared. "I ken what The Reaper looks like, and this is not the man."

Wotherspoon scoffed. "And what else would we expect his whore to say?" He grinned, but his eyes flashed, just as they had in the street, before he'd struck her.

Then she remember why he'd struck her and turned quickly to Ash and shook her head. "Doona give the devil so much as a pebble, do ye hear? He's not who you think! His son, Ivan, was at *Givet Faux!* The Scotsman, remember?"

The constable screeched and flew toward her with his claws raised. Thankfully, her soft-hearted guard thought to step in front of her.

"Givet Faux?" Ash repeated. "Wait," he said aloud. "Wait. Just a moment!"

The sheriff was suddenly on his feet. "To what are they referring, Wotherspoon? What is *Givet Faux?*"

The constable, having been thwarted by his own man, turned back to the large table and looked at the sheriff as if he'd just sprouted a second head. He took one measured step, then another, his head tilting to the right, then to the left. And in the face of such odd behavior, Blair had no notion what to expect, but if Wotherspoon were involved in the villainy of *Givet Faux*, along with his son, he was even more dangerous she suspected.

"If Lord Ashmoore is willing to cooperate, and he has. . .indelicate matters to confess," said Wotherspoon solicitously, "the least we can do is oblige a peer of the realm and clear the chapel."

"You suddenly trust him?" the sheriff asked.

Wotherspoon put a hand over his heart. "I do. After all, he has already confessed. His friends in London will know of his guilt soon enough. He is finished."

The sheriff shrugged. "Done." He turned to the man standing over his shoulder. "Clear the kirk."

With much grumbling, the population of Brigadunn filed out of the building row by row. Blair could feel their attention upon her as they went and imagined them gathering around the gibbet, waiting to see who would be offered to the nooses at the end of the day.

Wotherspoon motioned to Ash's guards. "All of you, out. Man the outer doors, of course, in case the earl changes his mind." To the man standing between himself and Blair, he smiled. "Ye as well, Farson."

Farson glanced at the sheriff, then at Ash, his dilemma clear. Ash simply nodded and moved to take the man's place. Her heart tripped with every step that brought him nearer. When he reached the box, he took her hand in his and gave her fingers a squeeze.

A moment later, the guards were gone. All that remained, besides Ash and her, was the constable, standing cheerfully to one side of the table, and the sheriff, standing behind it with his gray brows raised to his hairline.

Ash turned and faced her. In sotto voice, he said quickly, "No matter what happens, you get low and make your way to the side door immediately. No matter what, do you understand?"

"But—"

"No matter what." He then grabbed her by the shoulders and pulled her close for a quick kiss.

"Here, now," the constable complained. "I'll not have you getting on like cats. Step aside, Ashmoore."

Ash looked one last time into her eyes and turned back to the sheriff. "My lord sheriff, if I may. *Givet Faux* was a den of vipers who kidnapped many a man in the midst of the war in France. My friends and I liberated a number of these unfortunates, and with no reliable law in the immediate vicinity, we executed those vipers. It seems the constable's son was among them." He slowly stepped around the box to stand before it, shielding her. "I suspect Constable Wotherspoon was party to the murder of The Earl of Northwick's parents as they were in route to pay his ransom. No doubt Wotherspoon and his son had some larceny business on the side."

Wotherspoon kept smiling. "Turned a pretty penny, too, until you and your lordly friends came along and murdered my son." His voice grew hoarse as he said the last, and he didn't seem concerned in the least that the nervous sheriff was listening carefully.

He pointed a finger at Blair and a shiver when down her spine. "Ivan decided he wanted this fancy piece for a wife, fool that he was. But since she'd rejected him when they were young, he thought he'd keep Martin drugged and stupid, wait until she ran home, then he'd bring her brother to her. Play the rescuing hero. Thought she'd notice him then, the eegit. But she didna run home like a proper lass, did she? Likely murdered my son herself. There were six of them, all told, covered in blood."

"Thus the six nooses outside?" Ash tucked a hand behind his back. His gesture bid her to wait.

"Mm hmn," she murmured softly.

Wotherspoon glanced curiously at the sheriff then, as if just remembering he was still present. "I was hoping the rest of his friends might arrive, given time, and given their spy, who had to have reported my suspicious dealings. But alas, only the blond could be bothered to come. But Northwick lost his parents," he told the man, counting off a finger. "Punishment enough, for now." He waved an arm at Ash and her. "These two will hang in a moment." Fingers two and three. "And the blond will hang before word reaches London that he was tossed in jail. The title *Future Duke* was a bit premature, wasn't it?" Four. "That leaves only two others; your soldier/spy and a Lord Harcourt." Fingers six and seven. "Hardly fair, Milord Sheriff—six to suffer for taking three times as many lives. But it will have to do.

"I am certain I can run yer spy to ground before he leaves the glen," he told Ash. "Hiding at Brigadunn manor, I hear. Then perhaps I'll hie off to London. Harcourt will be an easy target at some memorial service in yer honor, no doubt. And poor Northwick will need to be put out of his misery."

"That leaves only one obstacle."

Blair was certain that obstacle was the sheriff, but before she could shout much of a warning, Wotherspoon had removed his pistol from the back of his breeches. Without a pause, he swung his arm around and pulled the trigger. The sheriff stood still for one heartbeat, then another. Then he sank to the floor and disappeared beyond the table's edge.

Get low and make your way to the side door.

Blair dropped behind the banister surrounding the box and shuffled off the edge, ducking between pews and heading to the right as she'd been told. She would follow her own instincts, but it was important Ash know where she was. She only hoped he had a plan for himself.

She suddenly understood how Jarvill and Coll had felt when she'd ordered them to leave her behind in Ashmoore's barn.

The narthex doors flew open and guards poured around the font and up both aisles.

"Cease him!" the constable shouted. "He's killed the sheriff! And find the whore! She is in here somewhere."

She reached the end of the pew and took a peek. The transept was but six feet away. The pounding of the guard's footfalls mimicked the hammering of her heart. She didn't have time to dally. She jumped into the aisle but at the sound of numerous pistols cocking behind her, she stopped, then turned. A shot in the back was no way for The Highland Reaper to end.

Four men stood scattered in the pews with their pistols pointing her way, though two of them looked sheepish about it. If it weren't for the stern-looking pair in blue, she would have turned and fled with no fear. Their size and the way they were dressed, however, pegged them as the sheriff's men. And with their leader slain, they were no doubt hungry for blood.

She held perfectly still.

Her eye was drawn by the flurry of activity in the rest of the nave as men stumbled over each other, still searching. Ash had gotten away!

"Come out, Ashmoore!" called Wotherspoon. "We have yer whore. Come out, or she will wish she were dead before she ever reaches her noose!"

"Nay!" she shouted. "If ye can hear me—"

One of the sheriff's men stepped forward and raised a hand to strike her if she continued. She looked him in the eye and grinned.

"Run, Ashmoore!" she screamed, then braced herself for the blow. But it never came. She opened her eyes when she heard the guard hit the floor, his grunt sounding quite like that of a pig as Ashmoore's weight took his breath away. A powerful fist to the guard's jaw took away everything else.

"That," Ash said to his victim, "is for thinking to strike my woman."

My woman? The words poured over her like warm water on a cold morning, but she had no time to dwell on it. Perhaps, if she lived the day, she would find the time.

The two less confident men shrank back, but the last guard was not so easily cowed. He side-stepped around his fellow's legs and stood at arm's length from Blair, his pistol aimed at her head.

"Hold, or I'll discharge my weapon, sir."

Ash raised both hands in the air and planted a knee in the oblivious guard's chest as he got to his feet.

"The constable shot your sheriff, young man," Ash murmured. "Offer him neither your trust, nor your back."

CHAPTER FORTY-THREE

With a rope, they attached the manacles locked around Blair's wrists to her left ankle. She could walk, but would not be able to run. Ash was then trussed up in similar fashion, but his hands were tied behind him since he had no skirt that might need lifting on the steps.

She was shocked when the sheriff's guards believed Wotherspoon's explanation of how Ash jumped him, took his weapon and shot their leader. She tried to point out the first man needing killing was the constable, and not the sheriff at all, but they remained unmoved. With no other authority at hand, Wotherspoon pronounced sentence and ordered Ash and her to be hung immediately. He sent four men to the jail to retrieve Viscount Forsgreen, their co-conspirator.

The villain paused just inside the kirk doors and leaned close.

"I've had an idea," he said quietly. "The three of ye will remain hanging until all six nooses are filled. I imagine yer spy will go collect Northwick and Harcourt for me. All he'll need do is tell them some madman has hung their friends, don't ye suppose? I needn't lift a finger."

Laughing, he lifted his odd hat onto his head and walked out into the misty rain waving a hand for them to follow.

~ ~ ~

Blair refused to give up hope even though they were being led to the scaffold. She imagined the six of them standing with their nooses lying limp against their throats, their bodies splashed with the blood of the fallen at Givet Faux. Stanley, Harcourt, and Northwick. Everhardt, Ashmoore and herself. Surely it was the same tableau Cornelius Wotherspoon imagined when he thought of his son's death.

But even viewing it from the constable's point of view, she could not see the justice in it. They'd fought their way inside the citadel to save others. They'd fought their way out for the same reason. Not a just court in the land would condemn them. Why, then, had she been so quick to condemn herself?

Half way there now. The crowd parted, though begrudgingly, as they were urged along.

She felt Ash's eyes upon her and turned to meet them. *Ash*. The man she loved. The man who loved her. A future she never dared hope for. A future that would never be unless someone intervened.

She searched the crowd. The familiar faces watched her, watched the constable. But none of them seemed too fashed by the fact she was headed for her death. Did they expect The Reaper to appear and save her?

But there was no Reaper. And it was time to share that secret, with Ash at least.

She turned to him once more, tugged on her lead to move closer to him. He did the same. They were two feet apart. It had to be enough.

"There is no Reaper," she hissed.

He looked at her sharply.

"There is no Reaper," she repeated.

He shook his head. She had to try again.

"I sleep with the Reaper, but I sleep alone. Do you understand?"

Ash's brows shot up beneath his mussed hair.

She gave him a wink.

He looked away quickly, then wandered toward the edge of the crowd. She did the same, scouring the mob on her side of the street. Just ahead, a man turned sideways, the hilt of a blade stuck out from his belt. If she wasn't mistaken, he'd shown her a' purpose.

Blair hurried forward, creating slack between herself and the man who pulled her along. Then she hurried to the side. By the time the rope jerked tight again, she had the blade in her hand.

She looked at her guards, but their attention had turned to Ash, who had stumbled. No one noticed her weapon, so she held it to her leg and pulled a fold of her skirt over the top of it. She looked over her shoulder and gave Ash a wink. The man allowed himself to be helped to his feet and kept walking.

Ten feet away, now.

She was so nervous, she feared she would never act in time. But she tamped it down. She was The Reaper. The Reaper was fearless. For one last time, she must be capable and fearless.

The barrel of a pistol pushed into the side of her neck and moved along with her. She dared not slow.

"I'll take that blade, ye wee bitch." The constable's breath caught her by surprise and she coughed. The pistol pressed harder. The metal bit into her skin.

Slowly, she let her skirt free and gently lifted the knife up for the taking. The man wrapped his fingers around the hilt and pulled it away, slicing open the meat of her thumb as he did so. Still, the metal remained at her neck. She could feel a tremor in it now, as if Wotherspoon were barely restraining himself.

"Come now, constable." Ash called. "There's no fun in hanging a dead woman."

Wotherspoon snorted and the pressure was gone.

"Harken ye, people of Brigadunn," the bastard bellowed. "Yer Highland Reaper has confessed. His whore shall hang beside him—"

The crowd laughed and whistled, as if he'd made a clever joke.

The fool frowned, then shrugged. "Yonder comes The Reaper's accomplice to join the condemned."

Again, they laughed.

Four guards made their way through the mist, as they neared, it was clear they'd brought no one with them. The rain spattered every face, setting the crowd to blinking, but none of them ducked their heads or ran for shelter. They laughed at the sky as if they'd all gone quite mad.

"Look!" a lad cried.

"The Reaper," someone whispered, and it was repeated a dozen times.

The crowd sobered. Sitting on horseback, an odd, shadowy figure with two heads nodded as it came down the road from the jail. Darker and darker it grew. And darker still when it became clear—a black-cloaked figure, its horse dark with rain. And upon his shoulder, sat a very wet Shakespeare. The ring of dark feathers surrounding the bird's face was unmistakable.

Blair wondered at Stanley's skill with her bird and glanced at Ash. But Ash was not looking at The Reaper. She followed his gaze to four other cloaked figures in the crowd standing close enough to intervene if necessary—Martin, Coll, and Jarvill. The last was a white-blond man whose hair was simply too unique to be hidden in a hood.

Stanley!

Then who is playing Reaper?

The mounted figure raised a fist to Shakespeare and the bird hopped onto it. "Hoo-hoot," it sang.

"Ke-wick," answered a female owl in the distance.

The Reaper dipped his fist and then flung the bird into the air. The fool had removed the owl's jesses. They might not ever see it again!

The mysterious figure now pointed at Ash.

"Who are ye, to claim my name?" he demanded.

A chill ran up her spine at the timber in the man's voice. Heaven help her, she knew it!

"He is not The Reaper," the man bellowed. Turning his finger toward Blair, "And she isna my whore."

"Shoot him!" Wotherspoon screamed. But none obeyed. The sheriff's men stood still as if they'd not heard the order. Exasperated, the constable lifted his own pistol toward The Reaper. But if he wasted his shot on the stranger, he would have no leverage if his men were no longer with him.

Blair glanced at the sheriff's man at Ash's back. He still held to Ash's lead, but his pistol was pointed down and away.

"Show yerself," the constable demanded.

The Reaper's horse shifted its weight, but the man made no move.

Wotherspoon's weapon, once again, swung in Blair's direction.

"Show yerself, I say."

The man took a deep breath, then lifted a hand to his hood and pulled it back.

A hundred people gasped.

CHAPTER FORTY-FOUR

The man in the saddle, Allen Balliol, had attention for no one but Blair.

"As I said, Wotherspoon, she is not my whore." Her father swallowed. "She is me daughter. And she has never gone a' reivin' with me. God as my witness, she hasna. For this is the first time I've laid eyes on the lass in a live long while. A pair of years, at least."

Daughter! He'd called her *daughter!*

Her body jerked forward, but she froze at the grip of a cold and sweaty hand on her forearm.

"Touching, to be sure," Wotherspoon spit. "But the court has already pronounced sentence, and the sentence will be carried out. It makes no matter yer father's found a costume. He cannot prove he is The Reaper."

"Auch, but I can, Cornelius." Her father grinned. "I can decipher the Riddle of The Witch's Vale. Only The Reaper kens it."

The constable snarled. "Ye're daft Balliol. Plenty ken the riddle."

"But few ken the meaning. Do ye understand it, Cornelius? Laird Ashmoore couldna decipher it when he went in search of Finn. Surely ye're more clever than the Englishman. Haven't ye been sayin' so to all and sundry since the man's shadow crossed onto Scottish soil?"

Wotherspoon only glared.

"What does it mean?" Ash's voice boomed across the top of the crowd. "Tell us, Balliol."

Her father grinned. He knew it! What clever stock she'd come from. But if he proved he was The Reaper, her father would hang! She would simply have to call on her people and beg them to see the truth, that if anyone was to hang, it should be the true Reaper.

Her father winked at her, then looked at Ashmoore.

"Turn left," he said, enunciating carefully. "That is what the riddle demands."

"I doona believe it in the least," Wotherspoon snarled. "Prove it."

Her father nodded. "Fine, then." He cleared his throat. *"Tic toc, a map before. A quarter less, or three quarter's more.*

"Tic toc—a clock. A map before—a map before yer very eyes, but only if ye're looking close-like. There are wee rocks laid in the shape of an arrow. There is yer map, but it is also the hand of a clock. A quarter less—take back 15 minutes. Or three quarter's more—add forty-five. Either way, instead of the clock hand pointing the way, pointing at twelve, or straight ahead, it points at the nine. It points to the left. If ye see an arrow, turn left and ye'll be on the right path."

Ashmoore laughed.

Her father grinned. "Tell me again I'm nay The Highland Reaper."

Wotherspoon's eyes bulged above a nasty grin. "Oh, aye, Allen Balliol. Ye've convinced me. So come down here so I can hang ye along with yer long dead daughter."

Her father straightened. "I doona suppose I will. Seems as though only one will hang today, Cornelius. The spy you keep at Brigadunn manor has had a change of loyalty, ye see. And as penance for his sins, this footman has explained the way ye and yer son have been thieving from the glen, leading the people to believe it was their Anglish landlords bleedin' the land dry, until The Reaper came and took everything ye meant to pocket. Then yer deeds turned to kidnapping soldiers and stealing from their families. It seems ye've been a curse to more than just our part of Scotland. But we're happy to remedy that.

"Cornelius Wotherspoon, you are hereby charged with kidnapping, larceny, murder, and misusing yer office. Since laird Ashmoore's freedom is in question and the District Sheriff has been murdered, I, Allen Balliol of the House of Balliol, hereby pronounce ye guilty and sentence ye to hang by the neck until dead." Her father grinned and looked around at the crowd. "That is, if the people of this town wish me to act as their temporary constable."

The crowd cheered.

"Any opposed?"

Someone laughed.

Blair dared a glance at Ash. He was speaking over his shoulder to the man behind him, but he was frowning at her.

A chill ran up her spine. He rolled his shoulders and brought his hands together in front of him and she jumped. He was free. And she was not. And the look in his eye promised he'd take advantage of the disparity.

She turned abruptly to the crowd and raised her hands in front of her in a plea for help. A man stepped forward and produced a blade, then he glanced over her shoulder and stepped back. She looked behind her and found Ash bearing down on her, a dark cloud across his face. A lock of hair hanging in his eyes.

She thought it wise to run now, free her hands later. Only she had to bend forward to do so because the rope tied to her ankle had little slack.

The crowd parted for her, but she stumbled on her sagging skirts. Arms reached out and caught her, then pushed her backward onto her feet and into Ash's reach.

"I was once told," he said, "that if a woman kept her skirts four inches short, she could run without tripping."

She remembered when she'd said those words to him—that first night he'd caught her in the woods—and she shivered.

"You couldn't have told me sooner?" His whisper sent a wave of chills up the side of her neck. The crowd became a distant buzz, easily ignored.

"What?" she said innocently. He could have been referring to a dozen omissions.

"*Turn left?* How long would it have taken you to shout two words as we were leaving to look for Finn? *Turn left.* Not long at all."

"Oh. That. Well, I couldna just hand the enemy a clear map to The Witch's Vale, now could I?"

He tucked his chin into the cleft between her shoulder and neck and she curled into him. "I was never the enemy," he said.

"A recent development, surely."

He wrapped his arms around her and pulled her roughly back against him. "And how long were you going to torture me?"

"Torture?"

"Yes. Torture. You think it was pleasant, believing you were The Reaper's woman?"

Her body sighed into him. She covered his arms with her own. She had no intention of letting him release her. "It tortured you?"

"You know it did."

Her smile grew. "Only a recent development."

"No, Scotia. I have loved you for years now. A thousand at least."

He pulled her hand up into the air, then slid the warm owl ring onto her finger.

"It will fall off," she warned.

"Not if you hold it like this." He laced his fingers through hers and squeezed. "Never let go."

"Never?"

"Never."

"What if I'd like to have a word with my father?"

"Not even then."

She laughed. His body was a warm blanket at her back. She could have worn him for hours like that, until their legs became weary.

The crowd grew silent. Blair turned, with Ash, to see what held their attention. Cornelius Wotherspoon was being dragged to the gallows. A rag had been tied around his head. A large knot poked out between his teeth. Whatever he meant to say was unintelligible.

"If yer prayin' to yer maker, Cornelius, I'm certain he understands every word. No need for us to listen." Allen Balliol nodded, still atop his horse, and two of the sheriff's men hauled the condemned up the steps and beneath a noose.

Martin climbed the steps and moved to stand before the prisoner.

"As I'll be acting as henchman today, constable, I ask yer forgiveness."

Wotherspoon snarled at him.

Martin straightened away from him as if he'd been insulted.

"I asked forgiveness, ye bastard. Just because ye didna give it doesna mean I won't enjoy it. But rest assured, it's a far easier death than those suffered at Givet Faux, by yer son's hand. Ye'll not rot in an oubliette, more's the pity."

Ash suddenly took Blair by the shoulders and turned her into him. He pulled her head against his chest and covered her exposed ear with his hand. Then he hummed a silly tune, as if the sight of a hanging was something that would upset her, as if she'd never been at Bergen op Zoom or Givet Faux. As if she were some delicate woman who might have nightmares. . .

She could barely hear the roar of the crowd. A moment later, someone grabbed her elbow and pulled her away from her sanctuary. She looked up to find her father frowning down at her.

"Forgive me, daughter," he said. A general command, but enough. "Forgive me."

"Oh, da," she wailed and fell against him, suddenly feeling every bit of ten years old, pouring her heart out on her da's shoulder over hurts she couldn't put a name to.

CHAPTER FORTY-FIVE

A hundred tears later, Blair was ushered into Stanley's lovely carriage and took a seat next to Finn, who had already fallen asleep. She tried to feel bad about soiling the viscount's cushions with their filthy clothing, but she was simply too weary. Besides, she was suddenly empty of emotion, having spent them all on her father's shoulder.

She glanced up at Ash, sitting across from her, and reconsidered. A riot of emotions began to swirl in her stomach, but thankfully, her eyes were dry for the moment.

Rain pattered on the roof. She wondered where her people would find shelter, then realized they all had homes nearby. Even her.

Ash frowned out the window. And continued to do so. Something was wrong.

Her heart sank to her stomach. Had he reconsidered so quickly? Had her tears disgusted him?

"Here, here, Miss Balliol. Do not fret, I beg you." Stanley put a hand on her knee.

Ash leaned forward and plucked the same hand off her knee and flung it back at its owner.

Stanley laughed. "You see? He is paying attention."

Ash huffed out a breath, then returned his attention to the window.

She thought it wise to do the same. They traveled in silence toward the east. The moon nudged its way between storm clouds and she thought she could at least do the same.

"What is it?" she asked firmly. "Why are ye angry with me?"

Slowly, he turned to meet her gaze. A deep breath. Then another. Then he slowly raised his hand. Between two fingers he held the owl ring.

When had she lost it?

She laughed lightly, for surely he could not be angry with her over the ring. "I told you it would fall off."

"And I showed you how to keep it from doing so."

She could not tell if he was still frowning. The moon had turned coward and run, taking its light along with it.

"Will ye show me again?" she breathed.

"If I do, Blair, there will be no going back," he said ominously.

"No going back? What do ye mean? No returning to The Vale? To being The Reaper?"

He shook his head. "No going back to being Blair Balliol."

Her heart sank again. "If ye wish to call me Scotia, do." She shrugged. What did she care what he called her? The ring could not mean marriage, not to an earl. And if he was going to offer to keep her as his mistress, there would be little need for him to use her name at all, since she would refuse him. And if she refused him, she could not very well live down the road from him, watching him come and go, wondering if he were going to see some woman who'd taken the position she had not wanted.

Heaven help her, she couldn't go home after all! At least not for long.

Stanley cleared his throat. "If I may—"

"You may not," said Ash.

His friend snorted. "Miss Balliol, I believe what he is trying to say—"

"Get out, Stanley." Ash knocked on the roof.

The carriage slowed. Stanley knocked on the roof, and it sped up again.

"I will not get out. It is raining. And the carriage is mine, old sock."

"Then shut up." Ash glared at the man.

"Then do it properly. I'll be damned if I'll—"

"Give me a moment," Ash growled.

Stanley laughed and turned his attention out his own window.

Ash turned to her, his eyes still unreadable. The carriage interior was eerily blue and gray with shadow.

"This would be much easier if you were sitting on my lap," he said.

"No." She hoped he understood everything she was saying no to.

Ash huffed again. Stanley snorted, but got an elbow in his ribs for his trouble. It only made him snort louder.

Blair simply wished the carriage would stop so she could climb out.

"Marry me, Blair," Ash said suddenly. "Be my Lady Ashmoore. Blair Merriweather. Not Scotia, not Blair Balliol. Take the bloody ring. Hold my hand tightly until I can purchase a proper one."

He couldn't possibly—

"Take the *bloody ring*?!" Stanley choked, then roared with laughter.

While Blair tried to convince herself she hadn't just imagined a proposal of marriage, the men across from her began to wrestle. Finn's ability to sleep through it all was nothing if not impressive. She wasn't certain whose hand it was that got free and knocked on the wall, but the carriage slowed and she was grateful. Perhaps without the wheels spinning, she could think clearly and perhaps catch her breath.

Ash reached over and opened the carriage door before they came to a complete stop.

"Here now!" Stanley complained, but then started laughing—high-pitched and out of control. He was laughing so hard, in fact, he couldn't defend himself when Ash pushed him toward the door. And with a foot to his backside, His Grace went flying.

Ash pulled the wee door closed and knocked again. The carriage sped on. Stanley's laughter grew hysterical even as it faded.

The carriage rocked along. Finn's breathing filled the air. Blair stared into the darkness where she believed Ash's eyes to be.

"Come here," he growled.

"Why?"

"So I might convince you."

Blair was already convinced, but she was so curious, she stood and turned to take Stanley's seat. But Ash pulled her onto his lap instead. She told herself she was simply too exhausted to fight him.

"Say yes," he said, and kissed her neck.

She couldn't say yes. Speech was impossible.

"Say yes," he said again, kissed her neck again. It was hardly incentive to give in.

She laughed. "Is this the extent of yer powers of persuasion? To bid me, over and over, to say aye?"

"Blair, my love, I will do and say whatever it takes to sway you. I have waited a thousand years. I can wait an entire minute more." He kissed her lips then. It might have been another thousand years before he paused. They might have been well south of London before his warm mouth released her. "Say yes."

"I'm hardly the right woman for an English earl."

"The perfect woman for me," he whispered against her forehead. "The only woman for me." He kissed her again. "And you owe me dearly. Marrying me will not cover your debt by half."

She placed a hand on his glorious chest and pushed back from him.

"My debt?"

"Two years of torture, without you in my arms. Impossible to name a fitting price."

She wanted to goad him further, to keep him talking, for the rumble of his voice against her hand was a bliss worth any price. Nearly worth her own two years of torture, and she told him so.

"Marry me, Blair. Be my bride forever more and I promise to never rest my tongue."

She suspected he'd completely missed the point.

"Say yes," he leaned forward and kissed her just below the collar bone. "I warn you, if you deny me, I shall simply purchase a stone tower and keep you anyway. Our children will grow up believing their father is an ogre."

"A chatty ogre?"

"If you prefer."

She laughed.

"Say yes, my precious Scotia. Cease my torment." He bent to kiss her once more, but suddenly straightened. "Say yes, my love," he ordered, "or I shall never kiss you again."

"Oh. Well. You should have said so in the first place. I'd have agreed straight away."

"Truly?"

"Aye," she sighed. "Aye, aye, aye," she said between kisses to his cheeks, eyes, and nose.

He laughed. "I only hope Stanley will forgive me. . .for not catching on much sooner."

CHAPTER FORTY-SIX

Blair woke in the chamber in which Stanley had locked her days before. When she was ready to leave the room, she found her brother lying across her threshold.

"Mornin', sister mine," he said cheerfully.

"High spirits with the sun still low, brother."

"Oh, aye. Seems my choice of pallet didna sit well with yer betrothed, and for some reason, it makes me smile."

She tried not to blush at the thought of Ash stalking about outside her door.

When she and Martin entered the dining room, her father rose to his feet, as did Ash, Stanley and Finn. She could not help but grow teary at the memory of the last time she and her family were all in the same room together, but she kissed each one on the cheek and blinked her eyes dry. When Stanley turned his head for a turn, Ash mumbled something about giving the man a chance to turn the other cheek as soon as breakfast was over. Stanley rolled his eyes, then gave her a wink instead of taking a kiss.

She stopped next to Ash. He frowned around the table and stooped to accept a kiss on the cheek. Then he gave her a look that promised he would need more later. She hoped they might run into each other in the larder. . .

"I was just pointing out to Ashmoore that it is down to Harcourt and me, and I refuse to be the last of the Four Kings to find a wife. And not any wife, mind you. I want a good one, like The Scarlet Plumiere or The Highland Reaper."

Ash took a moment to explain to her family about The Scarlet Plumiere, the woman who Northwick recently married.

Stanley sighed heavily. "I don't trust my own judgment anymore. Not after Irene Goodfellow."

Blair looked to Ash for an explanation.

He obliged. "Irene was His Grace's fiancée. Or rather, his former fiancée. She murdered Stanley's mistress."

"Murdered?"

Stanley nodded. "You see why I question my own taste in women?"

Blair smiled and looked at Ash. "If I were you, Stanley, I'd just keep tasting."

Ash smiled in return—a smile that promised retribution for every time he'd imagined her tasting another man's lips. He'd claimed that particular torture was what had turned two years into a thousand.

Oh, yes. She was going to pay.

Hopefully, for a good long time.

THE END

Other novels from L. L. Muir

The Curse of Clan Ross Series
Going Back for Romeo
Not Without Juliet
Collecting Isobelle*
What About Wickham?*

The Scarlet Plumiere Series (Regency romance)
Blood for Ink
Bones for Bread
Body and Soul*
Breath of Laughter*

The Secrets of Somerled Series (Young Adult Romance)
Somewhere Over the Freaking Rainbow
Freaking Off the Grid *
Arma-Freaking-Geddon*

Other stand-alones
Lord Fool to the Rescue (Regency)
Christmas Kiss (Time travel)
Where to Pee on a Pirate Ship (Middle Grade)

*at the time of printing, these books have not yet been released

Get my New Release Newsletter by signing up here:
http://llmuir.weebly.com/

Excerpt from BODY AND SOUL

The Scarlet Plumiere Series: Book 3

CHAPTER ONE

"I would very much like to murder your wife." Stanley bowed to his friend manning the receiving line at the first rout he'd attended since returning to London.

"Your Grace. Good of you to come." North bowed in return. "I would prefer you did not. Rather fond of her, you know."

Stan took a step to the side, lifted Livvy's hand, and kissed it. "Livvy," he said through clenched teeth.

"Your Grace." She grinned. "If you must murder me, would you mind waiting until tomorrow? This is my first role as hostess, and I would hate to bleed on my guests."

Stan turned back to North. "You noticed. She denied nothing."

North laughed. "Livvy is not the only one who knows how to place notices in the *Journal.* Anyone could have announced you were in the market..." North looked quickly about him, then leaned forward. "...to be in the market, so to speak."

Stan glared at the still-grinning love of North's life. "No one else was aware," he growled.

Livvy laughed and covered her mouth with gloved fingers. "Stanley, please. It was simple retribution for not locking Ashmoore in stocks until we could get to Scotland. Surely you knew how North would feel for missing Ash's wedding." She began giggling. "I had no idea you would become a prisoner in your own home."

Her laughing got the best of her and she was forced to bury her face against Northwick's chest to keep from drawing more attention. No doubt the entire population of London in full Season had heard of him having to don a disguise to escape his own home. A certain Lady Abernathy had set no less than three men to the task of stalking an eligible duke's every move in order to drop her daughter in his path at each turn. The fact that it had taken a woman's disguise to fool the stalkers was a detail he hoped to keep to himself. Considering Livvy's hysterics, it seemed that detail was a secret no more. At least it had not been included in the *Journal* gossip.

"North. As soon as you are free, I would like to discuss funeral arrangements with you in your study." He glared at Livvy.

Surprisingly, she made a concerted effort to calm herself. She even managed to stop smiling.

"Of course," North replied. "May I ask whose funeral?"

"I have not yet decided." He turned and entered North's home. The crier faced him and offered a low bow. "If you announce me, sir, I will cut out your tongue."

The man started to rise, but instead, bit his lips together and bowed again.

Livvy's laughter followed Stan up the stairs, along with a hundred eyes, he was certain.

Once inside the study, he stomped over to the wall. He took off his gloves and pulled the edge of Old Northwick's portrait. It opened on a hinge, as did a section of wall behind it. On the next layer before him were two knobs attached to small squares of canvas. He removed the square nearest him and peered out over the ballroom through a screen. On ballroom side of the wall, one might notice a shadow of movement within the painting hanging there. But only if one knew what to look for.

Old Northwick's father had installed the device in order to both enjoy his wife's soirees without the need to mingle with others, and to keep a close eye on his wife's dancing partners. There was also a bell-pull within reach that caused a small bell to ring beneath the musician's mezzanine, so he could send his wife a signal if needed.

When they were young, The Four Kings—North, Ashmoore, Harcourt, and himself—had been allowed to spy through the painting only when important guests were in attendance. But tonight, the highest ranking guest at the party was going to do the spying. Stan had no intention of stepping a foot outside the study until he was absolutely certain Lady Abernathy and her daughter were not lying in wait for him. And if Livvy's reputation as a hostess was damaged by his absence, then it served her rightly.

All's fair in love and war. Especially if theirs was a war *about* love.

The night he'd come to recount to North the happenings in Scotland, he'd tried to explain to his friend how desperately alone he felt now that two of The Four Kings had found the perfect women for themselves. He hadn't taken into account that Livvy, the woman perched on the arm of North's chair during that conversation, had once been the most notorious gossip in London. And now he was paying for that oversight.

The study door burst open and Stan started.

It was only North, but just standing next to the spy holes made him feel as if he were doing something he oughtn't.

"We have a plan," North announced and hurried to stand beside him.

"We?" he scoffed. "You mean yourself and that woman—"

"That woman *I love*, yes. We have a plan. Livvy is going to walk about the ballroom and strike up conversations with ladies to whom you might like to be

L.L. Muir

introduced. If you like the look of the woman, you pull the bell. Gently. She'll be listening for it."

Stanley gave a gusty sigh. "It seems rather like an animal auction."

North laughed quietly. "Of course it does. And just think of how the animals feel." He nodded toward the spy holes.

"If I am not interested in an introduction?"

"Then do not ring the bell. Look here, old sock. I will try to make a note of their names, but for the most part, we'll be relying on Livvy's memory, so we shan't choose too many."

Stan refrained from sharing his doubts about finding even one woman among the guests who might raise his interest. He wasn't searching for a woman to wear on his sleeve to balls and the like. He wanted to find someone like Livvy or Ash's wife, Blair. And neither of them were twirling around on ballroom floors when they were found.

It was possible the woman he was longing for was not even in London. Of course he wished to find someone suitable. He was a duke after all. But he refused to spend the rest of his days wishing his wife were more…adventurous.

That was it!

He'd suddenly struck upon a word for it. But he would keep it to himself for the time being. He certainly didn't care to read about it in the paper the next morning.

North moved close to the wall and revealed the other spying hole. When they were younger, they'd needed to stand upon chairs to reach them. Now they jockeyed their shoulders in order to fit in the opening.

"There she is." North pointed to the right. "She is waving."

Livvy wasn't exactly waving, but she was drumming her fingers on her lips. After a moment of perusing the crowd, and side stepping an older gentleman who looked interested in speaking with her, she hurried up next to a girl dressed in white, glittering from the crown of her head to the hem of her gown.

"A shining package," Stan half-whispered. "Perhaps to draw one's attention from what lies inside."

North reached for the bell-pull.

"Not on your life." Stan huffed.

North laughed. "She is jesting."

Livvy moved along, drumming against her lips as she searched again. North was enraptured with every move the woman made. After a moment, Stan wondered if his friend had forgotten the game.

While Livvy wandered through the crowd, Stan allowed his eyes to do a bit of searching of their own and his gaze was drawn to a woman in pink who was also moving through the guests but with much more focus and a bit more speed. Through the screen, it was difficult to see her features, but the way others watched her as she passed, he predicted she was a beauty. Of course her image was of little interest, but what did hold his attention was the seemingly lazy circuit she made around the perimeter of the room while actually making impressive progress. It was like watching a butterfly flit about a flowering bush—every movement seemed random until one realized the pretty thing had managed to successfully visit each blossom exactly once.

What was equally interesting was the bee-like creature following that butterfly around the room.

A dapper, intent looking gentleman, with a substantial widow's peak, remained a good ten steps behind the woman, whether by design or the fact he failed to keep pace, Stan could not say. But the man noted each person with whom the butterfly came in contact, as if he were keeping track.

"Surely this one," North murmured.

Stan tore his attention away from the imaginary garden and scanned the mob for Livvy's blue dress.

There. Livvy was laughing with a lovely, tall woman with dark hair, dressed in green.

Stan tugged the bell-pull so he could go back to watching the bee and butterfly.

North slapped him on the back, jarring his focus. "There is the spirit. See how pleased you have made her."

Stan realized his friend was referring to Livvy and found the blue gown again, noticed the way she bounced on her toes. Her drumming fingers could not hide her smile.

A pink cloud moved next to the blue.

The butterfly!

He found the bee, pausing, stopping, looking on.

Stan grabbed the bell pull, tugged enthusiastically, and heard an answering clang.

"Easy, now." North took the ribbon from his hand. "We do not wish to draw attention to the bell. Besides, you do not want this introduction."

Stan moved his face closer to the screen, wondering if he'd been wrong about the reason others turned in the butterfly's direction as she passed. If she was homely, it mattered little to him. He was merely curious about her and her bee. If he were introduced to her, he could work out the mystery.

Livvy conversed with the butterfly, but each time the woman in pink spoke, Livvy shook her head, as if in sympathy. But Stan was certain she was attempting to tell him what North had already said, that this woman was not for him.

Stan grabbed the bell-pull and tugged again, this time more gently.

Livvy's head shook faster. He could only imagine how she had to scramble to come up with conversation that matched her odd movements.

Stan laughed and pulled again.

The conversation between the women ended and the pink cloud moved on. Livvy glared up at the painting and shook her head sharply. The butterfly paused and turned back, noting the position of the bee. Stan was gifted with a clear look at her face…and a solid punch to his middle. The air was suddenly gone from his lungs and he gasped for breath.

"Dear Lord," he whispered.

He did *not* reach for the ribbon again.

About the Author

L.L. Muir lives in the shadows of the Rocky Mountains with a charming husband who makes her laugh, but does not make her do pans. Like most authors, she is constantly searching for, or borrowing pens. The best ideas always begin on a napkin.

If you like her books, please consider leaving a review. You can reach her through her website— www.llmuir.weebly.com , or on Facebook at L.L. Muir.

Thank you for playing!